TEMPER:
DEFERENCE

Lila Mina

TEMPER: DEFERENCE

Book One of the TEMPER Saga

Visit http://lilamina.com to discover the world of the TEMPER saga.

LILAMINA

Facebook: @AuthorLilaMina
Instagram: @lilaminaauthor
Twitter: @lilamina11

Copyright © 2019 Lila Mina
All rights reserved.
Front and back cover design: © 2019 Giulia Natsumi
All rights reserved.
Cover picture: AdobeStock
Back cover picture: Aleksandar Pasaric

Table of Contents

1 Just Another Manic Tuesday 1

2 Tempers Are Running High 11

3 Obedience and Respect 25

4 Losing Control and Denial 47

5 Attempting to Move On 63

6 Facing the Truth 77

7 A New Player in the Game 93

8 Mapping New Territories 103

9 Testing Limits and Accepting Them 125

10 Inside and Out 135

11 Taking out the Trash 147

12 Master and Apprentice 169

13 Rattling Her Inner Cage 185

14 A Lesson in Discipline 201

15 On Shaky Legs 221

16 Burnt Bridges 237

17 Creepy Encounters	249
18 Master and Mistress of the House	263
19 Memories Buried under Ashes	285
20 A Ladies' Night	301
21 Snarls and Teeth	315
22 Strange Neighbors	331
23 Two Sides of the Same Coin	343
24 Fighting Ghosts	357
25 An Offering of Blood	369
Glossary of Japanese terms	i
Loved it? Please Review!	iii
The TEMPER Saga Continues!	v
About the Author	xxvii

Fall seven times, stand up eight.

1

Just Another Manic Tuesday

"RICHARD, ARE YOU kidding me? No!" Lana slammed her hands on the desk in front of her and leaned over it. Her boss grimaced and raised defensive hands with a worried glance at the open door behind her. She didn't even bother to check if anyone listened in. The entire floor could hear her for all that it mattered. "There's no way I'll waste my time on this again!"

"Come on, Lana, take it down a notch. We all agree that you're the best one to handle Michelle and—"

"We? Who's we? You, Takemura and Yamamoto? Oh, color me surprised! Michelle's got all of you by the balls, hasn't she? She's on a witch hunt, and now you have no choice but get on your knees and lick her boots."

Richard's wrinkled face flushed red, and he stood up to lean over his desk. They were almost nose to nose now. "Watch it, Martin!" he spat from behind clenched teeth. "I'm fed up with that foul mouth of yours. I'm not asking you a favor, I'm telling you to do it. See the difference?"

With a snort, Lana crossed her arms over her chest, staring outside the windows behind Matherson. The sun was setting over the Roppongi business district and the Tokyo Tower was lit up. *Shit! It must be past six already, I'm going to be late at the dojo! Dammit, I've got no time for this kind of playground shit.*

"Oh, don't worry, I'm not daft. You don't have to add 'insubordination' to 'hysterical' in your little book—no, please, spare me the offended looks. I know what you all call me. Just because I like to call a rat a rat and won't sugarcoat it for you."

She gave the manager of their branch office a disgusted look. "So basically, I have to babysit her and do all the damage control for you. Right when I'll be wrapping up the executive report for HQ *and* during the final rounds of the Daihanko-Dos Santos talks. Neat!"

The middle-aged man moved his arms to mirror her posture before catching himself and placing his hands on his hips. It would have been a good power pose if only she didn't know he had nothing to back it up. It cast a cruel light on his posh beer belly though.

"Well, feel free to see it that way. *Or* you could take it as a good opportunity to gain points with our CFO. Could be useful the day you want to go back to Montreal or ask for a transfer to Rome. When was the last time you went home?"

Rubbing her temples, Lana took a deep breath. "I'm not leaving anytime soon, certainly not to Italy, and Michelle is the last person on Earth I want to please. Let's agree she's a bully, always doing her best to be unhappy with something just for the pleasure of burning down the house." Matherson grunted his reluctant agreement. "Okay, I'll be on my way. Any chance you'll send me something useful in the coming days? Whatever data that riled her up so much? I mean, she won't be here until the end of April, but I don't want to wait until the last minute to tackle it."

"Sure. Believe me or not, we don't want to let you hang out to dry."

Lana arched a dubitative eyebrow but bit her tongue. *Let's not start again, or I'll really be late, and sensei will go ballistic on me.*

Basic Japanese etiquette and strict martial arts rules frowned upon being late, but her instructor had zero tolerance for this. No need to start practice with a scolding, she'd endured enough aggravation for one day. After giving Matherson a curt nod, the bare minimum she could muster, she strolled out.

Back in her own office two floors below, her resentment still pumped adrenaline in her blood. On top of it, her heartburn was flaring again. With a heavy sigh, Lana grabbed a prescription bottle in her desk drawer and gulped down two pills with a grimace. The bottle was almost empty, she'd have to pay Dr. Stein a visit soon.

Richard Matherson. What a weasel. After all this time, his lack of spine still amazes me. No wonder he got promoted to upper management so fast.

A glance at her watch made her cringe. Time to get out of here if she wanted to catch the Express train to the Mitaka suburbs where her apartment and dojo were located.

After tying up her hair in a strict ponytail, she grabbed her duffle bag packed with her aikido *dogi*– her white training gear–and slipped her feet into a pair of red sneakers. Her black pumps would stay under her desk. No way she'd ride her bicycle between the station and the dojo wearing those.

"Oh, you're still here? Usually on Tuesday, you're out before six," a melodious voice called in Italian from her doorway. Lana glanced up and smiled at the beautiful brunette with startling green eyes who stood there. Her best friend Gabriella was a sight for sore eyes.

"*Cara mia*, consider me gone. I'm so late it's not even funny."

"I didn't see you." Gabriella chuckled and stepped out of her way. They walked in silence to the elevator. "What's going on?" she said under her breath after pressing the down button.

"Richard dropped Cruella on my lap. Third year in a row now. *Noice!*" she parroted Jake Peralta before clenching her jaw. Bursting another artery wouldn't help.

"That little shit!" Gabriella spat. Like Lana, she had a personality that often clashed with the more reserved attitude of their colleagues.

"This is getting old," Lana groaned. "Anyway, we're still on for many well-deserved drinks on Friday?"

"You bet we are! I can't get through this darn thirty-seventh birthday without plenty of liquid comfort."

"Hey, you'll see it's not that bad, it took me only two months to recover," Lana chuckled.

Gabriella turned serious again. "Lana, call me later if you want to talk about this, okay? You more or less lock it up, and then it's a nuclear apocalypse. Management sucks, but you need to let it go now and then."

Lana sighed and shook her head. Gabriella knew her so well. More than a friend, a sister. Their bond ran deep; they had gone through devastating pain and tears together. To have Gabriella by her side was a constant source of comfort even after all these years. Being dispatched together to Japan had been a blessing.

"I guess you're right. But don't worry, a solid hour of rolling on the mats and getting my joints twisted are just what I need to vent. That is, if I don't get burned at the stake because I missed the train."

"Girl, I don't know why you keep doing this. It doesn't even sound like fun! That overbearing sensei of yours—"

"Is a stickler for discipline but one of the best around, and you have no idea how good it feels to throw dozens of guys around after a day like this. See ya!" The doors opened, and Lana jumped inside the elevator with a happy wave of her hand.

The subway ride between Roppongi and Shinjuku was manageable, but the second stretch to Mitaka was a nightmare. Today, Shinjuku was obviously intent on earning its label of the world's busiest station. For sure, the average 3.5 million passing its gates had decided to gather at the same time, just to make Lana's day more difficult.

Without hesitating, she pushed through the throngs of commuters to the front of the line where she'd have at least a chance at boarding her train on the Chuo line. Acutely aware of the condemning stares drilling holes in her neck, a wave of embarrassment made her cheeks burn. She didn't have much choice. The train arrived, already full, and she squeezed herself inside, helped by dozens of people behind her trying to do the same.

The evening rush hour was the worst time of the day to board an Express train. On normal days, Lana used the Local one that stopped at every station. It would take some additional fifteen minutes to reach her destination, but at least she avoided being crushed against the door with the combined weight of a hundred commuters pressing on her back. Like right now.

Her hands against the glass, her bag digging into her stomach and hips, it was impossible to grab her smartphone to go online. But tonight, the majestic view of the Tokyo cityscape at dusk held no appeal. Instead, Lana closed her eyes to block out her surroundings. Thank goodness she wasn't claustrophobic and that her ride would last only sixteen minutes. It helped that the car was eerily silent, except for the recorded voice announcing the stations. Everyone attempted to do the same: retreat inward to forget how hellish going home at the same time as ten million other people could be.

Taking deep, relaxing breaths, Lana did her best to set aside her confrontation with Richard and what it would mean for her in the coming months. Instead, she thought about what awaited her in Mitaka.

Aikido.

From a passing hobby at first, this martial art form had become a real fixture in her life. The mental and physical discipline helped her manage the stress of her high-demanding job. It was the perfect outlet for the building pressure that filled her on a daily basis. Not to mention her exasperation on days like this.

"Next stop, Mitaka. Mitaka."

Lana's eyes shot open, and she readied herself. Getting out the train was as much a challenge as stepping inside. Thankfully, her bag was in front of her, not on her shoulder. She had almost lost it once, swallowed by the human wall closing on it behind her.

Outside the station, she ran to the bicycle parking, putting on her gloves to protect her fingers from the biting February cold. Ten more minutes spent slaloming in the back streets and she'd be there.

The best part of her day could finally begin.

2

Tempers Are Running High

SWEAT RUNNING DOWN her back despite the cold, Lana took off her shoes in the dojo's entrance. She dropped her bag and hurried to kneel and bow at the portrait of O'Sensei, the Founder of aikido, and the small Shinto altar affixed on the opposite wall. "Good evening," she told the group of aikidoka who were cleaning up the mats.

To her acute relief, their chief instructor wasn't on the *tatami* yet. She darted to a narrow and smelly locker room to put on her *dogi*. More a broom locker than anything else, it was the only place with a closing door, and so the women used it to change. The men were doing it in the open next to the *tatami* area.

The building itself was old, built just after the war, and was completely made of wood. With no form of insulation and no actual windows, only mosquito nets, it was freezing cold inside during winter and felt like an oven during summer. They were next to the huge park of the Jindai-ji Shinto shrine, and with the wildlife that came to life at night on the other side of the walls, it felt more like being in the middle of the jungle, not in one of the largest cities in the world.

Lana loved the place's timeless feel; the atmosphere was a big part of the pleasure she found in training. It couldn't get much more Japanese than this. It was a good dojo, with good people training hard to improve themselves at all levels, led by an outstanding instructor. It'd take an earthquake or a near-death experience to make her miss a class.

Not a weak man like Richard nor despicable office politics.

"Ahhh, *samui*," Naomi complained about the cold while dressing up as quickly as possible.

One of Lana's *kohai*, a fellow aikidoka with a lower grade, they had started together. Naomi had gone through two tests over the previous two years, making her a fourth *kyu*. "I heard it will snow tonight, I'm sure inside here as well!"

Shrieking *'samui'* all day long was the Japanese national anthem every year whenever temperatures dropped below 15°C. With its high humidity levels, February in Tokyo was brutal.

With a chuckle, Lana tied her white belt, the sign she was still a *mudansha*–a 'no-rank' practitioner. No colored belts for adults here; you were white until you turned black.

"Yep, it must be what, 8 to 10°C in here, tops? I can't wait for spring!"

After a double-check of her belt knot, Lana nodded in satisfaction and relief; the flatter, the better... and the safer. *Let's not do a repeat of last week. What an embarrassment!*

A pair of large pants, a white jacket and a belt – that was all the gear they needed. A martial art based on redirecting an attacker's kinetic energy to throw or immobilize them, aikido didn't require special equipment. It also meant no head, chin or chest protection. Getting thrown face-down on the ground could turn extra painful if a hard and unforgiving ball of cotton tried to drill through your navel. Something Lana had found out the previous week.

The two women jogged back into the main room. The next exam session was coming up, so the mats were crowded despite the numbing cold. She sat next to her friend Tim, and they exchanged a nod and a warm smile.

Spending time with her fellow aikidoka was a great source of motivation and pleasure. Like Tim, most of them had become friends over the two previous years. Ten years her junior, the American was nevertheless her *sempai*–upperclassman–because he was already *shodan*, a first-rank black belt. Lana was two tests away from that level.

This wasn't the time for chit-chat but rather for light meditation to clear their minds and center themselves, something she desperately needed. Silence settled down on their group.

At 7:30 sharp, Honda sensei stepped upon the tatami. Lana threw him a discreet glance. Broad-shouldered, tall and fit, he looked younger than his fifty-odd years. The traditional aikido uniform worn by practitioners holding a *dan* rank–flowing black *hakama* trousers tied at the waist–suited him particularly well. Not that Lana would ever confess it aloud.

She looked down before he caught her frowning at him. If possible, his mood seemed more somber than usual. While he always favored a scowl, there was no sign of a smile tonight. Fists clenched and unclenched on his lap while he sat in front for his usual greeting before class commenced. Something was up.

Her ability to pick up on those subtle clues wasn't a surprise: they weren't total strangers. Two years of aikido practice together and her excellent ability to read body-language, helped. On top of it, being a foreign made her extra sensitivity to the non-verbal clues of people around her vital. Especially in a country like Japan where corporal self-control was so highly valued.

She snapped back to attention when Honda signaled the start of the warming-up. After fifteen minutes, they began a special pre-exam session, focusing on free sparring to give everyone taking their test the chance to review their *waza*–their techniques.

Lana partnered up with Tim; after the ritual salutations, they got to their feet. Lana attacked him right away by grabbing his jacket at shoulder level. In a blink, he defended himself with the proper technique, but his pivot to her side wasn't perfectly timed and he couldn't unbalance her.

"Argh, *katadori menuchi* is my bane!" Tim muttered when his hand landed on Lana's shoulder and he pulled her down, putting too much strength into the move to compensate for his lack of technical precision. She grinned and jumped on her feet, eager to roll again as quickly as possible to get her blood pumping, build heat, work on that shape of hers, and above all get rid of her work-related tension.

"I hear you, it's one of the worst, but lucky me, I'm not the one going for second *dan* four weeks from now!"

Lana grabbed his left shoulder; right away, she blocked his strike to her head with her free forearm. For a couple of seconds, they remained face-to-face, each of them trying to unbalance the other, using their arms like swords. *Nasty bruises, here we come!*

This time, Tim's timing and movements were better. Pivoting on his side to make her stumble forward thanks to her own momentum, he ended up behind her, one wrist pushing down her attacking hand. He moved his arm in an upward spiral until his hand was right in her face while the other grabbed her collar. Unable to keep her balance, Lana stopped resisting when he flung her on the ground. She broke her fall with a backward roll.

"Johnson san! Your hip move! Wider now! Martin san, such a weak attack, push him back as if you mean it! Volleyball is on Saturday afternoon!" Honda's booming voice startled them and wiped their smiles off their faces.

"Yes, Sensei!" Tim and Lana replied as one.

She couldn't help a shudder and straightened up. *How does he even do it? We're over thirty tonight and still, I always light up his radar. Do I suck so badly?*

"Well... you heard the boss! Fire away!" Tim said, rolling his eyes discreetly. "Seriously, can the guy be any scarier?"

Lana went again at Tim with a more powerful strike. Her friend caught her forearm, and this time his general body movement was perfect. He grabbed her neck, and she saw nothing coming. She found herself again on her back in a blink, winded. *Wow, his* irimi nage *is so smooth and fast now! Can't wait to know how to do it like this.*

Jumping back onto her feet with a dangerous grin, her next attack was a frontal punch to Tim's stomach. He sidestepped, caught her wrist at the same time and twisted it backward, the proper form for a *kotegaeshi*. Lana let herself fall down immediately to protect her joint and limb.

For the next attack, she grabbed both his wrists. "You know how he is..." she whispered. "Old school and all."

To be honest, Honda's attitude made her blood boil. He was right to demand efforts and dedication from everyone, but her Western upbringing rebelled against his unforgiving way of teaching. So Japanese. Such a strict hierarchy. But he had one thing going for him that she would never give to a spineless guy like Richard: her respect. That single bolt of steel that kept her anger in check where he was concerned.

Tim pinned her on the ground, flat on her back, right arm in extension. Despite the pain shooting from her shoulder, elbow and wrist, she mock-punched him in the face from below, showing he had leaned forward too much. He rolled his eyes at his rookie mistake and muttered something unintelligible.

Of course, Honda hadn't missed it. "Martin san, on your feet! Attack him faster, faster! Your timing is wrong, do it again, again, again!" Later, in his coldest and most terrifying voice: "Your feet! Again! What kind of fall is this? Wrong, correct it!"

Bruises started showing up everywhere on her forearms where they collided with Tim's. Despite the cold temperatures, sweat burned her eyes; her breath came out short and ragged, and there was no break in sight. Her comrades, and Tim in particular, were now glancing at her, not bothering to hide their worry.

"Are you okay? What's wrong with the guy?" Tim panted, getting more and more agitated. "That's not how *mudansha* are treated!"

Lana ground her teeth and shook her head, looking for her breath. Her burning lungs felt as if she had run a marathon. "Hush, don't worry, it's hard but fine!"

Being on the blunt end of his criticism strained her nerves. But if she wanted to be truly honest, it bothered her more when he ignored her completely than when he ground her down. *Need for attention much? Grow up girl. You ain't fifteen anymore.*

Back on wobbling feet, she grabbed Tim's arm with both hands; he pivoted next to her and threw her away. Lana rolled forward and landed on her feet again, right in front of their instructor. *Ugh, did he beam himself over here or what?*

Winded, she straightened up and craned her neck, meeting his eyes; Honda had a good head on her. His sheer physical presence played a role in the overall sense of respectful and fearful awe he generated. That and his impeccable technique, which sent the heaviest and most skilled students flying, and made the reputation of their dojo so prestigious.

Something flashed on his unlined and tanned face. He held her stare longer than expected. Puzzled by his scrutiny, slightly out of breath, the shivers running down her spine startled her. But the impulse to reach out to touch his face was even more surprising. Out of nowhere, a blush crept up on her cheeks before she remembered dojo etiquette and offered him a belated, yet respectful bow. *Thank goodness I'm already purple, with any chance he missed that.*

"Martin san," Honda growled, and the fuzzy moment was gone. "Stop talking or leave and don't come back. This is not a coffee shop. You and Johnson san are not focused enough. His technique is messy, and your roll was... barely passable."

Before she could react, he invaded her private sphere like he was more and more prone to do. He extended his hand for her to grab, and she obeyed out of pure reflex. It was cold, yet his skin was warm to the touch, with only strong muscles, sinew and bones under it.

It was impossible to seize his large wrist properly with her smaller hand. Despite the rock-hard sensation, she couldn't help but appreciate the softness of his skin. This wasn't new. But until now, such contact hadn't sent sparks shooting to her core. *Careful, careful, slippery road here!*

She had no time to reflect on her reaction. Quick as lightning, he passed under her arm, turned, crouched down, took hold of her collar, and pressed her lower back with her own twisted arm before thrusting her away from him. A roll broke her fall, but it was another poor one, and she landed too hard on her back. It hurt like hell, but she gritted her teeth and stood up, hiding her irritation at his brusque way of proving his point.

"Your shoulder is still breaking your fall, when it is your arm that should take it. Go over there. You will do forward *ukemi* until the end of this class." Anger washed over Lana at what amounted to punishment in her eyes, but she did her best to hide it.

"Yes Sensei, thank you very much for your explanation," she said, her voice ice-cold. *Cool down. Keep it together. You know how it works here. No talking back. Smooth face. Emotions under a tight lid.*

Still tense, she bowed to Tim to thank him for their intense sparring session and jogged to where Honda had pointed. Thankfully, there were only ten minutes left.

Honda walked up to her side of the *tatami*. His looming presence couldn't be ignored, and the nice sensations flowing from her string of smooth rolls were a relief. Next on her to-do list: the spectacular high falls, the trademark of aikido. She'd get there. With a bit more work.

She got up at his feet and threw an upward look to confirm her self-appraisal was correct, but rod-straight, he stared off in the distance, checking on other people. His minute nod of approval quenched her burst of annoyance.

By the time the session came to a close, her head buzzed and her stomach was queasy. She dashed to the washroom and threw up bile out of sheer exhaustion. After washing her mouth and face, she stared at her reflection in the mirror after brushing back her dark blond hair matted with sweat from her brow. She didn't know whether she wanted to laugh or cry.

That was... intense all right. But I survived! I didn't give up despite all he flung at me! I'll show him, he'll see I can take it.

As she left the restroom, a commotion outside the dojo caught her attention. To her dismay, Tim and Honda were locked in tense confrontation.

"Sensei, please! You need to calm down with Lana, she has done nothing to deserve this treatment!"

"Enough! This is none of your concern."

"Of course, it is! She is my friend and *kohai*! It is also my duty to look after her, and you put her through hell!"

Honda stepped closer to the younger man and towered over him. "I do not have to explain myself to you. This is for her own good."

Exasperated, Tim threw up his hands. "What? Oh, that's just a joke!"

Lana couldn't stand it any longer. Making sure nobody else lurked around, she stepped outside and joined them. "Tim, calm down, there is no problem here," she said in English, placing a calming hand on her friend's shoulder.

But he shrugged her off. "Have you even looked at yourself? You're as white as a sheet, and your legs and hands are shaking. You don't have the level yet!"

With a happy and confident smile, she switched to Japanese. "It's tough, but I can handle it. I... need this kind of conditioning to make real progress."

Bewildered, Tim stared at her. "You're mad!" He turned to Honda. "Sensei, you should know better!"

Honda had reached the end of his patience. Clearly trying to reign in his anger at the other man's lack of respect, he narrowed his eyes at him. "Everything falls well within her limits. I welcome her strong desire to progress."

Lana bowed with gratitude. "Thank you, Sensei. Tim, all is fine, okay?" Her friend threw her a piercing glare but her calm attitude seemed to convince him. He grumbled, bowed to their instructor in a less than stellar fashion, and left them.

To her surprise, Honda made eye contact. Although his face was the usual blank mask that he favored, once again the intensity of his glare took her aback. "Stay behind for a while. There is something we need to address, you and I." His clipped words left no place for discussion.

Even though she longed for a hot shower and was more than a little hungry, Lana nodded, curious as to what this was about, and more than a bit anxious to clear the air.

Lila Mina

3

Obedience and Respect

After everyone had left, Lana joined Honda on the mats. As usual, he had folded neatly his *hakama* and sat now in *seiza*–the 'correct' Japanese way of kneeling so many adult Westerners find too difficult to adopt, legs underneath thighs, and buttocks resting on heels. This was his habit, but also what aikido etiquette required. Facing him, she mirrored his posture.

"Martin san, let's talk about your attitude, which is less than appropriate. There are basic rules in the dojo everyone is expected to follow, even foreigners."

Lana straightened, trying to smooth her face and hide her stupor at such criticism. "My apologies, Sensei, I never meant to cause offence. But I don't understand what I'm doing wrong."

Eyes narrowing, he leaned toward her. "This, for example. You should learn how to apologize the proper way."

She couldn't help a frown. *Apologize? For doing what?*

Time to play the language and culture card. Her professional Japanese was much better than her vernacular; it was easy for her to miss subtleties and hints.

"I am truly sorry, Sensei, is it the words I use? I don't know all the proper expressions... please tell me what I should say?" Her tone was even and proper, but the situation was ridiculous.

"No, not your words; your words are more or less fine. I am talking about your attitude. You are a student. A white belt. A woman. Twenty years younger than me. Bow! Lower. Your. Eyes! Don't look at me directly and assume you may challenge me!" he bellowed, barely containing the booming earthquake in his voice.

Unimpressed, Lana pinched her lips, and her fingers curled on her lap. The tension of her difficult day came back with a vengeance, sweeping away the benefits of their practice night. The man was infuriating but not the first to act like this with her. She led business negotiations every day with shark lawyers and hungry CEOs who assumed she was there to take dictation or serve them tea. She respected him, yes, but unconditional deference bordering on mindless obedience, because of who she was? *Hell no.*

"Sensei..." The growl in her voice was loud. Without thinking, she copied his move and leaned forward, refusing to let him invade her space with impunity. She could see now his quick pulse beating in his neck. Much too close for propriety, but they had other priorities.

His body heat washed over her, and she repressed a furious urge to inhale his scent. *Come on, focus girl, now is not the right time for that!*

"Yes, you are my sensei, and I should express my respect better, I guess. But I wouldn't grovel in front of my father, nor my husband, if I had one, and certainly not my boss. So, why should I do it with you?"

Lana knew she was out of line. She was supposed to nod and keep quiet. There was no valid excuse for talking back to your instructor or even your senior in Japan. A great example of cultural clash, but it was one of those days where she had to draw a line against cultural adaptation. *I shouldn't be the only one making the effort here, he could also be a bit more understanding and flexible, dammit!*

Honda's eyes blackened, and his next move caught her unprepared. With one hand, he grabbed the jacket of her *dogi* and pulled her easily to him, nostrils flaring; he was as strong as an ox and had decades of martial arts training under his belt. With a strangled yelp, Lana caught herself on his arm and leg to avoid crashing onto his lap.

Of course, she should have tried one of the dozen techniques she had learned to free herself, but she had no chance against him. Her mind wandered off track again at such close contact. *My goodness, it's not just his arms that are hard. That thigh is as solid as marble. How would it feel if –*

"This is unacceptable," he rasped, face inches away from hers. "Don't think natural skills and even less a pretty face can absolve you from your duties. You will not get a pass simply because you are not Japanese. You will learn your proper place in relation to me!"

She snapped back to the problem at hand, forgetting her ridiculous train of thought and overlooking his awkward compliment. The nerve of the guy! He had a temper for sure, but this was something else. It was ridiculous to ask this of her! Foreigners weren't supposed to master the art of 'mutual relation positioning'.

Social hierarchy between people in Japan, and the etiquette rules that differed in every relationship, even among family members, were much too complex to learn if you were not taught them from birth. This was outlandish.

A storm of frustration and exasperation, and something else she refused to name, snapped the last threads of her self-control.

"Really? And what is this place then? Please teach me because this silly little girl can't figure it out by herself..." she retorted with the low, calm voice she used with challenging clients.

Did she hear an actual growl coming from deep inside him? And was it only anger burning in his eyes? Her breath caught, eyes widening as realization struck. *No way! Is he also...?*

Still clutching her jacket, Honda jammed Lana on her back with one swift move, even though her legs were still under her. She yelped and slammed the mats with her open palm, requesting release. But against every rule, he did not relent, far from it. The next second, he was over her, one hand on each arm, a knee between her thighs.

"Here. Under me," he hissed, panting hard, eyes staring at her mouth.

There were ways to get out of his hold, but the feeling coiling in her stomach stopped her from trying.

Lust.

It was now evident in Honda's eyes too, but Lana didn't believe their confrontation would resolve peacefully.

What a particular way to make the first move! But who cares? This guy is one fine piece of alpha male, and angry sex... well, that's the best legal drug out there. But boy, you don't know who you've got under you. You're going to have to fight and show me your secret moves to keep me here! Not everybody gets to make me submit in bed.

Lana growled in return and bucked her hips, which ground him against her even more. It was the first time she felt a real sense of his weight and mass, and as fit and strong as she was, her full strength would not be able to handle it.

The tension running in his arms and neck, his hard panting, showed how much he struggled to keep himself in check. As infuriating, angry and aroused as he was, Honda was an honorable man and would not force himself upon her; her consent had to be crystal clear.

"I see," she kept cool and quirked an eyebrow as if they were chatting over coffee. Lack of shouting and wriggling would show him she was considering playing his game. She raised her head as much as her position allowed and whispered in his ear. "But what do you plan to do to keep me here willingly? Please be... convincing," she hissed before biting his earlobe.

A grunt passed his lips. He released one of her hands to catch her throat and bring her back to the ground. His grip was light enough that she could breathe, but it was a warning.

"I will show you, and then you will give me true obedience."

With a sharp intake of breath, she locked eyes with him. "I swear I will, but only if you make me beg," she rasped.

Months later, she'd wonder why the earth hadn't shaken or lightning struck when she had spoken those fateful words.

Honda's body relaxed as if her pledge untied a knot inside him. He thrust his thumb into her mouth. She licked it without breaking eye contact, a devilish smile fleeting on her lips. She was pushing it; she was trying her best to position herself as his equal in their tumbling game, and it was bound to make him even more frustrated and angry. This could actually be a lot of fun.

He brought his lips just over hers. "Oh, when I am done with you, you will. You will call me *goshujin sama*," he vowed with the first smirk of the evening.

Her eyes widened. He had used the highly traditional word for 'one's lord' or... 'one's husband'. That was pushing this game a little too far! But there was no time to come up with a witty reply. His mouth crashed on hers, his tongue invading her. He was rough; he was overwhelming; he went for the kill. But because the goal was to make her beg for more, he was also systematic.

Busy kissing her roughly, Honda untied her belt and pants, opened her jacket and pushed everything away to get plenty of access to her body. His hand wasted no time fondling her clit and pushing two thick fingers inside her. They slipped in easily as she was already wet, aroused by their verbal sparring. She couldn't help a low moan escaping into his mouth.

Still, Lana refused to relent. Granted, this had been a typhoon months in the making, but a pledge, her word, was at stake. She wouldn't offer him his prize on a plate. She launched herself in a battle of tongues to see if she could invade him in turn. Her hand grabbed his *dogi* lapel to pull herself up against him, to show him her matching desire, but also to get access to his skin.

His free hand pulled on her hair. Lana's abs screamed, the only muscles keeping her up. She ignored the discomfort. There were many more important things than pain at this moment.

His hand left her wet pussy to untie his own *dogi* pants. His hardness pressed against her entrance. Lana opened her legs as much as she could. Honda twisted her hair, broke their kiss and sunk his teeth into her neck. At the same time, he slipped into her.

Lana cried out, both in pain and pleasure. He was thick and long, hitting deep spots inside her. She let go of him and arched her back, giving him more access. Her fingers caught his sleeve; she twisted it hard to hold on to something. Her other hand landed on his chest, and gripped it, not caring if she hurt him. Given these new aspects of his personality he was showing her, pain had to be at least manageable, if not arousing.

As a form of retaliation, Honda kept on biting and licking the mark he had made, still buried deep inside her.

Hold it together, dammit, hold it! Don't give in yet! This single thought swirled in the back of her head. Her determination was nearly shot to pieces when he thrust at a fast pace. She couldn't move: his teeth still pressed her neck, the jaws of a hungry beast catching its prey. Her nails raked his chest, leaving deep and angry red marks behind. The tempest of emotions raging inside her left her panting.

Honda released her, sliding out and sitting up before grasping her hips to turn her face down. He pushed her until she was flat on the floor, squeezed between the mats and his body. She grunted, trying to get on her knees to gain leverage but he was much too heavy.

When he began pounding into her again, she could only let him have his way. His teeth grazed her skin once more, this time on her shoulder. His harsh bite drew blood, which he sucked and licked away. His sheer passion, his bare hunger ignited Lana's arousal as much as his primitive rutting.

How? How does he know? Why am I so turned on? Where does this perfect chemistry come from? It's crazy!

Heat shot from her core and, strangely enough, from somewhere right below her ribs. Her whole body was on fire, all rational thoughts evaporating like water under the midday sun. Sweat erupted on her back and chest. Unable to control her grunts and moans, she used the pain radiating from her shoulder to fuel her will.

He let go of her and easily caught her chin to turn her head toward him, claiming her mouth once again.

Tasting her own blood in his mouth, she decided to return the favor one way or another.

Her orgasm was building up fast, but it was his own release and feral growl in her mouth that pushed Lana over the edge. Her body started to shake, and her eyes rolled back when she let out a throaty shout. For a few minutes, he stayed where he was, his body a warm blanket over hers. Deeply satisfied, Lana hummed while tremors still made her quiver.

There was a problem, however, and they both knew it.

She had not relented. She had shown him her strength.

Without any comment, Honda straightened up, bringing her along to make her straddle him. Sweat trickled along her heaving chest to her navel. She swept her hair out of her eyes with her arm, where *tatami* burns already bloomed in large bruises. But she remained steady.

Honda caressed her face, glanced at his bite marks—purple and red, showing the indent of his teeth—while deft fingers pinched and twisted a hard nipple. A small moan escaped her; a hand slid up in his hair and gripped it, the other roamed on his powerful and smooth chest where she had left slight scars. Strong muscles rippled under his soft and taut skin. Not a trace of fat in sight.

Damn, it should be illegal to look so good at his age.

He pressed his mouth to her ear. "You are strong; I doubt you have met a man who could match you before me. But I know what it would take to overwhelm you."

Her anger soared up again. Lana licked her dry lips and wriggled on his lap. *Oh, you're so full of yourself! Making me cum once–even hard–doesn't make you the king of my castle yet!*

She bit back a nasty comment and a grin. He would undoubtedly need time to recover given his age. Instead, she chose a silent challenge: she licked his jaw from his right ear toward his mouth. Her nails dug deeper along his ribs, leaving new angry red marks behind.

This time Honda grunted in a mix of pain and pleasure. He pulled her head back. Their eyes locked. His intensity, his iron will, and the energy coursing under his skin made her shiver with renewed arousal.

A dark and raging tempest swirled inside her. An odd recognition tugging at her bones, like rusty old gears getting back into motion. She could tame this man, but deep down, submitting to him didn't sound so bad after all. She had never been so exhilarated and aroused, and certainly not so fast.

Honda pushed her down, but this time he kept her in his arms and moved with her, spooning against her back, his soft member against her ass. Her half-naked body was now exposed. In this position, there was no way to grasp him or hold him without exerting significant effort.

His hand roamed over her body, caressing and pinching her skin. He kissed and licked her neck, nibbling it now and then, sending shivers running along her spine. Sharp teeth caught her earlobe and pulled hard. She hissed and tried to move away, without success. He had wrapped himself around her limbs.

"Ready, little *mudansha*?" he purred. Her 'novice' pet-name warmed her heart.

She blinked in confusion, but then felt his fingers at her entrance. First, only two, then three, stretching her and going deep. Little electric shocks made her sigh and groan, but while it was nice and pleasurable, there was nothing extraordinary to it.

She closed her eyes to enjoy a more languid pace than before. He brushed her clit now and then and licked her burning and sweaty skin; her inner muscles clenched around him in response. The guy had technique and skills, well beyond aikido.

But when he added a fourth finger, Lana gasped and twisted her upper body to face him, incredulous. *No way! Is he going to... Just like this?...*

Face blank, he stared back at her, a silent challenge in his eyes. She opened her mouth to protest, but words turned to a snarl as he slid his thumb in, completing the fist inside her.

Lana hissed, and shut her eyes. Her nails dug in his arms to keep herself grounded in reality. He wasn't moving, but his hand was overwhelming. To her utter embarrassment, sobs built deep inside her and swam to the surface. It was painful, yes, almost too much so. Still, the intense growing pleasure mingling with a craving for more couldn't be denied.

Again, that pull, that tug. Deep inside her, something sat caged, and Honda, of all men, rattled its bars and nearly drove her mad.

Out of breath, sweating, half sobbing, she summoned all her strength to grasp his lapel again and pull herself close. "What... are.... you... doing... to... me?" Lana grunted through clenched teeth, not caring to hide her anger. The onslaught of pleasurable pain—or was it painful pleasure?—made her light-headed.

"Getting you to kneel at my feet. Demanding your allegiance of spirit and body," he growled back, turning his fist inside her, and pushing a little bit further. At his words, something exploded inside her and her vision turned black for a split second. She didn't groan; she roared and let go of his jacket to snatch his invading arm, but it was of course useless: his wrist was so thick her hand couldn't cover it entirely.

He took his time licking the sweat off her neck. "Shall I stop? Is this too much for you?"

And right then, she lost.

"No, please! I... beg... you, I... need this... Honda Sensei..." Her body shook with repressed desire.

"*Goshujin sama*," he reminded her with a short bark, taking half his hand out.

She hissed in anger and frustration. A sob wracked her body again, and she twisted his jacket, pulling herself against him once again. "Please, *goshujin sama*! Fill me and make me come hard..." she whispered, her voice low and tight, tears flowing on her burning cheeks.

It killed her to beg, but she couldn't bear to lose that feeling before completion. He pushed back inside her and started thrusting, in and out, slowly but with purpose. Her world disappeared, her mind blanked out, the thing inside her roared and broke free, and a crashing wave swept her away. She forgot her name, lost her bearings and finally consciousness for a few heartbeats.

Lana opened her eyes to find herself in his arms, face buried against a perspiring chest bearing the signs of her passion. His rapid heartbeat drummed under her ear, and for a split second, she wished she could remain there all night. Something wet and sticky covered her back.

She smiled against his skin, feeling smug and somewhat vindicated. *Well well well... look at that... bringing me down to heel made you hard and happy all over again...*

Their eyes met. She didn't trust her voice yet. To her intense satisfaction, his composure was far from pristine. Beads of sweat covered his hairline, and his breath was ragged. Honda gazed at her with narrowed eyes; her test wasn't over.

A new part of her wanted to be held and hugged, to be cradled. But the other part, more familiar and strong as steel, did not want to hear about such things. Cuddling and whispering sweet nonsense were for lovestruck couples; whatever they were, this wasn't it. *But what? What is this?*

Ignoring her sore body parts, Lana disentangled herself, and he let her go without any further comment. She put her *dogi* back in order. Though her legs and nether regions protested, she drew away from him and sat in *seiza*.

She had gambled and lost, she had to relent and concede defeat. Caught in her burning desire and voracious hunger, she had pledged to submit, and she wasn't one to go back on her given word. Above all in a country where this was taken so seriously.

She bowed her head to the ground, her forehead on her hands in front of her. "My deepest gratitude for this precious gift, *goshujin sama*, and my most sincere apologies for my behavior in the past," she intoned. She waited for his signal, but for a few minutes, nothing came. The only thing she heard was the rush of blood in her ears.

"Straighten up," he grunted.

Hands flat on her lap, she kept her eyes lowered to the ground, trying her best to school her behavior even though it was unfamiliar territory for her.

To her surprise, he moved closer, within her arm's reach. "Do you understand now what I expect of you?"

"I believe I do." Truth to be told, she was confused, and more than a little curious. To go from such an extraordinary intimacy to a businesslike interaction in a couple of heartbeats was new. It was quite different from past experiences, even one-night stands, because for a while there, they had exchanged something powerful.

Honda took her chin and lifted it up. He scrutinized her face, searching for clues hinting at rebellion, lies or hidden thoughts. She did her best to keep her gaze neutral and non-aggressive.

Fingers tightening on her jaw, Honda quirked an eyebrow, pointing at his chest. "You hurt me on purpose. Do you plan to repeat this in the future?"

Ah yes, my nails. That was fun! I wish I had drawn blood though... Then his question registered.

"You plan to do this again?" she blurted out, surprise and hopeful anticipation swelling in her.

Honda chuckled and didn't let go of her chin. "Anxious for more, aren't we? Teaching you how to check your temper and your quick tongue when it comes to me seems indeed to require more... practice. Answer my question."

Lana breathed in deeply, unsure of what would be the right reply. "It... would be my pleasure to do it again if you wish me to," she articulated. *Hot as hell would be a better word, but hey...*

"Better. And yes, I would have you do it in the future, as I will mark you again, in many ways. Your resilience is remarkable. It opens the door to many possibilities." His voice was calm and expressionless as if discussing some fine points related to an aikido technique, but his words sent new shivers down her spine.

"I thought you didn't want me to show strength toward you," she pointed out, face controlled, suppressing new waves of excitement at what he suggested.

His hand swept from her chin to her cheeks and finally rested on her neck. "Do not confuse obedient respect with weakness, or strength with childish opposition, Lana san. You will need all your resourcefulness of mind and body to handle my demands. Battle hard against me. I am not interested in dolls. You already saw a little of this today, didn't you?"

Again, some form of dark joy bloomed inside her chest. A kind of relief that left her wondering about her repressed desires. "Yes. So, does it mean you want to push me until I break?"

Honda tutted and clenched his hand on her neck, keeping it just below the threshold of pain. "No, I do not wish to break you at all. I want to make you stronger, to make you realize you can go much further than you think. But you need to put yourself into my hands, into my care, and accept I do know better, even when it comes to your body. You need to show me absolute obedience."

Baffled, Lana recoiled a little. *Hold on, where are we going with this?* "Forgive me, but I want to do it my way just for a minute." Time to test his willingness to respect her limits. He removed his hand from her neck, and she regained some freedom. Arms crossed, she moved into full business negotiation mode. "Will I be able to put an end to this if I want to?"

His eyes narrowed at her stiff and direct body language, but she didn't look away or back down. He had to understand she was willing to play this game only because she liked it, not because he was domineering his way through.

"You may decide to stop everything at any time. Of course, such a decision would not affect your aikido practice here, although be aware that I plan to raise the bar of my expectations, given your skills and potential for growth."

She nodded, happy that this was out of the way. Moving on to the most important part. "How much will my consent matter?"

"Your consent is key, and you must always express your limits. This is what I want: your willing obedience and sincere show of respect. We will decide on safe words and gestures you may use."

"And what would you call our... relationship?"

He hesitated. "Like the one we share in this dojo; a form of training."

Lana couldn't help a frown. Training? Of the sexual kind? Is that what they called friends with benefits, a submissive or a mistress here? Well, fluffier emotions were to be kept at bay. All fine in her book. She had no time for that.

"I understand, thank you. Well then," she said, taking a deep breath and once again bowing her head to the floor. "Then, *goshujin sama, yoroshiku onegai itashimasu*," she stated in a clear and strong voice.

This was an everyday polite expression of gratitude, but she had used the most formal register to increase their significance; this time, it went well beyond usual politeness. She was *literally* putting herself in his hands, in his care. Goosebumps broke out on her skin, and a sudden acute pain shooting from somewhere below her sternum made her grimace in annoyance. It wasn't a good time for acid burns.

Honda replied in kind and bowed to her in return, but not as low, because in his book his social status put him above hers. And now that they were into this dom/sub thing... he was even more entitled to it. While this still bothered her at some level, she had agreed to play his game. They straightened up again, and he bid her good night, leaving her to her own thoughts in the deserted dojo.

Lila Mina

4

Losing Control and Denial

TWO WEEKS LATER, on a sunny but cold Saturday afternoon, Lana stood in front of a hotel entrance. The establishment was fifteen or twenty stories high, and in the same district as their dojo and her condo. Maybe Honda lived nearby, too.

She cringed and double-checked the note he had given her. The address was correct. With its fancy façade made of fake European-style red bricks and blind windows, it was a love hotel. An upscale one, for sure, but it would be a big first for her. *Why pick this kind of place? Well, as if I would ask him! I guess we won't spend the night, thank goodness. Talk about... awkward.*

She had waited for their first real date with trepidation. Remaining aloof and professional during training wasn't an issue. And indeed, there had been no trace of innuendo or any dubious gesture hinting at something else. Quite the opposite: Honda had become merciless and relentless with her. Nothing had transpired, no arched eyebrow made her uncomfortable. The rumor mill was silent.

Their new dynamics outside the mats was another story. A string of meetings and deadlines at work hadn't given her time to dwell on it though. Maybe confiding in Gabriella would be a good call. Still, something kept Lana from doing it. She wasn't ready to hear hard truths about herself and the delicate position frolicking with her instructor had put her in.

"So, cold feet, hmm? Maybe he's not worth it, after all?" Lana jumped out of her skin and glanced around, frantically searching for the origin of the shrill voice.

What the—?

An old woman, with more wrinkles on her face than Lana had hair on her head, stood behind her, a large toothless smile on her parched lips. She was small—no, diminutive. Her back and legs bent unnaturally, certainly due to decades of hard labor in rice fields. Surprise quickly turned into irritation.

"*Obaa san!* Sorry, do I know you?" *Old folks! How come they always meddle in people's lives?*

If possible, the woman's grin turned even wider. But there was no glee in the piercing glare she threw at Lana, who shuddered. Goosebumps covered her arms.

"So flustered, did I hit a nerve? You've been gawking at the entrance for five minutes now. Either he's really bad at it or more than you can handle," she said with a loud cackle that followed her until she disappeared around the corner of street.

Lana remained frozen on her spot for a few minutes, rattled by the brief interaction with the old hag. Then her initial annoyance turned into aggravation. *More than I can handle? Ha! As if!*

With a vengeance, she strolled toward the hotel and stepped inside. In this business, discretion was key. No staff at the check-in counter, everything was automated. As often in Japan, the black marble floor was so squeaky clean you could eat off it. The walls and windows were spotless, and low-key jazz music played from hidden speakers. By far, not a shady motel.

The elevator brought her to the 8th floor. Several drink and food vending machines were lined up opposite the elevator, next to one with prepaid cards for video on demand. Even more revealing, another offered a wide range of condoms coming in all sizes and flavors.

Her odd meeting in the street forgotten, she gawked at the machine selling dozens of colorful sex toys, at a total loss with the impossible shapes of some of them. Her fingers hovered near the slot containing an extra-large double dildo, but a burst of shyness held her back. *Let's go empty-handed this time... I'll bring along weapons next time.*

Snickering at her poor martial arts joke, she walked down the empty hall saturated with bright pink and golden decorations running under the ceiling until she reached the door of room 812. A thought struck her, freezing her hand mid-air.

Would their room have any theme? The idea of finding him in a room filled with Hello Kitty memorabilia, or something tacky like leopard patterns had her suppress a fit of giggles. But she snorted loudly as the image of a dungeon-like, BDSM-themed room popped up in her mind, with Honda sprawled on the bed, wearing only crotchless leather pants and a spiked collar. Her explosive laughter would bring the whole affair to a trashy and painful end, and she would have to find another dojo.

Nerves, nerves! Get yourself together, girl. Lana took several deep breaths to clear her mind from those treacherous thoughts and knocked on the door at exactly 3 pm.

"Come in," came Honda's voice, and she stepped inside.

"*Ojama shimasu.*" She used the traditional greeting when entering someone's home, to apologize for disturbing them. To her great relief, it was a normal *tatami* room with nothing special, at least at first sight. No furniture except for a low coffee table he had pushed against a wall, and he hadn't rolled out the *futon* mattress, folded in a corner. Tatami *burns, here we come!*

She removed her shoes in the entrance before stepping up on the raised floor. She knelt and bowed in formal greeting, like at the dojo.

"Good afternoon, Lana san. I am pleased to see you here." His voice was neutral, neither warm nor cold. He was dashing in dark blue *yukata* pants and jacket. While not his aikido gear, it still spoke to his culture and fit his bulky body to a T.

Well, thank you, o ye local deities of lust and passion, I'm a lucky girl.

"Before we begin, is there anything else you would like to tell me about your training?"

She shook her head, declining the way out that he handed to her. "No, everything is fine. Harsh and challenging, but fine. I enjoy it."

Honda nodded, shoulders and jaw relaxing. "Very well. We do not have much time. Stand up, take off your clothes and then come sit near me, little *mudansha*." His use of her 'pet name' signaled formally that things were on their way.

"Yes, *goshujin sama*." She removed her jeans, purple blouse and white camisole, as well as her royal blue underwear, folded everything neatly and approached him.

With her dark honey hair and chestnut eyes, she was used to standing out in any crowd in Japan. Her looks weren't the only things singling her out. While not self-conscious, and happy with her well-toned and shapely body, she stood taller and weighed more than most Japanese women.

Of course, Honda had already shown he appreciated her body, but still. She wondered what he made of her broad shoulders, muscled arms, and strong thighs. She wasn't especially classy or feminine. He didn't make any comment though. No leering, no lewd comments. It was almost a professional, clinical stare, except for the low-burning desire emanating from him. A pleasing sizzle of anticipation raced up her spine.

Something else stirred, too. A thirst. A craving she couldn't deny.

Temper: Deference

"We will work with clear safe words and gestures. At any time, if you cannot proceed for whatever reason, just say 'red'. If you cannot speak, tap the ground or your chest, like at practice. Do not hesitate to do it, in particular in the beginning, as we are still assessing your limits and abilities. Is this clear?"

Lana nodded. Honda could overcome her without any difficulty, so it was important to clarify this. For now, he came off as less abrupt than at the dojo, and she appreciated it. *Was he really so mad at my attitude back then?*

"Let's begin by working on those marks you seem to like giving me." He took off his clothes but kept his *yukata* jacket on his back, merely untying the strings. Her breath caught; his entire body was massive yet shaped by his years of training and rigorous regimen. "Come here."

Lana obeyed, using *shikko*, the special form of knee-walking used in martial arts to approach people respectfully, without standing up. Before she knew it, he had swept her on her back, performing a form of *irimi nage* where the attacker was slammed down, pulled at the collar from behind. Honda held her now pinned to the ground. Before Lana could check herself, her anger flared, and a loud growl passed her lips. He was already hard, his erection pressing against her thigh.

Knowing he waited for it and acting on a fiery need to fight back, Lana raked her nails on his chest, leaving long red marks behind her. Honda grunted and checked her level of readiness by dipping two fingers inside her. She whimpered, welcoming the intrusion, and licked his chest to encourage him. The entire situation hit all the right spots and made her pussy wet.

Without any further ado, not bothering with more foreplay, he slid into her and began pumping into her at a slow but powerful pace. She held onto his upper back with all her strength; each thrust ripped a moan from her. The friction, the places he touched, the energy rippling under his skin made her lightheaded. Her desire grew with each passing second: to be at his mercy while driving him over the edge fueled her arousal and filled her with boundless energy.

"Harder," Honda uttered, showing he had to control himself to not pound into her. "Go deeper with your nails, make me bleed."

Lana dug her fingers harder in his shoulders until droplets of blood oozed out. Honda quickened his thrusts. Her moans turned into a single breathy lament and perspiration broke out on her body.

On an impulse, she locked eyes with him. Careful, methodical, she began to lick his blood, pressing her tongue on his skin, lapping the dark rich red liquid. She had never done this before. So filthy and decadent.

Her vision darkened, and a rush of arousal jolted her. She came hard, clamping his dick inside her.

He stopped moving and gave her a feral smile. "Good... you are learning... continue, dig hard and lick me."

With a whimper, Lana complied and soon she was lost again in the delirious pleasure of sucking his skin and blood, while his shaft continued to make her body shake. He sat down on his knees and brought her up. In this position, she could ride him and continue to lavish on his chest. She groaned, hungry pleasure blanking out any form of rational thought.

She ground herself on his hard member, but Honda stopped her and made them face the same direction, her back against his chest. He parted her cheeks and guided himself toward her tight asshole. Surprised, Lana hissed and arched her back; his strong grip made it impossible to move away.

"What is our safe word, little *mudansha*?" he whispered in her ear, his erection at her back, demanding entrance.

"R... red," she panted.

"Do you want to say it now?"

Lana moved back against him. "No... no," she whispered, eyes shut.

"All right, then relax, let me in..." His voice was deep and low, much like during practice when her shoulder was too tense to do a technique properly. She focused on her breath and created a mental picture of every muscle in her body. Time to uncoil them, to set aside any discomfort and anticipate the pleasure that would come afterward.

At first, there were only his fingers, massaging, probing, stretching, shooting electricity along her back. Then, after long minutes of delicious torture, with slow moves but without hesitation, he resumed pushing.

Once again, she moaned loudly, a new part of herself stretched beyond reason. But soon the burning friction became pleasurable, and she rejoiced in this absolute fullness. He started thrusting. It wouldn't be possible to hold it for long.

"Ah, this... this... is... hm amazing... ah, please..." She was babbling but couldn't care less. Honda twisted his hand in her hair and yanked her head. He pressed his lips to hers, and she gave him the taste of his own blood as he worked her ass. After a few minutes, he growled into her mouth and came long and hard inside her, triggering her own powerful orgasm.

A thin sheen of perspiration covered her. Her slippery and shiny body couldn't stop quivering, and tears blurred her sight. She couldn't believe how the man kept unlocking hidden vaults inside her, one after the other. It wasn't only about new positions. Why was it so easy to submit to this guy? *Careful, careful,*

careful girl... this can become a bit too addictive for comfort. Don't get lost, now!

She tried to get herself under control. Honda was still buried deep inside her and holding her tight. While she enjoyed giving him total control over their intense couplings, she was also intent in not revealing too much of her weakness toward him. *Don't expose yourself, don't let him rule anything else than this, don't give him power over the rest.*

Honda buried his face in her neck, below her hairline and... purred? But he was anything but a kitten. Rather a tiger, going for the jugular of his plaything. Her fingers traced invisible lines on his folded legs, then up along the hand and arm holding her fast. She wondered if he had other partners like her or a wife for that matter.

"You are thinking too much again," Honda growled against her skin.

Lana had to take a couple of breaths, lest she express her exasperation and renewed anger at his insufferable ability to read her. "What makes you say this?"

He pinched a nipple hard and smirked at her annoyance at the gesture. "Your shoulders tense and your jaw clenches when you are trying to figure something out. You do it at practice with new or more difficult techniques. You don't let your body take control, learn by itself and speak on its own."

"I don't do it so much!" But her protest was weak. Her face burned in embarrassment at his obvious criticism of her brainy attitude. She was proud of her many accomplishments and analysis skills.

"Every single time. And you are still doing it now. You fight against your body, you try to keep it under control. But you have so many things locked in your *hara,* trying to get out. You need to at least acknowledge them."

While he spoke, his fingers left her nipple. They moved lower to rest against her *hara,* the area below the navel that was the center of balance and inner power according to aikido and other martial arts.

Then something unexpected happened.

The second his hand pressed there—ever so softly— her throat constricted, her head swam and the second most powerful panic attack she had ever experienced overwhelmed her.

"R....red! Red! Just... Just let me go, now!" All pretenses of obedience flew out of the window as walls crashed down on her head and nausea swelled in her throat.

Honda released his grip and she rolled over, far from him. Head on her arms, eyes shut, Lana tried to get back in touch with reality. She felt completely disconnected. *Just like when...*

She blocked the disruptive thought. That cursed memory lane was a strict no-go. Rather, she tried to ground herself back in her surroundings like her therapist had taught her so many years before.

"Empty your mind, focus on your breathing," he instructed her from afar quietly; he had enough sense to not try to get near her.

It took her several minutes to get her wits back. When she was herself again, she straightened up and sat again in *seiza*, still facing away from him. Her sternum began to burn, and to her embarrassment, her hands shook.

"I... I apologize, I have no idea why I reacted like this." Lana avoided looking at him. "I don't know what happened."

It made no sense. How could his hand on her belly cause such a reaction? After his other, much more invasive and aggressive moves she had welcomed with pleasure?

"Truly?" Honda challenged her with a growl. "You have been through this before though."

Lana cast him a sharp glance. He didn't have the right to dig through her past. "Perhaps," she snapped back. "Still, I don't understand why your move triggered... it." She wouldn't use the word 'panic' aloud. Certainly not with him.

It was surreal to have such a conversation while stark naked, disheveled and covered with bruises. A testament to their respective levels of self-control, it didn't seem to matter. Lana couldn't deny it was tough to stare at him without getting distracted. She was already too much attuned to his sensuality and body for her own good.

"Well, I do." His arrogance floored her. "Like I said, you are repressing too much, and in time of great... release, this leads to impossible emotional pressure, to excruciating tension, and your body rebels."

Lana couldn't help her snarl. "So, you know what this means, you've experienced it? Well, I wouldn't be surprised given the close check you keep on your emotions. Must be fun when everything blows up!"

With an angry hiss, Honda knee-walked closer to her. It took her a lot to not step back, yet she tensed. She wasn't ready to resume their physical rounds. He stopped before he could touch her.

"Careful, little *mudansha*, mind your attitude and words. Even according to your low Western standards, you are treading into dangerous, disrespectful waters," he warned her.

Lana lowered her eyes and breathed through her nose. "My apologies, *goshujin sama*," she replied.

"Yes, I control my emotions, as well as my needs and desires, but I acknowledge every single one of them. I don't hide from them but decide whether or not to show them or act upon them. You understand the difference, right?"

Again, Lana shuddered. *Yes, of course I do. And you're too right for comfort. I can't do this. I love it, but I can't.*

As long as she wasn't clear about her own needs, she couldn't be sure she could avoid another panic attack.

"I understand the difference. As it is, I cannot continue what we began, I am truly sorry to admit it. There is much I have to address."

Honda tensed and remained silent for a while, lips pinched in a scowl. "I see. This is unfortunate. You could also let me help you confront this."

How tempting. "Yes, of course, but you are not my therapist, and I fear you might even be part of the problem. Or at least my reaction to you could be. I regret being so... weak. My apologies." Her stomach churned at the admission, and another burst of pain made her wince. "Please respect my decision and release me from our agreement." She bowed her head to the ground.

Honda hissed, frustrated, but nodded once. "I regret this outcome but will respect your decision. I hope you will not consider quitting your aikido training."

Lana bowed again. "Thank you very much for your understanding. As for aikido, I will not quit practice as I have much to learn from you, Sensei. In time, I hope to be able to address my issues."

They bowed to each other and Lana quickly put her clothes back on before taking her leave. When the door closed behind her, she let out a shaky breath, and her stomach whirled. A bottle of wine sounded amazing. The idea of confronting him the next day made her cringe, but there was no way she would dodge that. She wouldn't add 'coward' to her personal list of 'weak' and 'psychologically impaired'.

Dammit, that old crone was right. He's too much for me.

5

Attempting to Move On

SEVERAL WEEKS PASSED in a blur. To Lana's relief, relying on their mutual professionalism, training had resumed with no awkwardness nor discomfort. Honda's stern attitude and sour expressions hadn't changed, and his intensive regimen left her exhausted three times a week.

She didn't complain, welcoming this chance to progress the hard, traditional way in aikido. But her body wouldn't let her forget. Her mind still spun with newly unearthed emotions she had buried for far too long.

One morning, Lana received an invitation to attend the wedding of two of her sempai, Ryota Takeda and Miyuki Kinoshita, at the end of April. As the groom was one of the grandmaster's in-house students, having dedicated his life to aikido, they had invited everyone. Lana disliked going to weddings by herself though. She considered declining.

The wedding—and whether to go without a date—occupied her thoughts for weeks. In addition, fresh work deadlines distracted her. So distracted, in fact, she almost didn't notice Frank, one of the IT managers, when she entered their floor kitchen space to fix herself a cup of coffee. He happened to be one of the handful of native French speakers of their office, so they often chatted together when they met up like this.

Frank looked up from his coffee mug and threw her a large grin. "Lana! Hey, how are you on this bright and shiny morning?"

"Not too bad, thanks." Rummaging in the cabinet over the sink, she put her hand on the last clean cup available. "You?"

"Well, except that it's Monday, and I'm already in dire need of a break, I'm peachy! I spent all Sunday on the tennis court. Man, it felt good to sweat." He stretched his arms over his head, ostensibly showing off his flat stomach. "I should go easy on my right knee though."

Not impressed by his antics, she gave him a slide glance and a wry grin. "Really? From what you've told me, I'd say the number one risk is twisting your wrist emptying too many cocktails at the lounge club..."

The picture of fake offended shock, Frank made a 'who, me?' face before chuckling in his coffee and sitting at the round table. He wasn't ready to go to work yet.

Not in the mood for more meaningless chit chat, Lana was about to leave when an idea crossed her mind. From behind her mug, she gave Frank a hard look. If she had to be honest, he had never hit her radar. Tall and broad-shouldered, about her age, he was handsome enough, but they had never talked about anything besides work and generic topics. His college student attitude and self-bragging were more than a little annoying.

However, she had a no-date problem on her hands. A real big one. With her limited social life, fueled by her lack of interest in hitting bars, she was running out of time. *And who knows, maybe it's just his work façade, and he's quite a decent guy. If I'm lucky, something else could come out of this in the long run.*

Time to switch to more regular guys in any case. Clearly, bigger fish are out.

"Hm, Frank, don't freak out, but I've got a favor to ask you."

"Oh! Go ahead, shoot! Anything as long as it's not too illegal," he said with an exaggerated wink. She repressed a burning need to eye-roll.

"Nah, but could be a bit of a bother, pompous and all. I've got a wedding coming up two weeks from now, and no date. Would you be fine coming with me? If you're free, of course. You mentioned dating someone from accounting a couple of months ago..."

"It's your lucky day because I broke up with her last week. And a wedding sounds cool!" he grinned. "I'm always down for parties with pretty girls everywhere, and decent food and drinks! Send me the details later on."

"Oh, that's great! Let's do this." Lana gave him a warmer smile this time, relieved to have solved her problem so easily. "I have to get back to my desk now, but let's talk about this later, okay?"

"No problem! Thanks for the invitation."

Admit it, his smile is cute. As she sat behind her desk, Lana stared at the impressive cityscape outside her window. At her feet, the streets of the Roppongi business district crawled with the morning crowds as small as busy ants. This view was the only nice thing of her small office; that and the fact it had a door, a blessing in a country where most employees worked in an open space. Lana felt a bit bad and manipulative toward Frank but shrugged it off and dug back into her reports.

Later, Gabriella knocked at her door for their daily lunch date.

"*Ciao bella*, here is your fix of delicious bento box!" She put down heavy plastic bags on Lana's desk.

"My, my, thank you," Lana exclaimed, pushing aside her keyboard and two piles of documents she had yet to get through. She closed her curtains so that her friend wouldn't get blinded by the bright sunlight. "What day is it? Monday? So, I guess it must be *zaru soba* and shrimp *tempura*?"

"Yes! I finally recovered from my fried-food overdose. Can't believe it took me two weeks to get over that mountain of food you stuffed me with." Gabriella unbuttoned her gray business jacket, kicked off her high heels, and kneeled on the guest chair opposite to Lana's cluttered desk.

Lana swirled in her chair and snorted. "Oh, it's my fault now? How about that awful mix of cocktails you gulped down? Blame the cute barman who wanted to help you celebrate properly! But my shoes don't thank you!" They erupted in giggles then busied themselves eating their lunch in companionable silence.

"So, you remember the wedding invitation I got?" Lana said after pushing away her empty tray with a sigh of satisfaction. "Well, I've decided to go with Frank. I figured it could be a good way to solve my no-date problem."

"Frank... Frank Dubois?" Gabriella asked between her last two mouthfuls.

"Yes, from the IT department. The guy who transferred from Belgium last year I think. Quite tall and athletic, gray eyes, brown hair."

"Not bad looking, but I don't like the vibes I get from him. Be careful."

"Should I be afraid for my virtue?" Lana grinned.

"Tsk, virtue, what's that, girlfriend? No idea what he's worth in bed, but he's dubious date material."

"Why is that?"

"I saw him snap at our office ladies for no reason. And the other day, he was quite the arrogant ass during an in-house training session about our new CRM."

"Well, as long as he doesn't embarrass me in front of my dojo comrades and the rest of the school, I can manage him for one evening. Otherwise I'll just strangle him on the spot!"

"That's my Lana!" Gabriella laughed. Turning serious, she leaned forward, a spark in her eye. "Now, are you finally ready to spill it?"

Lana winced and her good humor went down several notches. "You never give up, do you? No, like I told you already twenty times now, I don't want to talk about it."

"Come on! You've been ruminating and on the edge since February. I'm all good with giving you slack, but I'm getting worried! Clamping down like this isn't your style. So yeah, I feel I've got to turn all pitbull on you."

"*Cara mia*, calm down. Nothing bad happened, I told you. It's too weird, personal and... emotional, I guess, so I want to process it on my own. Not the guy's fault, mind you. But you're right, it's been too long already, I have to snap out of it." She gave her best friend a strained smile. "I'll tell you about it over a drink sometime. Let me get this wedding thing behind me, okay? Douche or no douche, hanging out with Frank will help get me back on track."

"Never hesitate, all right? We need to take care of each other, especially when it's tough."

Lana squeezed her friend's hand. "You're right. We'll get together soon. But let me warn you, it's not for the faint of heart," she chuckled.

"Really? Now you have to tell me! Gosh, and I don't have a thing to report..."

"Be careful what you wish for... Anyway, do you have time tonight to help me shop for a dress?"

"Girl, you're asking the shopping queen!"

The day of the wedding came. After spending her Saturday morning cleaning up her two-bedroom, kitchen and living apartment, Lana stood in front of her vanity mirror and gave herself two thumbs up. Her cream and light gold dress fit her curvy figure like a glove. Her favorite hairdresser had outdone herself this time: Lana's straight hair was now a crown of curls adorning her head in an airy updo, freeing her neck.

With only light foundation and powder, her natural makeup illuminated her rosy face. She hated lipstick, even for formal occasions, so she went with a simple dark gray eyeshadow and black mascara to highlight her eyes. She counted her blessings, because for once, she didn't have too many bruises on her forearms.

She frowned at her reflection. Something was missing, some nice final touch. Ransacking through her drawers, she smiled, triumphant, at the gold and white pearl hairpin bought ten years earlier in Rome. It offset her black pearl earrings and necklace perfectly.

At 4 pm, Frank was at her door to pick her up. When he saw her, he whooped and took a bow.

"Lana, you look amazing!" he exclaimed with a large grin and a sparkle in his eyes. Lana smiled back. The guy didn't hold back on compliments.

"Thank you, Frank. You're handsome as well." Frank looked impressive in a formal suit that had a clean cut. Her trained Italian eye told her it wasn't cheap. He had told her he practiced tennis three times a week. She appreciated the muscles under her fingers when she took his arm.

"Shall we go, then? The car and the chauffeur are waiting."

"Wow, Frank! That's true VIP treatment."

He let her step inside the car first but, to her slight annoyance, sat right next to her on the middle seat. She would have preferred to have more space between them; she wasn't the kind to cuddle. The car took off to the trendy and high-scale Yoyogi area, between Shinjuku and Shibuya districts, to the five-star hotel where the wedding would take place.

"So...uh, what movie have you seen most recently?" Lana said to start the conversation. This felt like being a teenager all over again. Still, it was safer to start off on some neutral ground, far from any company gossip.

"Ah well, I'm a bit of a sci-fi buff," he replied, excited and animated. "I saw *Star Wars* a couple of weeks ago."

"Ah, yeah, to be honest, I stuck with the original trilogy and didn't want to watch anything else. I loved those three so much, I always feared ending up disappointed..."

Frank laughed. "Well, I don't want to start an endless discussion about that, so let's agree to disagree. Any interest in the *Avengers* series?"

"Sure, now and then, blockbusters are always fun to watch," Lana replied, while she leaned against the car's door to put some additional room between them. Frank seemed to like invading her personal sphere a little too soon in their date. "But, uh, how about Japanese-made movies? I'm a samurai drama fan. Did you see *Nobunaga Concerto*? It was hilarious."

"Ah, to be honest, my Japanese sucks, and without subtitles, movies are a pain. Also, I don't know... it's always the same stories..." Lana struggled not to snort but let it pass. "By the way, your Quebec accent is so cute. I love it when you say '*oui*'. But it's weaker than... I don't know... Patrice's from accounting, for example."

Lana sighed and tried to keep her smile in place. Such a typical, Old-Continent, condescending microaggression. "I could say the same about yours, you know? You must be from Brussels. I swear, some Belgian people could have been born and raised in Quebec," she retorted. "But, well, my father spent most of his adult life in Europe. I guess my ten years in Montreal later on made my accent come back."

"Woah, don't fret! That was a compliment. A cute way of saying things in the lovely mouth of a beautiful girl," Frank replied, hands raised to appease her.

Lana took a deep breath and gave him another strained smile. She was no 'girl' anymore, but he was trying to compliment her. It wouldn't work if her temper got in the way. Gabriella's words of warning made her too hyper-sensitive. *He's trying. He's super awkward, but he's trying. Give him a chance. You jumped into the bed of an overbearing guy with an ego the size of an elephant; you can go out for dinner with a superhero fan.*

"Ah, well, thank you... I'm... not so used to this anymore. It's been awhile since I was twenty, you know?" She chuckled, hoping he would get her hint that 'girl' wasn't appropriate.

"Well, you sure look like you are," Frank said with a large grin. Lana rolled her eyes and forced a laugh, swatting his hand away playfully as it was again a bit too close to her thigh.

To her relief, thanks to their driver's impeccable sense of traffic, they arrived ten minutes later. Ten long minutes of heavy flirting that drained her energy and rattled her nerves. Once in the hotel, staff ushered them inside an enormous ballroom, with burgundy walls, a lush, deep red and black carpet, and illuminated by six large crystal chandeliers. Several dozen flower arrangements complemented the opulent settings and the hidden speakers offered low-key classical music. Many guests had gathered around oversized round tables; Lana estimated there were thirty of those.

Most weddings in Japan were less a joyful celebration for two happy individuals, and more a formal affair joining two families after months of discussions involving third parties. Even in less rigid contexts, priority was given to your boss, colleagues and friends of the parents. Family and friends of the newlyweds were at the bottom of the list. Thankfully, in this case, friends and colleagues were the same; the mood was more easy-going than usual. They found their table, and Lana was happy to see Tim and his wife Yurika already sitting there.

"Hi, guys! Great to see you're at our table," Lana greeted her friends. "Frank, Tim and Yurika are my aikido sempai and good friends. This is Frank Dubois; we work at the same company."

Tim extended his hand toward Frank with a large and welcoming smile. "Hi, Frank. Nice to meet you."

Frank appeared relieved to find a fellow non-Japanese at their table and shook his hand energetically. But then he winced, and she hid her smile. While Tim was rather short and lean, his strength was above average. As he was friendly and even-tempered, people underestimated him, unaware that under his good-natured attitude was a man with a spine of steel and crushing muscles to match.

"Delighted to meet both of you," Frank replied through his teeth, flexing his hand discreetly. Lana frowned; he hadn't bothered to hide his annoyance. "What do you do besides aikido?"

"Please excuse me for a few minutes," Lana piped in before anyone could reply. "I need to find the ladies' room before settling in."

The restroom was at the end of the main corridor outside the reception hall. To her relief, not too many people stood in line. But just as she headed back to the main room, her heart jumped in her throat, and she nearly did a U-turn. Only years of working in a tough business environment kept her from cursing loud and clear. *Oh, that's not fair! Come on, you've got to help me here!*

Lila Mina

6

Facing the Truth

HONDA STOOD BLOCKING her access to the reception hall doorway. That he was also a guest wasn't a real surprise, but to think it would be like every week at practice had been a terrible mistake.

On the mats, she could handle it because plenty of other priorities called for her attention. But to her growing horror, seeing him outside the dojo was another story altogether. And what he wore didn't help. At all.

He was dressed in a *montuki*, a formal kimono made of black silk, worn as tradition required with black *hakama* pants and a matching *haori* jacket on top. The outfit made him appear even taller and broader. Three white *kamon*–family crests–at the level of his shoulders testified to the formality of the event.

A discussion with fellow members of their dojo held his attention. Salt-and-pepper hair neatly cut, his stern face, unlined and tanned, made his air of authority undeniable.

To her dismay, her treacherous body reacted to this vision of male perfection. Heat flared in her belly and painted her cheeks red. Memories of their fateful afternoon flooded her–not only its disastrous ending but also all the juicy and incredible aspects that led to it.

Adding salt to her reopened wounds, Honda had the loveliest Japanese lady at his side. Slightly older than Lana, somewhere over forty. Her extraordinary light blue kimono, patterned with golden cranes and pine tree designs below her waistline, was priceless; her attire also showed three *kamon*. This was an *irotomesode*–a type of kimono only worn by married women. Her poise spoke of high education and elite background. Inner grace and beauty shone through her graceful posture and delicate frame.

His wife. No doubt about it.

Rocked by a wave of self-consciousness, Lana felt ridiculous, gauche and stocky in contrast. The tag price on her dress didn't matter; her expertise and degrees could never match a lifetime of polished skills ingrained from birth.

"What are you doing, stupid cow?" Lana muttered, staring blindly at her smartphone to give herself a semblance of countenance. "There's no competition. You were never an item, it's over! You walked out, remember? Get a grip!"

What were her options? Leave Frank and everyone else behind, claiming stomach cramps or something? Turn on her heels and hide in the restroom and then hope that her table was far from theirs? Or treat the problem like a hostile business confrontation, with the strength Honda had assumed she possessed... until she proved him wrong.

Fate decided for her. Right then, she glanced up only to meet Honda's piercing glare.

With hindsight, she'd sometimes wonder what *truly* pushed her to jump and meet head-on his silent challenge to stay put. She could have played it cool and safe; she could have waited it out and let them walk inside. But far from making her cower, the dark tempest brewing in his stare ignited something inside her.

Defiance, desire or something else, unnamed and unseen – she would never be able to explain what compelled her to act that day. And maybe, this time, it had nothing to do with him, but with *her*. The first inkling of an invisible pull. The third piece falling into place.

And so, on that fateful day, Lana locked eyes with Honda. Chin high, she pasted a confident smile on her lips. Tapping into her inner strength and rebelling against any concept of respectful deference, she walked up to his group. After all, she had every right to join them. No way she'd let him dictate where she could go and what she could do.

To her smug satisfaction, his jaw tightened, and his eyes widened. Her smart dress was doing its job.

Lana turned to his companion, who stared right back; to her surprise, the woman seemed to appraise her. Face serene, her discerning eyes traveled up and down Lana's body.

Such an open assessment made Lana blush, but she kept her composure, switching to a polite smile. *How much does she already know? How much is she figuring out? She can't miss the pool of sweat at my feet!*

"Sensei, good evening. How nice to see you here tonight."

"Martin san, good evening," Honda replied in low tones. Not a growl but still different from his usual professional voice. He was as bothered as she felt. For a few heartbeats, nobody spoke. Awkwardness lay thick in the air. "May I introduce my wife, Yuki?" Honda added, as if an afterthought. "Yuki san, this is Lana Martin san, the *mudansha* at my dojo I told you about."

Lana took her most respectful bow, not surprised by his use of honorific in relation to his wife given his conservative behavior. She thanked all local deities she didn't have to shake hands. Sweaty and cold palms wouldn't have sent the right message. They exchanged the ritual sentences of self-introduction.

Now that she was so close to Yuki, her classical beauty took her aback. They were of the same size, but their resemblance ended there. Jet-black hair piled up in a complex hairdo and held in place by silver pins framed her perfect ivory face. A steely strength emanated from her, and Lana would have bet she also practiced a martial art. A delicate perfume surrounded her.

Lana blinked at the sensual vibes assaulting her senses, and she clamped down the need to lick her lips. Something shifted inside her. *Uh, what's going on here, girl? Since when does this fire you up?*

"Martin san, it is a pleasure to meet you. My husband has told me all about you. He forgot to mention how beautiful you are, however," Yuki said with an unreadable smile.

It took Lana the last threads of her nerves and self-control to avoid blushing; she didn't dare assume anything about what the spouses confessed to each other. Who knew what their kinks were? But even if his wife knew everything, she should be giving her at best a cold shoulder, at worst scornful despite. Not compliments and warm smiles.

Unsure of where she stood, Lana went with self-deprecating humor. "Ah, well, I don't wear designer dresses at the dojo, and the cut of this one would make a bear look slender."

Yuki's smile broadened, and her sincere warmth caught Lana by surprise. "Oh, don't be so hard on yourself! But thankfully, *dogi* aren't flattering. Otherwise, practice would become a real challenge, no?" Her mischief was plain to see, but before Lana could come up with a witty reply, Yuki continued. "Have you come alone tonight?"

Lana did a double take. *Is she trying to figure me out? Is she flirting with me? And why am I fine with that?*

"No, I am with a colleague of mine, Frank. He is already inside." She felt compelled to add, "It is our first date."

Yuki raised an eyebrow and gave her another strange smile. "Oh, how sweet! Hopefully a good omen."

Lana couldn't help a half chuckle, half snort. She avoided glancing at Honda but increasing levels of tension and annoyance poured from him. Yuki also seemed happy to ignore her husband.

"Ah yeah, I mean, yes, tha... that's right... but I am n-not so sure about it..." She was supposed to try harder. Not be so transparent about her lack of real interest in her date. But she couldn't help it. "It's early to say, as we don't know each other well." *And given how I am reacting to your husband, and now also to you, it looks like it won't go anywhere.*

"Hm..." Yuki tilted her head. "Well, please drop by our table later on. I don't have many opportunities to speak with women from foreign countries, and I would love to hear about your life in Japan."

To any neutral third party listening on, all of this was reasonable and normal, but to Lana, it sounded more like an excuse. Honda seemed to be of the same opinion, given the black look he threw at his wife and his increasing broody mood. Lana's respect for her grew with each passing second. *Alluring wife: 1, kinky husband: 0.*

Lana played along; she had something to settle with him for turning her sex drive upside down. "Oh, with pleasure. I would love to know where this wonderful *irotomesode* comes from..." Painfully vapid but her short-circuited brain had failed to come up with anything else.

"I will tell you all about it," Yuki replied with a husky voice and then reached out to squeeze her hand so briefly that nobody else noticed it. A bubble burst inside Lana.

She was saved by attendants pressing everyone still standing in the hall to go inside. Their surreal conversation stopped, and she fell in line with the large group of guests going in. As she passed the doors, pressed and surrounded by dozens of people, a warm and large hand landed on the small of her back.

"I would suggest that you stop your little game with my wife. If you could not handle me and my demands, you will find it hard to manage her... and even less, the two of us together," Honda whispered in her ear.

Lana strained to make out his words. She shivered and straightened up, her familiar annoyance with his know-it-all behavior rising. Not glancing back, she pushed aside the powerful desire his words rouse inside her. "I don't know what you are talking about,

Sensei. I am pleased to get to know her... given she knows much more about me than I would have ever imagined."

His hand turned into a grip on her hip. "She knows enough but not everything," he retorted.

"Well, I'll make a quick social call later out of politeness. You don't have to fear anything else from me."

Honda chuckled. "You do not understand. You are the one who should be careful. She is a force to be reckoned with and will not be denied if you open that door. You should be ready to battle and might not like the outcome. But I would enjoy having you in my bed again."

Before Lana could reply, he was out of the crowd, and strolling to his table.

Her nerves tingled, along with other places inside her. Breathing deeply, she walked back to her table and dropped on the seat next to Frank. It was crystal clear she stood at a crossroad. For the sake of her conscience, she had to give her date a chance. She had to try a normal, sane, healthy relationship, as acceptable as it would get according to social standards. Even if her body screamed another story.

"Ah, you're back!" Frank told her with a big smile in their native French. "What took you so long?"

"Endless lines in the restroom and in the hall. A real traffic jam. I also ran into other friends. Everything going well here?" she asked in English to include the other couple and derail the conversation.

"Perfectly well! Tim and Yurika were telling me about their trip to Guam last month. Ever been there?"

Dinner started while Tim and Yurika graced them with pictures, videos and funny stories about their scuba diving trip. Formal speeches honored the bride and groom and their families. Friends and colleagues of the couple raised toasts, but Lana kept a strict control on her alcohol intake and limited herself to two glasses of wine. To her chagrin, Frank didn't have the same discipline.

"Frank, why don't you have a glass of water or oolong tea?" Lana tried to be as courteous as possible, but it was hard not to be harsh. He was her guest, so she was responsible for his behavior in the eyes of everyone around them.

"What? Oh no, I'm fine, don't worry. I'm just getting started. I'm Belgian—I can handle my beer!" he replied with a raucous laugh.

But as time went by, Frank neither slowed his pace, nor handled his liquor well. Frustrated with a behavior more fitting for a frat house party than a wedding, she turned her back to him. Her gaze wandered around the room and found the table where Yuki and Honda sat.

To her surprise, Yuki was staring at her with another enigmatic smile that reminded Lana of the Mona Lisa. She discreetly raised her glass next. Lana's cheeks turned red, but she returned the gesture without looking like a fool.

"What a hot chick," Frank mumbled on her left.

Bewildered, not sure she had heard correctly, Lana twisted on her chair to see at whom Frank gawked. Honda's table. "Excuse me?"

"That woman, the one who just raised her glass," Frank continued, oblivious to her shock. He was speaking in French so didn't bother whispering. "Kinda old, but still hot. Look at her face and figure! Who is she?"

Come again? What kind of guy felt fine to talk with his date about another woman–or like this in any circumstance? "She is my aikido instructor's wife, he's sitting on her left, and I would advise being more respectful. You wouldn't like what he'd do to you if he knew how you described her," she snapped.

Frank snorted. "She's married to that guy? Wow, talk about an age gap. Does he ever smile? He must be filthy rich to have landed a girl like her or seriously good in bed. But he should keep her on a tight leash. With the smoldering looks she's throwing around, she looks like she's open for some action." His fingers mimicked penetration in an awful and lewd gesture.

His vulgarity left her speechless, but her shock turned quickly into red-hot anger. It was not only about the identity of whom he bashed and disrespected. The excruciating lack of manners, of respect shamelessly veiled by the language barrier, fueled her aggravation.

"Will you stop?" she hissed, trying to keep a blank face so that no-one would catch that something was wrong. "This is my sensei you are talking about, and I happen to respect him a lot. I don't know much about his wife, but you're acting like a child!"

Frank snorted in his glass and put his arm around her shoulder. "Oh, come on! Don't be a killjoy. Why are you overreacting?" he whispered in her ear. "It's fun to make fun of your boss or teacher." He inhaled deeply and caressed her neck. "Hm, I love your perfume. I can't wait to show you the room I booked..."

Lana gritted her teeth and clenched her fists against the urge to punch him. Frank's heavy breath reeking of alcohol made her queasy. "You... booked a room for us?" she said and withdrew from his clumsy embrace. This was getting old fast.

"Of course! I've got so many plans for the after-party..." he slurred in her ear, giving her goosebumps, but not of the good kind. "Tell me, what are you wearing under this? I hope you also prepared a nice surprise for me..."

Lana closed her eyes and counted until ten. "Okay, I think you and I need to talk, Frank. Do you mind coming with me outside?"

Frank was so drunk that he didn't catch the warning tone in her voice. "Sure!"

Grabbing his hand, she jumped on her feet to lead him out of the room. He interpreted it the wrong way and made a hopeful face to their fellow table companions. Two men snickered; she saw red. She stared ahead, not even daring to look at the table where Honda and Yuki sat. Thankfully, people had started moving from one table to another, so they didn't stand out.

Outside the ballroom, she brought Frank to one side of the empty hall. "You should leave now."

"What are you talking about?" Frank exclaimed, going from smiling like an idiot to angry shock.

"You heard me. You're making a fool of yourself, and me, in front of everyone. On top of that, you're being rude. I'd be shocked even if I didn't know those people, but I do, and I can't believe what you're saying. Also, it's our first date! You can't expect me to follow you to a hotel room like that." *I'm the queen of double standards, all right, but no way I'm ending up in a bedroom with this ball of slime.*

"You must be kidding! Where do you live, the 18th century? That room costs a fortune! If you didn't mean to spend the night with me, why the hell did you dress up like that? Fuck that shit!" Frank snarled. "I should have known you'd do this to me, what with your reputation and all. Jonas warned me."

She stepped toward him. "What? What are you talking about? Jonas, from the marketing department?"

"Yeah, he called you the frigid queen, you know?" Cheerful, Frank seemed delighted to throw an insult at her face and oblivious to her rising anger. "You're always so bossy and snobbish at work! I know you ditched him even though he treated you like a queen. I thought it was because he was a sore loser, but you're just an attention whore!"

Lana had to call on her self-control and aikido principles to refrain from jamming him against the wall. "I don't give a shit what Jonas called me." Her calm voice made him flinch, and he gulped down hard. "Now, you little prick, let me be crystal clear here."

With one more step, she invaded his comfort zone and stared him down. "Let me tell you something. If you, Jonas or anyone else bashes me online or at the office, I'll make your life so miserable, you'll wish you'd stayed back home and never left your mom's basement. Don't think for one second you can harm me just because you can't handle your frustration and you let your dick do all the talking. Do you understand?"

"You bitch, you're crazy..." he muttered, voice trembling a little. "You couldn't do all that."

"Oh, trust me, that wasn't a threat it was a promise," she replied with a dangerous smile.

He stepped aside, brushed his hair, turned on his heels and was out of the hall in a few seconds. Lana pinched the top of her nose. Come Monday, she would have to make sure that the little shit kept his word. *What a douche! Thank heavens I could see that awful part of him so soon! Let it be my last and formal warning to stop going out with co-workers.*

"Well, that sounded like an unpleasant conversation."

Yuki's voice came from behind her, and Lana rolled her eyes. *When it rains...*

Turning around, she gave the newcomer a smile cooler than she deserved, since she was still attempting to reign in her flaring temper. "Yes, highly unpleasant. It's no big loss though." Lana shrugged.

"I will not pry, don't worry." Yuki gave her the same indecipherable smile as before. "I guess now is not a good time, but I was hoping that we could have a little... chat, you and I?" Her hands were open as a kind of invitation or peace offering. Given their circumstances, perhaps both.

Lana nodded. Flirting or not, they had a man-shaped elephant in the room to address. "Certainly. In one of those rooms over there?"

7

A New Player in the Game

YUKI LED THE way, opening the doors of a small and windowless meeting room with a couple of sofas around a low table. Both took a seat. It reminded Lana of the start of a business negotiation. Yuki being older and holding the higher moral ground, Lana remained silent and let her do her scrutinizing.

She used this chance to better observe her counterpart. Yuki was beautiful, but more than her looks, it was the strength, intensity, and sensuality pouring from her that made Lana fidgety, and not just with nerves.

"First, may I call you Lana?" Yuki began.

"Of course," Lana replied smoothly. That was direct, and so atypical for a Japanese woman, especially of Yuki's station.

"Thank you; please call me Yuki." Again, silence filled the room for a few heartbeats as the two women appraised each other.

Lana's mind raced in all directions, trying to anticipate where they were heading. *He said I should be ready to battle... Are we two lionesses fighting over the same turf? Ha! Who am I kidding? I'm a rabbit she's about to gulp down. I have zero sway here! I can only pray she won't make me walk the road of shame in public.*

"Lana san, please excuse my rude behavior, but we have little time, so I will be blunt."

Lana took a deep breath. *Here we go... If only she could stop smiling like this! Is this a disarming technique or what?*

"A few months ago, I noticed changes in *goshujin sama*'s mood. He was even more short-tempered than usual. It lasted for a while. Then one night, he told me he had obtained the willing submission of one of his most promising and strongest students, in the most delightful way. His mood improved dramatically, to my sincere pleasure. It's my wish and duty to meet all his desires and needs."

Lana fought hard to keep a smooth face. She knew Honda had spilled the beans. Still, to have this brought into the open, with no anger or accusation, was a shock. On top of it, Yuki was using *'goshujin sama'* to talk about Honda. Of course, in her mouth, it meant 'my honored husband', but still it hit too close for comfort.

"And then, two weeks later, he came home frustrated. He said you requested to be freed from any prior agreements." Yuki sighed and shook her head. "Since then, he's again often lost in thought and quick to lose his temper."

Yuki fell silent for a few seconds, and then a full smile bloomed on her lips. "Until now, I thought it would only take time and more dedication. But tonight, fearless, you walked up to us and confronted me in a respectful, yet powerful way. You're indeed strong on top of being a delightful beauty, so I'm not surprised you're still in his mind. And I'll confess that since we talked, I've been wondering about the taste of your lips."

Taken aback, Lana blushed crimson, and her breath hitched. Yuki's smile broadened, and she played her advantage. "*Goshujin sama* ordered me to stay away from you. He fears I'll make you flee rather than bring you back. I disagree because I sense you're receptive to me. I'm willing to risk his wrath by doing this... although punishment will be harsh."

That perspective didn't seem to trouble her. Either Yuki was so dedicated to her husband's well-being that self-sacrifice was nothing, or she enjoyed punishment at his hand. Or both. Lana swallowed her moan at the flash of racy images her mind conjured. Words kept failing her. *All right, all right, I like this a bit too much, oh boy...*

"It's clear to me you still desire him, but given the kind of steel you're made of... I'd like to enjoy what is so special about you that makes him lose his focus."

This time Lana had to close her eyes and bite her lip. Yuki had gone for the kill. Perspiration trickled down her neck. The small room grew increasingly warmer.

"Yuki san..." Lana whispered, eyes still shut to grasp her last threads of control. "Are you sure... Do you really think it's a good idea? I mean, you are beautiful, my head is spinning in all directions right now, but what about-?"

"Yes, all of us can get what we desire if you're willing to give it another try." Yuki's voice had turned into a husky whisper, full of red hot promises. "If you do, *goshujin sama* will be of course your master, like he is mine, but I'll ask that you heed to my desires and needs, and I'll take care of yours in return. In short, you would call me *oku sama* in an intimate setting. What do you say?"

Oku sama? *Well, she's his wife after all.* Lana opened her eyes, caught by surprise again. The other woman had silently moved to her side. Her warm and soft hand rested now on Lana's neck, and her breath caressed her face.

Lana was pretty sure that Yuki could see her rapid heartbeat pulsing in her neck and was aware of her panting. *A rabbit. A helpless rabbit offering her throat, that's what I am. But it's not the kind of slaughter I expected.*

"I say... well... I say you are full of surprises, although your husband did warn me that you are persuasive." Lana cleared her throat. "Sensei told me our relationship would be a sort of intimate training, with no room for more personal emotions. I was fine with this, because... he tends to infuriate me. Outside aikido practice, I am either turned on or mad at him... or both."

Yuki chuckled, and Lana fidgeted in her seat. "I don't know if I can offer him what he wants from me or accept what he gives me. At some point, he managed to get in touch with some deep-level feelings, and I... well... you could say I panicked, which is embarrassing, to say the least. Instead of facing it, I fled and decided we were done. Ah. Obviously, I am not."

Lana stared at her folded hands on her lap. *And now I look weak–and I just confessed it to someone who wants a piece of the action under her own conditions. That's not how you keep the upper hand, girl, but how the heck should I do it?*

"Yuki san, what you are proposing is tempting, but I am afraid. Of liking it too much. Of... of losing myself somewhere down the road." Lana fell silent. The language barrier had never seemed so high. Her thoughts kept derailing with Yuki's agile fingers stroking her forearm.

"At the same time," Yuki said softly, "if the three of us are satisfied, if everyone communicates their expectations and needs, why can't this work?" Her smile became less carefree, and something serious sparkled in her eyes. "Accepting him as your master to your physical needs doesn't mean giving up your free will. Don't forget this kind of relationship requires much more trust and mutual respect than what normal relations have at the beginning."

Yuki shifted, and this time, her body nestled against Lana's. "*Goshujin sama* should have been clearer about this, Lana san. Maybe he thought he had more time. Or perhaps, in a typical male fashion, he didn't explain it well enough. But now that I am also a part of this, I hope you can believe it."

Temper: Deference

Lana gazed at Yuki, the impulse to take her and kiss her warring with the acute knowledge she was Honda's wife. *Would it be all right for me to take the initiative here? Gosh, I'm a mess! I usually have a better grip on the situation!*

"I hear you, Yuki san, but this scenario is brand new. You're asking me to jump, yet I don't know what's at the bottom, much less if I have a parachute. And, well, how do you know this is a solution your husband will accept? He didn't propose this in the first place."

Yuki laughed again, and to Lana's dismay, she found the sound soothing and delightful. The woman then kissed her neck softly, sending goosebumps all along her spine. "He might not show it or act like it, but anything that makes you come back to him will satisfy him. As for the rest, well, it would also be a first for us. *Goshujin sama* has never cared for the women I've taken to my bed. If he allows me to be with you, together with him or simply the two of us, it will be a great, treasurable gift."

Her warm voice held so many promises that Lana couldn't resist anymore; she welcomed tempting and sensual lips, letting her desire overrule her need to be in control. Both moaned, and the kiss deepened. Yuki's fingers climbed up Lana's thigh, teasing and caressing her soft and hyper-sensitive flesh.

Yuki broke their passionate kiss before they got carried away. Her cheeks had turned to a lovely pink, but Lana knew she was crimson herself. Yuki took a plastic card from her small purse.

"Here is our room key. Take your time to think about it. We always book a room when we attend weddings. If you wish, please join us later in room 1710. If you don't, it's not a problem of course. *Goshujin sama* and you will talk about it without me. The choice is yours."

Lana played with the magnetic key, trying to collect her thoughts. *My choice. My call. My desires. It'd be so much easier if I didn't enjoy the sound of her voice already. But... two masters? Can I handle them when he's already a handful on his own? When I'm so new to this kind of game? But enough running already! Since when do I flee and hide? That's not who I am!*

She glanced up at Yuki and gave her a smile that thankfully didn't falter. "I believe I will join you later on, and this will be settled in one way or another for good."

"Wonderful. Let's go back to the reception; we've been too long already."

Lana put her clothes and hair back in order. They parted ways and went back inside the banquet room using different doors.

"Lana, here you are! We almost gave up on you," Tim exclaimed with a grin and a wink when she sat back at her table. Lana offered her friends an apologetic smile and hoped against hope her cheeks weren't as crimson as they felt.

"Sorry guys, I had to help Frank hail a taxi. I guess Belgians' reputation for alcohol tolerance is overrated," she said with an exaggerated grimace. Throwing some serious shade at Frank was the least he deserved. Everybody around the table winced and chuckled.

"I'm glad you stayed!" Yurika said with a kind smile.

Lana shrugged. "A hard decision, but Frank understood it was important for me to stay until the end," Lana lied through her teeth. "Anyway, what were you guys talking about?" she asked, hoping to lead the conversation away from her awful date and back to safer grounds.

The next hour seemed to drag on forever. She tried to relax and not let excitement cloud her head. She avoided Honda's table. What was now the oddest wedding reception ever in her book came to a close, to her relief. Everyone got up to congratulate the newlyweds and their families, who stood in rank to thank every single guest. Lana was quickly out the door, and Tim and Yurika, along with other dojo comrades, caught up with her in the hall.

"Hey Lana san," Yurika called. "A group of us are going to Shibuya to the new joint on the top floor of the *Hikarie* building for more serious partying. Care to join us to forget your awkward date? It's next door from here."

Lana managed not to smirk. *Sorry, I have other plans that include our scary sensei and his temptress of a wife.* "Thanks, it's a great club, but this evening was a bit rocky for me. I'll pass. Have fun, everyone!"

"Okay, no problem, see you at the dojo! Oh, don't forget all classes are off this week because of the holidays!"

Lana waved everyone goodbye and retreated to the other side of the hotel. Time to be strategic and avoid rushing upstairs. At the hotel's bar, a gin and tonic helped relax her fraying nerves. She stuck her nose into her phone, trying to drown her whirling thoughts in the blue-white wash of her screen. After one hour, she decided the time was right.

8

Mapping New Territories

IN THE ELEVATOR, the magnetic card unlocked the access to the guestrooms. Lana found herself alone in the long corridor of the 17th floor, and the lush deep blue carpet muted the clicking of her heels. This was definitely not a love hotel. She chuckled—what an upgrade to first class. Once at their door, she waited a few seconds before knocking to allow her racing pulse to slow down.

The door opened to reveal a smiling Yuki. The sophisticated woman had changed into a green *yukata* suitable for inside. It shimmered in the dim light of the hall, managing to be both sexy and conservative.

"Lana san, welcome. Please come in."

"*Ojama shimasu*," Lana whispered and removed her shoes. She discovered a *tatami* room, twice as large as at the one at the love hotel. Honda sat near a low table by the window. Behind him, the vast expanse of Yoyogi park and the pulsing lights of the Shinjuku district and skyscrapers in the distance. He hadn't changed clothes, and his sheer awesome presence gave her chills. Lana took three steps before kneeling in *seiza* and bowing her head to the ground.

"Good evening. Please excuse my intrusion." She used the most formal register she had learned. She was unsure of his appropriate title until things were clarified between them; the formality also helped hide a burst of nerves.

"Good evening, Lana san; I am surprised to see you here tonight," he replied, voice as neutral as his expression. His stare was evaluating, assessing her intent. He had told her he would welcome her back, but his guarded body language told another story. Yuki moved to sit by the table, removing herself from the conversation.

"So, you would like to reconsider your decision regarding our training sessions, and you would not be opposed to including my wife. I wonder if you are truly ready for this." Although not mean or patronizing, his challenge was clear.

You and me both, buddy. "Indeed, we had a lengthy discussion. I am ready to resume what we begun and go even further. This is why I am here tonight: to apologize for fleeing the difficulties I faced last time, and to ask you if you would agree to take me back under your tutelage."

Honda kept silent for a while. She remained in *seiza*, lowering her eyes, trying to project deference on top of strength.

"It is true I regretted your decision." He extended one hand in her direction. "Before going forward, let's take a closer look at your issue. Attend me."

Lana agreed. Her own perception of her mental state and its reality were two different things. Walking in *shikko*, she approached him. It was hard to relax, but she took it upon herself to look at him in the eye, to express her trust.

"Let's do this step by step."

One hand cupped her cheek firmly, preventing her from looking away; the other moved between her legs, glided up her thigh and landed on her crotch. He went around her tights and underpants to slide one finger inside her while the palm of his hand pressed against her clit. Her eyelids fluttered, and she bit her lower lip, a low moan escaping her. Her body jolted, and something inside her, wrapped in knots all over the past weeks, uncoiled.

Oh. I missed him.

He worked her for a while, and a new jolt coursed through her every time he changed angles or added a finger. Overwhelmed, she lost her balance and clutched his lapel; her head leaned heavily on the hand cradling her face. Her low moans filled the silence of the room, and the scent of her arousal permeated the air. Then Honda turned her head and caught her throat between his teeth. With slow but relentless pressure, he continued until the combination of intense pleasure and sharp pain ripped a climax from her.

He pulled her back against him and gently placed his hand below her navel, right where everything had gone wrong three months before. Body still quivering, Lana buried her face in his neck, inhaling the alluring scent of his skin she had missed more than she'd care to admit.

A whirlpool of emotions swirled inside her. Panic and anxiety surged, as the same drowning sensation that had undone her weeks earlier grew inside her. And that burning feeling in her sternum, again. More irrational thoughts. *Such a calming, caring gesture can't be real. It has to be fake. There is no peace to be found anywhere, only fight and violence. This is a trap and he will destroy me!*

A desperate sob rose in Lana's throat; she suppressed it and squeezed her eyes shut to call upon what years of therapy had taught her. Pushing back what her traumatized psyche screamed at her, she replaced it with cold, hard facts and her first-hand knowledge of the man holding her. Instead of letting the monstrous wave swallow her, she built a mental image of herself surfing it until she could reach the shore. The bubble of anxiety subsided and vanished.

"You have indeed addressed it, little *mudansha*. I am glad," he whispered in her hair. Lana smiled and placed her own hand over his.

"So am I, *goshujin sama*," she said, acknowledging him again as her dom. A burning desire to touch his skin, grab him, lick him, bite him in return, grew inside her. With each passing second, her body reminded her how much she had enjoyed the strength of her lust, her raw need. Yet, she had to wait for his signal.

"Yuki san, come closer," Honda ordered. "Help me remove my clothes. Lana san, stand up, take off your dress and free your hair."

Lana hesitated for a few heartbeats. *Here we go, on the next level. So far, so good. Oh, should I go with a striptease?*

The fiery intensity shining in Yuki's eyes told her that she wouldn't mind the show. But the controlled, stern gaze of Honda, along with his frown, made her doubt his appreciation of lighter games. *Right. Training. Better wait a bit before going with the call-girl act.*

With controlled, calm moves that didn't reflect her mounting excitement, she unclasped her complicated hairpins to let her wavy hair flow on her shoulders. Then she unzipped her dress and removed her tights and black underwear. Doing it in front of Yuki brought no shame, no embarrassment.

Meanwhile, eyes downcast, Yuki peeled away with delicate, yet precise gestures the complex layers of her husband's clothing. Honda watched each move with rapt concentration. It was not an easy task: first the *haori*, then the *montsuki* and the *nagajuban*–the long under kimono protecting the more precious outer garment from any contact with the skin–and finally the hakama pants. All the clothes had to be folded neatly, following particular rules.

Long minutes went by, in complete silence, adding to Lana's increasing frustration. She stood in front of them, naked, and for all that she knew, almost forgotten. Yuki's perfect choreography hypnotized her, and she couldn't tear her eyes away.

Seeing her so subdued, Lana wondered if Yuki was being punished for disobeying him earlier. Her slender fingers brushed her husband's exposed skin now and then, and each time she made contact, he couldn't help but shiver. *They are so much into each other... why am I even here?*

Her train of thought derailed when she once again faced Honda's large, powerful chest and enticing belly. Her breath caught, and she dug her nails hard in her palms.

"Good memories?" Honda smirked, breaking the heavy silence that had settled in the room. "Why don't you refresh mine? Yuki san, stay here. You may watch but do not touch yourself, understood?"

"Yes, *goshujin sama*."

Honda grasped Lana's hips and brought her with him as he reclined on his back. She ended up straddling him. It was a new position for them, but she didn't assume she called the shots. This gave him a perfect view of her body.

"I do remember there was something in particular you enjoyed doing to me..." he growled, his own arousal plain and throbbing against her nether regions.

Lana bit her lip. She decided to take a risk. She avoided his erect member. Sliding her hands upward from his hips, over his chest to his shoulders, she started licking him, beginning from his navel and moving at a leisurely pace, enjoying the texture and taste of his skin.

Extremely tempted to position herself on him and let him slide inside, she decided, however, to go with the second best thing when it came to sex with the man. As soon as her tongue reached the lower side of his chest, her caressing fingers became claws. She dug her nails on each side of his chest, leaving deep red marks on his smooth brown skin, enjoying the tremors under her fingers, the tightening of his muscles, the shortening of his breath, the low growl building in his chest. His grip on her hips became painful.

Never stopping her lavishing tongue, Lana met his steely stare. Many things shone in her eyes, but not deference. Defiance, challenge, hunger, a reflection of her volatile temper. If she had to become addicted to this man, so be it. If she had to submit to him and see to his needs, she could do it. But somehow, he would have to heed the consequences of rattling the cage of what was buried inside her.

Maybe, just maybe, this was what he had seen in her. Maybe, just maybe, this was why he had not been able to move on. Maybe, just maybe, he wanted to be the one to wake it up and tame it. How arrogant of him. How arousing to meet someone willing to try.

Her mouth moved on to his right nipple, alternating between sucking and gentle bites. She created a contrast between the softness of her mouth and the pain caused by her nails which kept on digging, drawing blood now. But even as Honda enjoyed her ministrations, he wasn't one to remain idle. His right hand left her hip to part her cheeks. A finger pressed against her rosebud, then moved lower to collect some of her flowing juices to bring them back where he wanted to explore next.

Reacting to the burning pressure, she raised her hips, encouraging him. She would be open, inviting; this was what she wanted. She groaned against his chest when the invading digit pushed further in; one, then two knuckles slid inside. Her body heat rose and perspiration broke out on her back and chest, making her skin glide against his. Leaving his nipples alone, a new climax building up, she decided it was time for some aftercare.

Her tongue found the red tracks on his left side and cleaned up the droplets of blood pouring from the wounds. She welcomed the iron taste and moaned at the decadent pleasure blooming inside her chest. Honda's response was quick: with a grunt, he inserted a second finger that went in easily. Lana melted, her juices flowing out of her pulsating pussy.

She switched sides and applied the same treatment on his right side. His strong and rapid heartbeat and his solid grip on her hip told her all she needed to know about his rising tension. Lana didn't try to repress her sighs and cries of pleasure. But just as she was about to reach her peak, everything stopped: Honda took his fingers out and pulled on her hair.

"Not too fast, little *mudansha*," he grunted, his eyes hooded. "I will have my pleasure first, do you understand?"

"Yes, *goshujin sama*," she replied, accepting the challenge; still, she pouted a little in frustration and licked her blood-tainted lips without thinking.

This seemed to be too tempting: he pulled her up by her neck and crashed his mouth on hers, kissing her hard before releasing her. In one fluid movement, he brought her on her back and found himself on top again. The next second, he was inside her pussy in one swift move, his balls slapping her ass. Her breath left her, and she bit his shoulder hard to stifle her scream. Even though she was wet and relaxed, he was large and long.

As a merciless Honda pounded her, she dug her nails in his shoulder blades, relishing his hard body and being powerless under him. It became increasingly difficult to control herself and tears of frustration spilled on her cheeks. She bit him even harder to refrain from begging for release and in harsh retaliation. The blood on the tip of her tongue mingled with his sweat and the taste of his skin, more intoxicating than any hard liquor. To her intense satisfaction, hints of passion and arousal cracked through his stoic mask.

Yet, he wasn't on the edge and frustration creeped in. She clenched her jaw and shut her eyes, attempting to keep her climax under a tight lid, but to her despair, she was losing ground in this battle of wills, and knew she was about to come. Finally, after what seemed to be an eternity, he tensed and emptied himself with a guttural growl.

Relief washed over her. She let herself go, arching her back and screaming out loud, her body wracked by shattering earthquakes. Honda held her tight until her body stopped shaking. Then he sat back in *seiza* and turned to Yuki who had remained by their side without moving or making a sound.

"Yuki san, you may enjoy her now," he said, voice gruffer than usual. His wife took a deep but somewhat shaky breath. The level of self-control she had to exercise was off the charts. Yuki bowed until her head touched her folded hands on the floor.

"Thank you, *goshujin sama*," she replied.

Lana lay on her back, still limp from her powerful orgasm. Yuki approached her and their eyes locked; neither of them spoke. Honda's looming presence couldn't be denied but now, it was supposed to be about the two of them. A whole new story.

Yuki pulled on her purple sash and let her *yukata* fall from her slender shoulders, revealing round and firm breasts with long and erect brown nipples. Her waist was thin, and her flat stomach revealed chiseled abs.

Lana had never been attracted to a woman before. Still, their previous flirting and current high state of arousal, enhanced by the power play already established between them, easily pushed open those new doors. Lust coursed in her blood and she felt adventurous, but it was up to Yuki to dictate the pace and design of this dance.

Lana's breath hitched when her new lover's hands began exploring her body, starting with her breasts. Yuki pinched and then twisted her nipples, softly at first and then harder. Lana arched her back, begging for more. Then Yuki's mouth and warm tongue latched on, and Lana saw stars behind her closed lids. She had to fight against herself not to press her lover's head and remain passive as long as she wasn't told otherwise.

Yuki's fingers dipped into her pussy. She scooped some of her husband's cum and spread it on Lana's breasts before licking it with slow, methodical strokes. Lana shuddered, her own juices flowing out. Yuki repeated her gesture, digging deeper inside her wanton lover who groaned.

This time, she brought her sticky wet fingers to Lana's mouth and pushed them inside, staring her down. Without breaking eye contact, Lana welcomed the invasive slender digits and licked them clean one by one. Yuki's pupils dilated. Her mistress brought Lana's hand to her own pussy.

"Show me what you can do with your fingers and agile tongue, sweetling. Be creative," she instructed.

"Yes, *oku sama*," Lana replied in a low voice before moving down on Yuki.

Her lover lay on her back and spread her legs wide. Lana admired her trimmed dark bush, already glistening. Relying on her instincts and what she loved, she parted cherry-colored nether lips, pushed two fingers inside and then curved them to hit that rough patch, rewarded by Yuki's gasp and moans. Then Lana left a trail of kisses on her lover's stomach, one inch at the time until her teeth caught the tiny bundle of nerves standing out.

For the few next minutes, Lana made it her mission to make Yuki come again and again, and somehow, through her skills, regain the upper footing. She added a third finger, alternated her pace between long, deep strokes and quick, short scissoring.

Her tongue found wet lips and moved lower to rim Yuki's smaller hole, making her hiss and cry out. Lana had closed her eyes to better focus on her task and sensations, but when she opened them, it was to see Honda kissing his wife and fondling her breasts. She was stroking him, and he was already half hard again.

Lana's heart beat faster, and she pushed her tongue a little more inside Yuki's ass. This brought her lover over the edge again, and her body convulsed. Her husband pushed himself up on his thick legs and slid his shaft inside her mouth, muting her screams of release. Yuki began to jerk him while slurping on his head. Lana's juices flowed anew at this incredible erotic image.

Yuki stopped her blow job and turned toward her younger companion. "Sweetling, come here and sit on my face. I wish to lick both of you." Lana happily complied and positioned herself in a 69 position, offering her fleshy ass and liquid core to taste.

At first, Yuki shifted back and forth from Lana's dripping pussy and tight asshole to Honda's shaft next to it, but then, inspiration struck her. As her husband was now erect again, she rimmed Lana and then placed his member on their lover's back door.

"*Goshujin sama*, if I may suggest, why don't you enjoy both our asses?" Yuki's humble tone of voice was markedly different than with Lana. "I know how much satisfaction this brings you, and it would please me to see you take her hard like you do with me."

Temper: Deference

Her husband grunted his approval and pushed inside Lana easily thanks to Yuki's careful preparation. Yuki pivoted on her back to face Lana while giving Honda access to her own ass. She grabbed her lover's head and licked her juices on Lana's chin. Lana began to shake, her senses overwhelmed by the combined assaults of her masters.

"Ready sweetling? He will be rough, this is how he likes it, but you know it, right? That's how you want it, isn't it?" Yuki asked in a sultry voice while Honda pushed. Lana moaned, head spinning. Dirty talking was a major turn-on, but it didn't feel right to do it with Honda, who had never used such language. But if his wife was into it...

"Yes... yes... I... love that... hm uhn please... *goshujin sama*... ohhh... harder..." With a victorious smile, Yuki kissed Lana deeply, sloppily, swallowing her moans and grunts. She locked her legs around Lana's hips and added mutual stimulation by gliding their clits together. Lana's eyes rolled back. Both women were now covered in perspiration and other fluids; their bodies slid against one another.

"You are so beautiful when you are wild like this," Yuki whispered in a tight voice, panting hard. "Hm, can you imagine? *Goshujin sama* can enjoy the view of our four welcoming orifices, all wet and begging for his attention. What a great gift... Take him entirely. Open yourself. Welcome him. This is how you can serve him best..."

Yuki's alluring words and Honda's relentless pounding pushed Lana over the edge again. Her arms began to spasm, strained by her position as she couldn't crash on the floor with Yuki below her. As if on cue, Honda wrapped his arm around her to support her, and bit her shoulder hard.

Just as Lana peaked again with a throaty shout, he slid out and aimed at his wife's tight hole. It was Yuki's turn to moan and jerk. She dug her fingers hard in Lana's biceps, shuddering against her husband's strong assault. Getting some respite, Lana took her time to enjoy Yuki's blissful expression of extreme pleasure mixed with pain. She fantasized about pushing large dildos inside all of Yuki's orifices, making her beg and lose her mind. The powerful image made her groan.

Eyes shut, Yuki muttered nonsense under her breath. Tears glistened on her long eyelashes, and Lana licked them while applying more friction on her clit. Yuki opened her eyes and smiled. Lana's breath caught; she was so beautiful. Although her body reeled against the continuous assault of her husband, Yuki managed to slip two fingers inside Lana's pussy. The younger woman groaned and reciprocated the gesture.

Temper: Deference

At some point, Honda grasped his wife's hips to get better leverage. Lana sat on the side and continued to finger her new mistress while Yuki enjoyed the double stimulation. Bold, Lana leaned against Honda to kiss and caress his large chest, her other hand roaming all over him to get a better sense of his powerful body. She raked her nails on his chest and then toward his flanks where his abs were salient.

"Careful, little *mudansha*," Honda growled without slowing nor looking at her; her indiscretion had been noted. "Don't think that because you serve us well, you may already step out of line..."

He didn't tell her to stop, so Lana took that as an implicit green light to take the initiative. Her fingers and teeth dug harder while her perspiring body glided all along his side. With a roar, Honda came hard inside his wife, before collecting her thrashing body in his arms with loving gestures.

Confronted by this intimate, caring scene that reflected the more tender feelings flowing between the married couple, Lana squirmed and looked away. The mood had turned, and suddenly she felt like an intruder. *That's... not for me. It's their dynamics, not mine. Let's not slide down the emotional road.*

The formal context–*martial*, if she had to be honest–of her relationship with Honda wouldn't go away. It was for the better. Her job was to act more like a disciplined soldier than a lover.

As for Yuki... she's a whole new story.

With no instruction nor express dismissal, it wouldn't be a good idea to go to the bathroom. She moved away from the couple who now whispered together and sat in *seiza* by the window. She focused on her breathing, going through all she had experienced since stepping inside the room.

Just as she was about to doze off, Honda straightened up, grabbed his *nagajuban* and put it loosely over his shoulders. He covered Yuki's sleeping form with a blanket and then approached Lana, fastening his sash along the way. She shook herself awake and shivered. Sweat and other fluids had cooled down on her body, but she didn't want to complain about it. A shower sounded wonderful but this, too, would be kept silent.

Honda assessed her from head to toes, his gaze lingering on the large bruises he had left on her body. Lana was pleased to see her own handiwork on his chest and arms. "Are you in any particular discomfort?" he asked in a low voice.

"No, *goshujin sama*," she replied in kind.

"Show me your back," he said with a grunt, brushing her throat and upper left shoulder where he had bitten her the hardest. "This needs to be taken care of," he commented before standing up. "Follow me," he added, reaching for her.

Lana blinked. Sitting in *seiza* was a challenge, having come to practice it only as an adult; after so much time, she wouldn't be able to stand up easily, even less walk. Of course, he would know it. He wasn't buying her tougher-than-thou act and called her bullshit by offering his assistance.

Muttering words of excuse for the bother, Lana took his proffered hand and pushed herself up. She grunted in pain when her protracted calves, knees, and ankles rebelled, and blood started flowing again. She swayed and to her embarrassment, lost her balance. A strong arm slid under her waist.

"Never hide your discomfort again, whatever the cause," Honda whispered sternly, holding her against him. "It could be dangerous. You are strong, but like everyone, you do have limits. You should recognize them instead of trying to deny them. I will not accept this and will not hesitate to put an end to everything if you cannot comply. We may enjoy ourselves in extreme ways, but safety is paramount. This is not where you should test my patience."

Shame made her face flush red. Like at the dojo, it was his duty to make sure she was safe. She gulped down her pride and straightened up to look at him squarely. "My most sincere apologies, *goshujin sama*. It will not happen again."

Their faces were so close his breath caressed her skin. Her eyes dropped to razor-thin lips. A strong urge to crush her lips on his stern mouth swelled inside her. *But it's not your right. It's the prerogative of the woman sleeping right at your feet.*

She looked away, stomach churning.

His hand moved from her back to her neck, cupped her cheek and gave her the authorization to proceed. This time, Lana threw caution out of the window. Her shackled alpha self pushed through, and something below her ribs tightened, almost to the point of pain. She kissed him hard, in a possessive way that had nothing to do with submission, or respect of hierarchy.

That's how she handled her lovers, and a grunt of satisfaction escaped her. To her surprise, Honda let her in. Her body molded itself against his, reveling in the physical contact and the contrast between her coolness and his warmth. He wrapped her in a full embrace. At the end, she broke their heated kiss, panting for air, a familiar rush spreading from her core.

While he was also short of breath, his blank mask was again in place. He pinned her with a gaze so stern she couldn't hold it and had to look down. She needed a couple of deep breaths to get herself under control once again. It would take time to adjust to this new kind of dynamics. He released her before heading for the bathroom without another word.

On the way, he picked up a standard *yukata* provided by the hotel as well as an amenity kit. Inside the bathroom, he made her turn around without a word. Foraging inside a black purse next to the lavatory, he took out some disinfectant and cotton and began to clean her wounds. She hissed but clenched her jaw. When he was done, she turned and silently asked him if he needed the same treatment. He declined and pointed at the bath area.

"Take a shower, but don't put any water on those wounds. Then you can use this *yukata*."

"You don't wish me to go home?"

Honda quirked an eyebrow. "Certainly not at this late hour. Join us when you are done," he added before stepping out of the bathroom.

Lana remained where she stood for a while. She gave a hard look at her disheveled face in the mirror. Her fingers grazed swollen lips, erect nipples, angry red teeth marks on her shoulder and dark blue fingerprint traces on her hips and legs. She let everything sink in.

Honda had been right. It was quite another challenge to handle two demanding lovers when she couldn't call any shot, except when it came to drawing the limit to what she would accept. But she had done it and passed a first test. Pride, excitement, and trepidation warred inside her. Where would this road bring her? Was she too eager to please?

She yawned and shivered. Her body reminded her of her basic needs, and she proceeded. The dead of night wasn't the right moment to dwell on those questions. She stepped into the shower and bath section, sighing with pleasure under the stream of hot water.

When she stepped back into the room, her eyes took time to adjust. It was dark, save for a dim light in the entrance. Honda had brought out a third *futon* mattress from the dedicated closet. He rested on the one in the middle, asleep or awake, she wasn't sure. She blinked in surprise; she would sleep next to him. Nervousness washed over her, and she snorted.

There was nothing to read into that; she was spending the night with the two of them because it was the logical thing to do. *Yes.* It was a one-time thing only. *Yes.* She wouldn't move in with them by next month. *No.*

She crawled under the cover and tried to set aside the strangeness of her predicament. She would sleep, wake up first thing in the morning and leave before breakfast. With so many thoughts swirling in her head, Lana feared at first sleep would never come but exhaustion overcame her.

9

Testing Limits and Accepting Them

MORNING CAME, AND before Lana had even opened her eyes, she became aware of someone's presence. Not only behind her—holding her firmly—but also in front.

Yuki was there, a warm smile gracing her beautiful face that, much to Lana's chagrin, didn't require any makeup to look fresh.

"Good morning, sweetling," Yuki whispered kindly, and the coals of envy in Lana's chest cooled down. "Such a nice surprise to see you stayed overnight. How are you?"

Lana cast a glance over her shoulder; Honda was still fast asleep. "Good morning *oku sama*," Lana whispered in return. "I'm fine, thank you, yourself?"

"Never better. It's been a long time since I saw *goshujin sama* sleep so well. We took good care of him, don't you think?" Yuki asked with mischief in her eyes.

Lana's cheeks turned a darker shade of pink, but she smiled back. "That we did. Thank you for your attention toward me, *oku sama*."

"It was my pleasure. Thank you for serving us so well; it was delightful and inspiring. I would like to give him special thanks, as he was so generous and energetic. Will you assist me?"

As if she would say no. "Of course, let me get out of here..." Lana carefully raised Honda's arm and rolled away from him. Yuki caught her in her arms and kissed her with a touch of aggression. Lana's head buzzed thanks to a sudden rush of blood.

"Oh, sweetling, you taste so good," Yuki whispered against Lana's lips. "Come, let's give him a proper morning greeting."

Honda was still in a deep slumber. Yuki set aside his cover, untied his sash and opened his *nagajuban*. Then she gestured to Lana to take care of his shaft, while she focused on his large balls. Lana sat on his left side, Yuki on the right. With gusto, Honda's wife put one, then both balls in her mouth, wetting them with saliva. Lana followed suit to swallow him whole.

He was large and long even at rest, but she tried to relax to take him as deep as possible. Her hand stroked his base, and his member stiffened under her ministrations. Closing her eyes, she focused on finding a good rhythm and approach, enjoying his taste and musky smell. A strong hand grasped her neck, but she didn't stop, only looked up.

Now awake, Honda enjoyed the show they were performing for and on him. Their eyes locked as he hit the back of her mouth. She relaxed her muscles and pressed even further, overcoming her gag reflex. The look of stormy bliss and satisfaction crossing his face was her reward.

She was about to touch herself when slender and warm fingers slipped easily inside her wet pussy. This sudden stimulation made Lana moan. Honda grunted and tangled his fingers in her hair. It wasn't comfortable, but Lana was so pleased to make him react like this that she didn't mind at all. Anything to make him lose his self-control and show his arousal was fine. The next instant, he moved to his knees, and both women had to move to accommodate the new angle.

"You two temptresses," Honda growled, breath coming out shorter than normal, "you tried to catch me unaware?"

Lana didn't know if he was humoring them or not, but Yuki gave a muted laugh. Lana kept swirling her tongue around his shaft. With another grunt, he pushed up on his toes and further down her throat. Lana had to grasp his thighs for balance and focus on breathing through her nose.

"Little *mudansha*, you thought you would try and pass another test? I don't know if you have enough practice, however... Hold yourself now, relax completely." The joke was over. This could become unpleasant; she had a nasty feeling that Yuki had set her up. The thought fired her up; failure wasn't an option.

He rose, forcing Lana to kneel to keep up. "Yuki san, come behind me and attend me there," he ordered.

His wife complied and began to apply her agile tongue on other sensitive parts of his anatomy. Honda grunted and grasped Lana's neck, effectively locking her in place. Then he started to thrust with the same intensity he had used with her pussy the previous night.

Caught unprepared by his speed, tears welled up in her eyes and saliva dripped over her chin. She stopped doing anything else except focusing on keeping her jaw relaxed. A moan of discomfort escaped her; the same helplessness that crippled her all those months before built up in her belly. Her head swam, and her vision blurred when something unpleasant tightened in her stomach. *I can't keep up... this is too much... I'm going to puke...*

With a muffled groan of frustration, Lana slammed her hand on the *futon*. Honda let her go. Panting, she dropped on all fours to hide her embarrassment, shame at her failure, and anger at his lack of consideration. Acting so forcefully for a first attempt had been totally unnecessary. *Why did he do this?*

She used the sleeve of her *yukata* to wipe her face as discreetly as possible, refusing to face him, to face them. The urge to run away was again powerful, but she tried clamping it down.

Busy managing her emotions, Lana got caught off guard by a hand cradling her cheek. Sitting once more in *seiza*, Honda pulled her to him by the hips. That reminded her of when he corrected her *maai*–proper distance–on sitting techniques. Yuki sat now next to him, looking at her with a sympathy that did nothing for soothing her nerves. Quite the opposite.

"Why this frustration?" Honda asked calmly, not even hinting at the fact that because of her inability to perform, and her breakdown, he was left with a raging erection. Again.

"Ah... my apologies, I failed," Lana replied with a broken voice, as her throat still hurt. He had the audacity to grin; it took all her willpower not to snarl back.

His next words deflated her irritation. "I am pleased you did not try to go beyond what you could. This was also part of the test, and you should not apologize for drawing a line. Ever."

Glancing away, Lana took a deep breath to release her inner turmoil and untangle the knots at the pit of her stomach. "Ah... Yes, I understand, *goshujin sama*." Her finger pointed at his member. "How shall I make up for this?"

A large smile bloomed on Yuki's lips, and the older woman leaned to kiss her neck just behind her ear. This gave Lana goosebumps, and she shivered, her forced smile becoming more heartfelt.

"Do you have anything in mind you would like to show us?" Yuki purred in her ear.

This woman was extraordinary, almost surreal. She enjoyed all of this too much for it to be a mere way to satisfy her husband's whims and fulfill her twisted marital duties. Conceding her the higher ground remained a challenge though. Honda had gotten hooked with her for a specific reason, something he couldn't find in his wife. For now, Lana wasn't ready to give up her advantage entirely.

All of her attention switched back to Honda and his shaft. These power games were a big part of his pleasure. Time to get back to it. She licked her lips and lowered her eyes.

"If I may..." her low voice whispered while her *yukata* fell off her naked body.

Honda's hand on her hip tightened to her utmost satisfaction. Yuki and Lana were as different as night and day, to the obvious pleasure of their master. While Yuki was far from fragile, she was much slender with lighter bones, slimmer legs, smaller breasts and narrower hips, and weighted easily ten kilos less. Lana had to remind herself he hadn't picked her to be a porcelain doll but because he enjoyed a good fight in bed.

"Proceed," he growled.

Lana put her hands on his thighs and leaned forward. By reflex, he grabbed her wrists and the next second, they were caught in a sexy variant of *kokyu ho suwari waza*, a sitting technique requiring breath and core muscles to take the balance of one's opponent without relying on arm strength. Straining her abs, she kept pushing until he relented and reclined on his back, still keeping a hold on her hands at the level of his hips.

Unable to use her hands, she placed her generous breasts on each side of his shaft and rocked her hips to gently massage him. He let out a groan. She dipped her head and licked his head every time it moved up again. Her wrists started to hurt as his grip tightened. Her pace quickened, and after a few more strokes and licks, Honda grunted, pushed forward and came hard inside her mouth. As much as she swallowed, she couldn't help spilling a good half of it on her chin and breasts.

Panting, Honda didn't release her as he straightened up, pushing her back up. "Yuki san, go ahead and clean her up," he ordered.

"Thank you, *goshujin sama*. You know how much I love your taste," Yuki whispered.

First her tongue licked Lana's face. Then she inserted herself between her husband's stretched arms. Their eyes locked over his wife's head while she lapped his cum on her lover's nipples. Short of breath, Lana did her best to hold his gaze while pulses of pleasure shot through her body. Yuki once again sidetracked her, pulling up and cupping her face in both hands. Yuki gave her a deep French kiss and pushed cum back into her mouth; both women groaned as their tongues met.

Honda grunted his satisfaction. He released Lana and moved to sit next to them, running his fingers through Lana's wavy and honeyed hair. Yuki let go of Lana's lips and gave her a satisfied smile. He tied his *nagajuban* back into place and went to the low table near the windows. Yuki sat down opposite to her husband.

"Well, your demonstration was more than satisfactory, little *mudansha*. It is time for breakfast though. Will you join us?"

Lana put back her own *yukata* and didn't reply right away. Once again in *seiza*, she looked at her companions–technically both her masters–sitting against the clear backdrop of the rising sun, the crazy urban landscape of Tokyo spreading behind them.

She took the scene in and sighed; while trivial, eating breakfast together was above her strength. This role was still too alien to her as far as Yuki was concerned. Bowing her head to the ground formally, she tried to find the right words to excuse herself.

"I am grateful for your kind offer, but I should be on my way now and not disturb you and *oku sama* any longer. Thank you for your attention and hospitality. If you would be so kind to give me leave..."

Honda's face remained as passive as ever, and he nodded once. "Of course. Please use the bathroom if you need to."

Lana bowed one more time. "Thank you very much, *goshujin sama, oku sama*. I wish you a pleasant Sunday."

Lana didn't waste time cleaning herself up and getting dressed in the bathroom. In the entrance, she offered them a last bow before closing the door behind her. Leaning against it, she couldn't decide whether she was relieved or sad, satisfied or frustrated.

She needed help.

10

Inside and Out

ON THE TRAIN home, Lana sighed with relief. Thanks to the Golden Week holidays, she wouldn't have to face Honda before the end of the following week. She'd be able to mull over what she wanted and sort out the mess of her conflicting desires, with Yuki jumping into the fray on top of the rest.

Time to talk with Gabriella. Asking her in confidence would help even if it meant losing feathers and getting her ass kicked. Her dear friend was never one to mince words when it came to shake sense into her.

The next morning, after the weekly debriefing of her department, she knocked on her friend's office door. "*Ciao bella*, do you have two seconds?"

Gabriella waved her in. "Always. Close the door—let's have a *cafè*."

Lana crashed down on the plush leather couch Gabriella used when she pulled an all-nighter and let out a big sigh. Gabriella snorted and went to fix them two espressos on the coffee machine she'd brought over from Italy, extra costs be damned.

"My, my, you look exhausted! Busy weekend? Busy nights? We're not twenty anymore, right? So, how did it go with Frank?"

Lana winced and buried her head in her hands; the moron had slipped her mind. Gabriella's eyebrows shot up, and she smirked. "Oh, so bad? Gosh, I hate being right sometimes... Here you go, lady. Seems like you could use two or three."

Lana accepted the cup with gratitude and gulped down the bitter, scalding beverage. She sighed with pleasure. "Hm, you make the best espresso on this side of the world. Yeah, you can send me your bill: he turned out to be a real ass. But thanks for reminding me to make sure he got my message straight and doesn't babble around."

"Wow, it went down the drain fast! No worry, I'll keep an eye open, my ear on the ground, and smash anything down that could come up. But what did he do?"

"Ah, let's not talk about it. He's not worth it. I wasn't that much into him anyway, but it's not what I wanted to talk about. Rather, it's about that thing that affected me a while ago."

Gabriella's eyes opened wide in surprise. "Oh! Finally! But why now? What happened?"

"Well... over the weekend things got back into motion and kind of... made a complete flip, with a serious twist on top."

Gabriella rolled her eyes and wagged an accusing finger. "That's really cryptic."

"Bear with me, please. It's kind of trashy and unusual. It's also a long story, and we, or at least I, will need a couple of drinks. We have tomorrow off, so what about going out tonight to the Miyoshi building lounge bar? I love the city view and their mojitos."

"Booze and chatting about scandalous sex! My favorite combo!" Gabriella joked to help her friend relax. "I'm in! I'll book a table for 7pm. Will that work for you?"

"Oh, yeah, I intend to be done with the Tanaka case and the executive report for HQ by then."

"Yikes, that report! When is Cruella coming over? This week already?"

"Yes, on Wednesday, for forty-eight hours. What a joy," Lana replied, sarcasm dripping.

"Another reason to drink tonight! Okay, I'll drop by your office at 6:45."

At 6:45 sharp, Gabriella was at her door; at 6:50 they were out on the street, crossing over to the next skyscraper. In the express elevator to the top floors, Lana unfastened her hair clips. A headache was coming up, and the complicated pins holding her hair weren't helping.

At the lounge, the *maître d'* showed them to their table, next to the large floor-to-ceiling windows that offered one of the most prized views of the capital. Hundreds of buildings sprawled out at their feet. The iconic red and white Tokyo Tower lined up with the skyscrapers of the business districts around them, with the Rainbow Bridge over Tokyo Bay in the distance. This view made Lana fall in love with the metropolis every time.

As soon as their drinks were on the table, Gabriella turned on the heat. "So, spill it! Who is this guy who haunts your days and nights, who's so outrageously skilled you squirm in embarrassment?"

Lana buried her face in her hands. "Okay, it's bad. Let me talk first, and then you can throw your glass at my face."

And for the next fifteen minutes, Lana gave a clinical version of what had transpired first with Honda, and then with Yuki, over the previous weeks. She left the hardcore details out because she didn't kiss and tell. Still, she didn't hide the domination/submission aspects of the relationship, or gloss over the fact she was now the lover—to use a kinder word than *pet*—of a married couple. When she was done, she drained her cocktail in one shot and stared out of the window, unable to meet her friend's eyes.

Gabriella broke the silence, chewing thoughtfully on an olive. "That... that's something else entirely, that's a whole new level, *cara mia*, even for you."

Lana threw her a pointed glare and shrugged. "A new low, you mean?" she retorted, full of self-derision.

"No, not at all, but it's so complicated!" Gabriella chuckled. "You're in an all new world of mess. The sexy stuff sounds amazing—by the way, you're such a lucky girl, you have to tell me more later—but it's not the problem. You're already in a deep emotional quicksand and let's be honest: he's not going to dump her to ride with you into the sunset."

"I can't deny it's complicated, but hey, don't put words in my mouth! I'm not in love! I don't even know him—well, except in the Biblical sense of the word," Lana chuckled. "In any case, I'm not looking for a sweeping romance, or doe-eyed love. You know I can't go there anymore, right? I burned that bridge." she said with a pointed glare. It wasn't the first time they had had this discussion.

Shaking her head wistfully, Gabriella gave her a small, sad smile, and both friends got lost in the bloody memories that had cemented their friendship forever a lifetime ago.

Hating the needles that pricked her eyes all of a sudden, Lana cleared her throat. "I wish it could be a simple case of pure lust, but... yeah, once the hot stuff is over, I get a bad case of angst attack. It moves too many things inside me, it meets too many needs. Truth is, it feels good, so I don't want to stop, but I'm not blind. The risk of getting too involved is huge. Problem is, *cara mia,* it's not an infatuation, but something else. And I can't believe how I've become so addicted to it so quickly. On top of it, she's molten lava and doesn't mind me getting ambivalent toward her husband. At the same time, he drives me mad with his contradictory signals. I mean, he cares in his own way, so it's not just a mindless fuck." She let out an exasperated sigh. "Gosh, look at me! A headless chicken running around!"

Gabriella groaned and finished her drink. "If I wanted to be mean, I'd say she's a manipulative bitch and he's a typical bastard trying to have everything without bothering to choose."

Lana shook her head, taken aback. "Now, that's unfair, Gabriella..."

"No, no, don't defend them!" her fiery friend cut her short. "Do you know their background story? How honest they are with you? You've got no clue what he thinks—that's the entire issue. And you say you don't believe in 'love' but you do wish to have someone by your side when you get sick and old, don't you? Don't you mind getting increasingly involved with people who maybe care a bit, but not so much? Don't you think you deserve more?"

Lana fidgeted in her seat. Her face made Gabriella laugh and relent a little. "*Cara mia*, of course, I've never met them, so it's only my outsider opinion. But whoever they are, and however honest they are with you, wherever this goes, there's one bottom line. You will be Mrs. Number Two, forever in the back, giving *her* precedence and *him* more than he ever will give you back."

"Number two... being number two would already be something." Lana's voice trailed off; even to her own ears, this sounded outlandish. Number two was hard to swallow. "I don't even know if he's thinking about this. It wasn't his initial plan. He didn't expect her to get involved. The situation delights her, but then, maybe it's because she doesn't feel threatened at all."

"Lana, stop. Listen to yourself. You don't fool me at all. Deep down, it's not her who makes you want more, even if she knows how to lick your clit, if I may be blunt. You need to talk with him, and I mean talk, not stare at him for a few minutes before you happily fuck like rabbits. A constructive discussion where you lay down your expectations. Not with his wife, with the actual guy."

Gabriella sighed, took a sip of her drink and went on. "I can well imagine it's not the easiest thing to do, him sounding like a textbook obtuse older, Japanese, hyper-controlling guy? The kind of man who barks three words once every blue moon. To me, he sounds addicted to your guts and strength. To other things as well, who can blame the poor soul," she smirked. "Use this and draw a line. He can't be worse than Cruella, or that insufferable CEO of Konuma Industries you nailed to the wall last week."

"Right, but what line?" Lana threw her hands up in exasperation.

"That's for you to find out, *cara mia*," Gabriella replied. She reached over the table and squeezed her friend's hand. "Hey, I'm not telling you to pull out all the stops. Enjoy this as long as you find it satisfying. But get your priorities straight. Like figuring out how to be with him, how to be with both of them while remaining true to yourself? How does that sound?"

Gabriella chewed a handful of peanuts thoughtfully. Lana became subdued as every word hit their target. "Don't forget Japanese people are the masters of compartmentalization. Try to do the same, and don't allow them to change you so much you become alienated from who you are, please. I'm not kidding, if I ever see this, I'll slap you and send my hellhounds on his heels, aikido master or not."

Lana groaned and pressed her palms on her eyes. "*Honne* and *tatemae*, *omote* and *ura*, right?" It made sense. Juggling between the open and hidden sides of people, things, concepts were key to Japanese society and cultural mores. "Okay, so you, the dreadful, reasonable voice of my conscience, are telling me to grow a pair, do my job and shake him up..." She pulled at the sleeves of her pale pink shirt to smoothen nonexistent creases. "You win. I'll try to get in touch with him, but I don't have his number. Do you mind if we call it a night? I'm sorry, it's still early, but right now I need a hot bath and a good night of sleep."

"No problem, let's get out of here."

Lana grabbed her bag and her jacket, and they headed out. The 41st floor, where their bar was located, was cut in two. A huge and popular reception hall occupied the west side of the building. Their company often held corporate parties there at the end of the year. That evening, something was going on, and a large crowd milled inside and outside the hall.

"Uh, did you see that banner and the posters? This is a kind of fundraising organized by Nakazawa Holdings. Seems big!" Gabriella pointed out as they walked toward the elevators.

"Yeah and look at the number of foreigners mingling... not your usual company evening," Lana added.

"Nakazawa Holdings is still a family-owned company, right? I hear the patriarch Nakazawa Toshiro calls the shots on almost everything and shareholders bow in fear and tremble in their pants when he gets in a rage. He's so powerful and, well, rich. Do you want to bet they wouldn't survive a competent external audit?"

They snorted at the idea of applying international compliance rules to such a behemoth and old-fashioned group. Lana pushed the elevator button and sighed. "Well, thank you for this drink. I needed some sense drilled into my brain. It's hard to think straight when volatile emotions get in the way."

Gabriella smirked. "Not to mention specific parts of someone's anatomy..." It was painfully true, and Lana was so tired and hyped by her drink she broke into a fit of giggles. The elevator bell rang, and she had still a goofy smile on her lips when the doors opened. The first two people who walked out were the cause of her emotional roller coaster.

Lila Mina

11

Taking Out the Trash

Hysterical laughter bubbled in Lana's throat. *Why am I not surprised! A girl can't get a break, right?*

With an impressive *tour de force*, she kept her composure. Her lips froze into what could pass for a surprised smile.

"Lana san," Honda uttered, so shocked he dispensed with formalities. "I didn't know you were on the guest list."

"Sensei," Lana croaked, doing her best to ignore Gabriella who was quick to add two and two. "Good evening. I'm sorry… the guest list?"

"Oh, Lana san!" Yuki exclaimed as she stepped out of the small group of people with a beaming smile on her lips. "How wonderful to see you here. What a surprise! Why didn't you mention it yesterday?"

Lana blinked twice, doing her best to maintain her composure. She felt like a child caught shoplifting candy. No doubt her purple-red face gave away every little dirty detail of what they had been doing together!

"Good evening, Yuki san. To be honest, it's just a coincidence. I came here with my friend Gabriella to have a drink at the lounge bar, and now we are leaving."

Yuki had a good look at Gabriella, assessing her with her intense stare; a faint blush painted the brunette's cheeks, but it didn't surprise Lana. Her friend's own appreciation of beautiful women was no secret.

Yep, beautiful and intense. Not so easy to handle, is she?

"I see! Well, it's not so late yet, so why don't you and… Gabriella san? Join us for a while. Many international guests join us tonight as we are celebrating the launch of a new program with our overseas branches. We even have the honor of welcoming the Spanish and Italian ambassadors."

"We...?" Lana blanched. "You work at Nakazawa Holdings?"

"So to speak." Honda's smugness made her want to throttle him. "Yuki is Nakazawa sama's eldest daughter."

Lana's smile never faltered. Behind her, Gabriella coughed to hide her unladylike snort, enjoying the added layer of complications messing with her friend. Of all the couples, of all the husbands... *What next? Is he a member of the imperial household, or the head of a yakuza clan?*

"Are you all right?" Yuki asked Gabriella, missing how Lana had turned two shades of gray.

Gabriella nodded, red faced. "Yes, Nakazawa san. It's just my asthma, my apologies. A trigger in the air..."

"Oh, you poor thing. My name is Honda now, but please call me Yuki. That's what Lana san calls me, anyway. Where are you from, Gabriella san?"

"Italy. Lana and I are childhood friends."

Yuki smiled at Lana. "You are Italian? I thought you were Canadian."

"Italian on one side of my family and Canadian on the other," Lana replied under her breath.

"Oh, I see! We should get to know each other better, don't you think?"

Is she pulling my leg or what? "I agree. There is so much we should discuss..."

"Then join us! Many of your fellow Italian nationals are here tonight, and it would be my pleasure to introduce you," Yuki continued with enthusiasm.

"That is—" Lana began.

"So kind of you, Yuki san," Gabriella finished with a smile which was much too bright.

Lana threw her a burning glance. *What are you doing? Why are you playing along?* Was she the only one who thought this was not the best idea? Gabriella smiled at her and switched to Italian.

"Calm down, Lana, it's for the best. Get used to it if you want to go ahead. Inside and outside, remember? You need a push, I'm doing you a favor."

Turning her back to the couple, Lana faced her friend and threw her a sharky smile, the one that made elder businessmen shudder. "Sure, *cara mia*, go ahead, but I'll get you back for this one, traitor." They could have been discussing the weather.

"I'm sure you will, naughty girl, but you will also thank me later on," an unfazed Gabriella replied with her airy and sexy laugh, the one that made men's heads turn from the other side of the street. They had been friends for too long to be affected by each other's antics.

Lana bowed to the couple. "We accept with great pleasure, Yuki san."

"You speak Italian, Lana san. What a lovely language! It suits you well."

Gabriella's smile turned voracious. "Oh, it's the language of love and seduction, all right! Maybe it's its rhythm and sounds, or because we Italians are such talented lovers."

This time, Lana couldn't suppress a groan. Even outside their particular context, this was borderline in a polite conversation, in Japan or elsewhere.

"Gabriella..." Lana began with a low level of warning in her voice, but stopped, shocked, at the sound of Honda's chuckle.

"I would go with the second alternative," he said, staring straight ahead. Lana turned beet red and stared at him; Gabriella laughed.

"Sensei, you are the first person I've ever met able to render Lana speechless, which is a feat. Trust me, the list of people who wished they knew how is long," she added before giving him a deep bow.

With a wry glance for her husband, Yuki patted Lana's hand. "It seems like everyone is enjoying making you uncomfortable. I am sorry for that. Come, let me offer you a drink."

Lana took a deep breath. "Thank you. I will be with you shortly. I need to refresh myself first."

"Please, take your time! Gabriella san, will you come with me? Let's find His Excellency, Ambassador Borghi."

Without another word, Lana turned on her heels and headed for the restroom area of the floor. She needed water on her face and some light meditation to cool down.

Gabriella was infuriating but right: she had to learn how to handle public situations where the three of them were together. She needed to relax, enjoy herself and... his company. She closed her stall door, sat on the toilet and did her best to empty her mind.

After five minutes, she stepped out, fixed her makeup, and stared at her reflection in the mirror like she had done two nights before. *Do I really want to do this? Yes. Or, at least I want to give it a try.*

By far, she had never dared jumping into something so exciting, at least since that fateful summer so many years before. Honda and his wife were giving her the opportunity to walk a new road. She had to keep a lid on her reactions, work on her nerves, talk with him and learn how to navigate this new land. All of this. In that order.

Lana stepped out of the bathroom and ran into Honda himself. "Sensei," Lana greeted him. Outside a bedroom, she dared not call him anything else.

He nodded back, as calm and composed as ever. "I want to make sure being here tonight with us isn't too hard for you. Things are perhaps moving too fast?"

This new demonstration of thoughtfulness caught Lana by surprise. "Thank you for your concern, but it will be fine. It surprised me to meet you tonight, and I already had a couple of drinks, that's all. But since you are here, I'd like to ask a favor..." Lana winced. *It's not a favor, it's normal!*

"What is it?"

"Do you have time for lunch this week? We should talk."

"I agree. This Friday at the Oaktown, one block from here? They have a *washoku* restaurant on the first floor. 12:30 pm?"

Lana blinked. *That was fast!* "Yes, thank you very much."

"Good. We should go back now before your friend gets overwhelmed by Yuki."

For the first time since their affair had begun, Lana laughed in front of him. He stared at her as if she had grown a second head. "Oh... I'm sorry, I meant no disrespect, but I wouldn't worry at all. Gabriella is always at her best in front of an audience. She is a party queen. I'm pretty sure she could teach even Yuki sama a trick or two about wrapping people around your little finger."

Honda fought not to smile but failed; Lana hated that it made her heart beat a little too fast. She wanted to become intimate with him, physically and mentally, while keeping a strong emotional barrier up at all times. Easy breezy.

The couple stepped inside the reception hall and spotted Yuki and Gabriella, surrounded by four men. She recognized the Ambassador from pictures shared by the Italian Chamber of Commerce. There was something vaguely familiar with one of the other men, but she didn't remember if she had ever met him. Yuki saw them and gave them a broad smile when they joined her group.

"Gentlemen," she began in passing English, to Lana's surprise. "May I introduce my husband, Naruhito Honda, and another Italian lady, Lana Martin. This is His Excellency Ambassador Fedele Borghi, the Honorary Consul of Osaka, Dr. Daniele Spazio, Mr. Luca da Madene and Mr. Alessandro Maggio."

Lana did a double take at the last name, and stared at Maggio, recognizing him. *Oh. Oh! That's bad, very bad indeed!*

As she plastered a smile on her face and shook hands, she shared a glance with Gabriella who also looked distressed. Yuki didn't seem to notice their reactions and pale faces and went on.

"Mr. Maggio just informed me his family company is considering opening business discussions with Nakazawa Holdings in Italy. This sounds highly interesting, and I will be delighted to mention this to our President."

All sorts of red alerts sounded in Lana's head; even the Ambassador didn't hide a painful wince. Then she caught the way Maggio was gawking at Gabriella, and an idea popped up in her head. A bad one, but still.

Right then, the Ambassador excused himself; all four men were going to take their leave and join another group when she jumped in.

"Oh, Mr. Maggio, please, one more minute of your time. This is such a nice coincidence. Gabriella was telling me the other day how much she had enjoyed the exhibition of your company's collection in Rome last year. Could you give us more details?" If looks killed, she would have died on the spot with what Gabriella threw her.

Maggio beamed in delight. Lana had read him properly: he was smitten with her friend. "My sincere pleasure! May I first bring you a drink, *signorina*?" he asked with a voice so sugary it made Lana's teeth ache. He was awful.

Gabriella gave him her fakest smile and nodded. "Oh yes, please, champagne. And one glass for my friend if you don't mind."

"Naturally," Maggio replied and left to go the bar area to pick up their drinks.

As soon as he was out of earshot, Gabriella grabbed Lana's arm. "The hell, Lana?!" she uttered in an angry whisper. "You recognized him, he is a sleazy, awful ball of slime!"

"Yes! That's precisely why we need to throw him out of here. We have to play it like in '98 in Milan!"

"'98... Milan...?" Gabriella took a step back, disgusted. "Oh no, you won't make me do this! At least back then, that guy was good-looking! I'm sure you didn't want to throw up in your mouth!"

"Gabriella, please!" Lana begged, but her friend shook her head with vehemence.

"What is going on here? Lana san, explain yourself!" Honda's stern whisper interrupted the two friends' glaring match. Lana switched back to Japanese.

"My apologies, but we have little time before he comes back. Yuki sama, Maggio must never, ever meet your father. He must not compromise his company by associating with the Maggio family. They are..." she continued in an urgent whisper. "They are organized crime, hidden in plain sight under layers of nice and clean business or charity groups. Their pockets are deep and they own too many politicians. And this guy... his own father doesn't know what to do with him, so he sent him as far away from Italy as possible. He hangs out with members of far-right groups, he molested countless women, including underage girls. He is *poison*."

Yuki blanched and clenched her jaw. "How do you know this? How can he be at the ambassador's side?"

"It's common knowledge in Italy. His family is powerful enough, well-connected enough, to make sure the Ambassador cannot push him away, even if he wants to—and believe me, he hates that man. I beg you, Yuki sama. I'm sure your father wouldn't associate himself with the Yamaguchi *gumi*, right? So, he shouldn't do any business or entertain any relation with the Maggio family."

"Here he comes," Gabriella warned, another fake smile pasted on her lips. There was no risk the man understood one word of Japanese.

"Sensei, please play along," Lana had just the time to add, sending Honda a pleading glance. He grunted, his face tempestuous.

"Here you are, *signorina*. And, of course here is another glass, for another beautiful lady," Maggio told Lana with the greasiest expression she had ever seen. She gave him her most professional smile.

"*Grazie mille, signor* Maggio," Gabriella said with a ten-thousand-watt smile.

"Oh, call me Alessandro, please." The brunette let out another airy laugh as if she was already drunk.

"All right, Alessandro. So, how do you like Tokyo?" Gabriella pretended to care, shuffling closer to him.

Honda moved right behind Lana. "What is she doing?" he whispered in a strained voice. Lana smiled and turned toward him, pretending to translate the conversation.

"Gabriella will respond to his ridiculous attempts at flirting with her. She will hit on him hard. We'll take him out of this room and the building then put him in a taxi before he can talk with anyone else here. For the sake of your company, nobody in Japan must realize his family is interested in the holding. The simple association of the two names would be disastrous for any expansion plans in Italy."

Honda pinned her with his steely gaze. "It seems like a familiar strategy to you."

Lana's smile widened. "We first used it in 1998 when we were students. I was the one who had to pretend to be interested in a real douche bag. Unfortunately for Gabriella, this man is worse than the guy I had to fool back then. Please come with me when I ask, sensei, because I might need your physical help."

Lana stared back at Honda, communicating her intent but also her need for help. With rats like Maggio, only true muscles would drive the message home. Honda grunted. She bowed and turned to Yuki.

"Yuki sama, my apologies for this situation."

Yuki shook her head. She was struggling to keep her composure. "No, don't apologize. I am grateful that both of you are helping us out here by not making a scene, but if your plan doesn't work, I'll call security."

Gabriella now had her hand on Maggio's forearm and pretended to laugh at a ridiculous joke. The man leered at her in the most disgusting way and was close to groping her ass. Lana approached the pair and smiled.

"Oh, look at who just came in!" Lana pointed at nothing, making a wide move with her arm. Her glass of champagne hit Maggio's suit, and everything spilled on him. He jumped back and cursed, enraged.

Good, you pig. You're showing your true self.
"Ohhh, I'm so sorry!" Lana exclaimed in a shrill voice. "I'm so clumsy! Let me help you!"

"No no, Lana, I'm taking care of this." Gabriella took over with a fake giggle. She brushed Maggio's suit, and pressed her hand on dry and clean, yet strategic areas between his legs. "Alessandro, please come with me, we're going to the restroom," she added with heavy innuendo.

This calmed him down, and a repugnant smile bloomed on his lips. "With pleasure. Show me the way, my dear." The pair saluted their group and headed out. Lana watched their retreating backs and glanced at her watch.

"Lana san..." Honda growled.

"Yes, I know, one minute... All right, let's go, let's rescue Gabriella from that swine."

Honda and Lana hurried up outside as fast as possible without attracting attention. They walked back toward the bathroom area and turned a corner. The disturbing sight of Gabriella playing her part to the end met them. Pressed against the wall, she tried weakly to push back Maggio.

His tongue down her throat, a knee between her legs, he held her hands on each side her head. Lana and Honda grunted in anger, but she put a restraining hand on her companion's sleeve. They had to make it as non-threatening as possible.

"Oh Gabriella, again? What would your husband say if he saw you?" Lana exclaimed, with feigned annoyance. Maggio stepped back and turned toward her. His social façade disappeared, and his angry scowl distorting his features showed them his true, sick nature. In another context, Lana would have been scared. Here, rage fueled her resolve, backed up by Honda's reassuring presence.

"It's none of your concern," he sneered. Lana was close to hitting him in the nose, and Honda's body language made it clear he struggled to keep himself in check. It wasn't necessary to speak Italian to get Maggio's meaning.

"Oh, but it is, Alessandro," she replied as if nothing serious was happening. "Her husband always asks me to keep an eye on her, because when she drinks, Gabriella becomes too affectionate. For her sake, let's pretend this never happened, shall we? *Cara mia*, come with me, it's time to go home. Lorenzo doesn't have to know…"

Maggio grabbed the hand Lana had extended to reach Gabriella. "Get lost! Don't ruin my fun, bitch. She's drunk, which is even better because she won't remember a thing."

Lana dropped all pretenses. She twisted back his wrist, then pushed it down in an unnatural position. Something snapped under her fingers, and he crumbled down, howling.

"Your feet and hips!" Honda exclaimed from behind her, exasperated. "Had he been more focused, he would have hit your back easily."

Lana threw Honda a bewildered glance. *A lesson here and now? Talk about priorities.* "Uh, duly noted Sensei, thank you. If you could now bring him to the elevator and make sure he gets in a taxi…"

"With pleasure," he growled. "Take care of your friend." Honda leaned down and picked up Maggio. He almost had to carry him. The Italian nursed his wrist, sobbing aloud. Lana figured she might have broken it.

Oh, well. The little creep wasn't going to tell anyone a woman had done it.

She turned back to her lifelong friend. "Gabriella, are you all right?"

The brunette made retching sounds and headed for the restroom. "Oh, shut up, of course not! I had his awful hands on me, his horrid breath in my nose and his slimy tongue in my mouth. I need to throw up, brush my teeth, take a shower and throw up again. Any other stupid question?"

Lana winced and joined her in the restroom. "I'm so, so sorry Gabriella. I owe you big time."

"And then some! Gah, the horror! Well, at least it worked."

"Yes, they owe you too."

Gabriella grunted and spit the water she had been gargling. "There is one good thing that came out of tonight: I confirm you have great taste in picking up dark, brooding and powerful men and their dashing, sexy and flirting wives," Gabriella said after a while, disgruntled. "It will be a mess but forget about being careful. Go for it and have fun. They are a walking disaster for anyone with an active libido. And I want all the lurid details, to have something to spice up my lonely evenings! Just be careful, okay?"

Happy to see her friend had her priorities straight, Lana snorted. "Well, you know what? I got a lunch date with him, to talk. Really."

"Good for you! I hope you won't be alone in the room with him, because I can't imagine him talking to you with your clothes on. He's drinking you up—don't tell me he's only here for a 'teaching experiment.' Both of you are cute if you believe this. You got under his skin, and he's making this up just because he can't face it."

Lana made a dubious noise. "If you say so... He's doing a good job at hiding it. And don't forget I still need to figure out how to handle her, for all her attractive assets and positive inclination toward me. Anyway. Come now, let's go home. I've had enough excitement for one night."

"Look who's talking! Next time, you get to let Awful Guy grope your ass."

With a hearty laugh, Lana took Gabriella by the arm, leading her back to the hall and reception room. "Sure, sure, I'll be the one making the ultimate sacrifice next time."

"Be sure not to do it in front your new 'personal trainer.' I can't see him reacting well to that."

Lana tried not to snort again. "Yeah, well, he doesn't have to know everything either. Our days of mayhem and doing stupid things aren't over, *cara mia*. I'm not marrying him."

"Good to hear!"

As they were approaching the entrance to the main room, Yuki came out and gave Gabriella a critical glance. "Gabriella san, are you unharmed?"

"Ah, Yuki san, don't worry at all. As usual, Lana had my back. I was ten seconds away from making that big bad boy cry. She beat me to it, to her great satisfaction, I'm sure."

A sparkle in the eye, Yuki threw a knowing smile to Lana. "Dangerous *and* lovely then." Lana managed not to blush.

"I would say, in dire need of practicing her *taisabaki* on *katatedori kotegaeshi*," came the stern voice of Honda from behind them as he walked out of the elevator. "We will work on it as soon as practice resumes."

Lana stifled a witty retort about his amazing sense of timing when it came to offer aikido lessons. He was right: her body movement had been more than approximate on that defense and being childish or temperamental in front of an audience wouldn't go well. She went with a deep bow, acknowledging his rebuke.

"Oh good, Honda Sensei, you could get rid of that pig?" Gabriella chimed in, aware Lana's nerves were being tested.

Honda cast Gabriella a piercing glare. "I put him in a taxi and gave strict instructions to the building's security team. I will also make sure he is denied access to the company's offices throughout Japan. We will also conduct some additional background checks."

"Excellent." Gabriella nodded. "Please tell us if you need more information from Italy about that family and their network. They are unfortunately smarter than him."

"Yes, I'll share this information with you, off the record," Lana added. "Let's be careful and not leave any electronic trace. I'd recommend increasing your information security, not only at the IT level but also training your employees on how to handle sensitive data stored on physical support. Please do not assume that your data being in Japanese protects you."

"I need to talk with my father," Yuki told Honda with a deep frown.

"I agree, tonight."

"Okay, *cara mia*, I'm ready to go now," Gabriella said. "And don't forget whom you've got to entertain the day after tomorrow: Cruella in the flesh!"

"Well, thank you for reminding me of my personal hell. But yes, we should take our leave."

Yuki quirked an eyebrow at Lana. "Nothing too serious, Lana san?"

Unable to hide her annoyance, Lana shook her head. "Don't worry. An overbearing and annoying member of our senior management comes every year to Tokyo to grill our office and make everyone miserable."

"Yes, and our dear Lana here, would you believe it, is the only one among us with enough guts and spine to take a stand against her. Even our general manager folds down against that difficult lady. So, to protect us all, she needs her rest and beauty sleep, don't you, *cara mia*? No overtime, no extraneous activity, nothing, just rest."

Exasperated, Lana stared at her friend. Gabriella's lack of subtlety grated on her nerves but made Yuki laugh. The woman was incredibly relaxed about this entire situation. She didn't seem to mind for an instant that the brunette was in confidence. Honda looked aggravated, but it was his default mood. They were similar in that, to Lana's chagrin.

"Well, off you go!" Yuki told the two friends while patting their lower backs. "Thank you again so much for your help. What a blessing to meet you here tonight. Gabriella san, thank you for your extra efforts. I hope to see you again."

"Oh, trust me, you will. I'm always hovering around Lana. You know, never far from her, checking on her..."

"Okay, that's it!" Lana exclaimed in Italian, pushing her friend away. "Can we not make this more obvious than it is?" Switching back to Japanese, she bowed respectfully to Honda and Yuki. "Honda sensei, Yuki san, if you will please excuse us, we have already taken too much of your time." Gabriella was already walking to the elevator, laughing out loud, enjoying her sweet revenge for the events of earlier.

"Good night, Lana san, we will meet on Friday," Honda replied, and Lana could have sworn he was smiling. In the dimly lit hall, it could have been a trick of the light though.

"I'm looking forward to it, Sensei. Good night," she answered before catching up with Gabriella, who held the elevator doors.

Once the doors had closed, Lana sagged against the wall. With any chance, not all of their interactions would turn out so eventful... at least outside a bedroom.

Lila Mina

12

Master and Apprentice

ON THE FOLLOWING Friday, Lana left her office to go to her lunch date with Honda. They'd need two hours at most, so it wasn't necessary to clear her afternoon. Just another business lunch. At 4:45 pm, she had a conference call with their Dublin office, so she'd be back at her desk with time to spare.

The restaurant was one block away, so she walked there. It was a good way to transition from her pile-up of work-related worries to the important discussion ahead of her. Like for any top-level business talks, she had to come out of it with two results: a better understanding of their own dynamics, and how to handle Yuki. She had a nagging feeling he'd never agree to let her take the lead as far as Yuki was concerned, but she had to try.

She sighed in discomfort as she crossed the last street before the building where the restaurant was located. The weather channel said the rainy season was nearly here, way too early for May, and she turned too hot and sweaty for her own comfort. Lana let out a breath of relief as cool and dry air greeted past the venue's sliding doors. *Wait until July hits...*

A quick glance at a mirror reassured her. No perspiration stains on the back of her pearl-gray business dress in sight, hair held in place. Honda had seen her in many states of disarray, but she wanted to look perfectly professional during their discussion.

The *maître d'* led her to a cozy private room, where Honda already sat at small table for two.

"Sensei, my apologies for keeping you waiting." He remained in his seat and returned her deep bow with a smaller one, pointing at her seat.

On her left, a large window revealed a beautiful and serene Zen garden, with a pond where golden and red carp swam leisurely. They wouldn't be disturbed, however good manners dictated to wait to address the reason for their meeting.

"I trust your week went well?" Honda asked after they placed their orders.

"As well as expected with the visit of our CFO. She is a... challenging lady to handle, but nothing out of the ordinary happened."

He raised an eyebrow. "Ah yes, the woman your friend mentioned. She said you were the only one who could handle her. What does it mean?"

She offered him her most predatory smile. "It means nobody speaks ill of my team and their work or tries to challenge our results with no valid reason and walks out of the room with all their toes. She's a bully who thinks she can substitute competent management with downright intimidation, and it is always my pleasure to crash her party."

"And your management is fine with your attitude toward her?"

"My management counts on it. So far, they have deflected any of her attempts at getting me fired."

"Still, good people skills aren't enough. You must excel at your job for them to value your temper and your natural aggressiveness."

Her eyes met his unreadable stare; she didn't flinch under his intense scrutiny. When it came to her career and professional skills, she wouldn't excuse herself or downplay her achievements. She had worked too hard for that. "Yes, I am. We've got a saying in French. We say it's impossible to get rid of your natural tendencies, as they always come back to bite you at full speed. I'm making efforts, but I don't eliminate those traits."

"An interesting way of putting it, but it defeats the whole concept of self-control, discipline, and self-improvement. Tell me, little *mudansha*, how will your natural tendencies affect our training sessions?"

This time, she accepted lowering her eyes in acknowledgment of the shift in their conversation. "*Goshujin sama*, when it comes to you, I will express them as much as you want me to," she said, careful to pick the right words.

"How elegantly put," he chuckled. "I see why your management will not let you go. So, when it comes to me, hm? Just as I thought. You seem to have other plans regarding my wife, then."

Her shoulders and jaw tensed; she had to glance out of the window to collect herself, trying to find flimsy threads of composure in the quiet scene of the Zen garden.

"Well, about her..." Her voice trailed off when the right words failed her.

"What is it? Don't tell me you cannot handle her. Don't say you don't appreciate her either—you proved the opposite convincingly. So. What is your plan?"

His pushy manners were so annoying! "I have no 'plan,' I assure you," she replied with a colder voice.

"Granted, this situation is challenging; being number two runs against my nature. However, Yuki sama is your wife. She has every right to—" His impatient hand gesture cut her off.

"Stop right here. Yes, she is my wife, and yes, she has decided you would submit to her. Your submission is what she wants, this is how she has been with her other lovers, and they have followed suit. But it is not engraved in stone."

Lana didn't hide her bewilderment. "I beg your pardon, but I... I have no legitimate grounds to—"

"I am the head of my household and I am the one who decides what is legitimate or not as far as it is concerned," Honda growled.

Reclining in her seat, Lana crossed her arms, taken aback by his choice of words. *Your household? Ah, yes, such a traditional way to talk about your family. But I don't belong to it, do I?*

He continued his scolding. "Being my wife or not is irrelevant. Both of you are dominant women. Yuki saw it right away when she first met you. Anyone with such a sensitivity does. She decided to play, to test herself and her capacities when she chose to insert herself into our relationship and ask you to accept her as your mistress. Frankly, I would have preferred her to let it go and stop interfering with my training. It is a bet, but depending on what you will do now, she could lose."

Lana's head swirled, and she didn't reply right away. She picked her chopsticks up to eat a few bites of her grilled vegetables and fried tofu before emptying her cup of tea.

"Why are you telling me this? Why do you want me to turn the tables in relation to Yuki sama?"

"There can be only one dominant woman in my bed, and I will always enforce her position, whoever she is. Yuki knows this, and also perceives you struggle accepting her as your mistress. But as long as you allow this to persist, there is no reason for her to change her behavior and not treat you differently. It is up to you to decide whether or not to accept this, but I will not tolerate indecision much longer. Make a decision, or the three of us will stop seeing each other."

When Honda leaned across the table, not for the first time, Lana found she couldn't look away. Her heart pounded wildly. He was in charge of the conversation, and she saw no opening to counter him. Downright infuriating and... challenging.

"And now, let's talk about us. What I am about to share is highly personal, so pay attention. Our marriage was set up, negotiated and concluded without either of us having a proper say in the matter. This is as it should be, as the interests of our families required it; it was our duty. We found our own path and are satisfied with it, but Yuki didn't choose me. I didn't choose her." His voice became a low grumble. "When I decided to train someone at a more intimate level, in a way that matched my needs, I chose you."

She blushed against her best judgment. *He chose me? Is this...? No, impossible.*

"I admit I find it challenging to understand what this 'training' means in your book."

"We are not in a standard relationship, and despite your language and cultural skills, I realize there are gaps that can lead to misunderstandings regarding my expectations. You should not try to apply your usual references. Like I told you from the start, you are free to leave at any time. Do not blame me, or even Yuki, for any frustration. Embrace what I am offering you or walk away from it."

Honda must have seen something flashing on her face because his eyes narrowed. His voice took a steely edge. "This is not a level, equal relationship. Accept it. I am training you, I am your master, and you are my apprentice. When we are together, I demand your obedience, self-discipline, respect and loyalty, and control over your body, passions and desires to meet my needs. In exchange, I give you what you crave and meet your needs as well. I will help you become even stronger, like I told you on the first day. I will be demanding and harsh, but never abusive or humiliating."

He stopped and seemed to be resting his case. But after a few seconds, he continued with a softer tone. "Do not expect it to transform into something else down the line. Do not compare your position with my wife's. I am expecting different things of you, as you have different roles to fulfill. As strong as she is, Yuki will never be tested as hard, nor required to give me as much. I am not your lover, not in the childish, emotional sense your Western culture portrays it. There is care, yes, but only because there is loyalty and obedience. You will learn, step by step, what this entails."

Her breathing had turned shallow and fast. Lana lowered her eyes and tried to regulate it while pondering his statement.

Well. This was what she had been hoping for: an open conversation about the situation. His approach seemed to be another expression of *bushido*—the warrior code of ancient samurai—with its range of complex intricacies in terms of discipline, authority, devotion and mutual respect between a master and his student, a lord and his retainer. It permeated not just all martial arts but also other aspects of life in Japan.

It was now up to her to determine if she wanted this, regardless of Yuki. The delicious sensation spreading from her core told her the picture he drew didn't scare her.

"Thank you for taking the time to explain this. This sounds good. Now—"

He stood from his seat. "If you are in agreement, then we are done here. The next part of this conversation will take place elsewhere."

Dumbfounded, Lana looked up and gaped at him. He was now right next to her, his face a blank. She blinked and shut her mouth to avoid looking like a fish out of water. Where he wanted to go was crystal clear, but ending up locked in a bedroom all afternoon hadn't been on her agenda, and there was that call...

"Well? Is there something you don't understand?" He was on the verge of losing his patience at her slow reaction time.

Lana got on her feet, shaking her head. "My apologies, *goshujin sama*, but this is unexpected, and my professional agenda for this afternoon is already—"

Quick as lightning, Honda nudged the chair between them out his way and stepped forward until she had her back against the panel window. "What part of 'obedience' is so hard to understand, little *mudansha*?" His voice was a dark purr.

Frustrated but attempting to hide it, Lana tensed, yet didn't cower. The rush of blood to her head and elsewhere told her she liked his attitude a little too much.

The rush of blood to her head and elsewhere told her she liked his attitude a little too much. She shifted on her feet to face him squarely.

"Again, let me apologize, *goshujin sama*," she replied with just enough deference, but not breaking eye contact. "It was a lack of foresight on my part. I need to find a solution regarding an international conference call at 5 pm where my presence is required."

His hand went to rest beside her head on the window, and he was now so close that even with no contact, all his body heat radiated on hers. To her surprise, she reacted right away; it took her a lot not to moan and mold herself against him.

"Yes, find a solution. We can arrange a break if it is so imperative, but you will not leave the bed until I say so. While you are at it, if you had any plans for tonight, cancel them."

A wave of annoyance and anger washed over her. So now she had no longer any control over her social life and agenda? She clenched her jaw, trying to find the right way to protest.

Honda smirked as he saw through her poor self-control. "Temper, little *mudansha*. Such a fiery and volatile temper. I absolutely love it in bed, but outside, you need to work on it. You do understand I demand shifts in your priorities, don't you? I am not asking you to give up your job or your friends, but you will attend my needs when I require it."

Lana breathed through her nose and looked down. "Yes... I understand. Give me five minutes to arrange the situation."

Honda nodded and stepped back. Lana hated how much she missed his physical presence. She was addicted, and it clouded her judgment. Pushing those thoughts away, she took her purse and speed-dialed Minohara Kyoko, her assistant, who picked up right away.

"Good afternoon, Martin san. How are you?"

"Hello, Minohara san. I'm fine, thank you, but something has come up, and I won't come back to the office this afternoon."

"Oh, is everything all right?"

"Yes, yes, everything is fine. I'll take the conference call with Jeb and Christie from my smartphone, no need to reschedule it."

"Okay, but do you have everything you need with you?"

"Yes, it won't be a problem." Lana was about to hang up, but she paused. Something was wrong. Kyoko didn't sound as cheerful as usual. "Minohara san, are you all right? You sound disturbed." Lana avoided looking at Honda. She wouldn't apologize for making this call longer than necessary, not when something was wrong.

The other side of the line went silent for a few seconds, except for a distinct catch of breath. "Ah... well... no, Martin san. It's... I'm so sorry." To Lana's horror, her composed and skillful assistant broke down in tears on the phone.

Lana put aside any thought of Honda to focus on her assistant. "Minohara san, what's going on? What happened?"

"It's Johnson san. For the past hour, she has been calling me every 15 minutes with dozens of questions about the minutes of your meetings, asking about you, insulting you, calling me incompetent because I wouldn't answer..."

"*La salope!*" Lana exclaimed in French, swept by a burst of anger. "She's calling you from Montreal? But it's 1 am over there! Stop answering her calls. I'll take care of this now."

"I am so, so sorry, Martin san. I thought I could handle this, but you know how she is!"

"Yes, I know exactly how she is." Cruella had never been a more suitable nickname. "Don't worry, she won't bother you anymore," Lana vowed with a deadly calm voice. "Take a break, have a tea or something, and relax. This is unacceptable."

"I am so sorry for the bother..."

"Trust me, it is no bother at all. I'll call you later, bye." Lana hung up and switched her smartphone to silent mode. Honda was watching her, an eyebrow hidden in his hairline.

"I need to make another call," she explained, unapologetic. "It's not about me but about my assistant who is being harassed because of me. I have to set things straight."

Honda raised a hand before taking back his seat. "Go ahead." As expected, he understood her responsibility to take care of her staff.

"This will take only a minute." She looked up Michelle Johnson's number.

The phone rang twice, and her nemesis picked up. "Lana. You've got guts to call me at this ungodly hour," Michelle's icy voice assaulted Lana's ear. She spoke English, as Johnson was from Vancouver and wouldn't speak two words of French even if her life depended on it.

"Don't play this game, Michelle," Lana chuckled. "I know for a fact you were up and busy, since you have been harassing my assistant for the past hour."

"Ah, that empty-headed idiot? I wanted to talk with you, but you seemed out of reach. Taking some time off? You thought it was fine to go on holiday?"

"Stop right here. You have my number, so nothing stopped you from calling me if that's what you wanted.

I think you just wanted to play some disgusting power game with my assistant who is too kind and polite to tell you to stop. I am neither kind nor polite, so I am happy to say it to your face: back the fuck off. If you call her one more time, even only to ask about the weather, I'll call Donagan and file a harassment complaint so thick one box won't be enough to contain it. He will hand you your ass."

"You little brat. If you think you can threaten me, you are dead wrong. Your team is just like you: a group of incompetents with oversized egos who will bring your branch to its end because you can't add two and two. I'll have your neck! Just wait until Monday to see what happens when anyone tries to go after me!"

Lana laughed. The woman was unreal. "Oh please, be my guest! I can't wait to see it. I look forward to bringing you to your knees. It's been my great displeasure working with you!"

Lana hung up. She turned back to Honda and gave him a cold smile. "Thank you for your patience."

"I could not catch everything, but I understood enough. Nothing scares you, right?" he asked, thoughtful.

Lana tensed and threw him a dark look. "You know better," she replied slowly. "But... no, not people like her." She took a deep breath. "Forgive me, I need to calm down a little."

Honda chuckled, and got up again from his seat. "No, you don't. Let's make good use of your adrenaline surge." This time he strolled out of the room, not even bothering to check if she followed him. Doing her best to clamp down her powerful arousal, Lana hurried after him. Access to the guest rooms was possible from another aisle of the hotel.

Lila Mina

13

Rattling Her Inner Cage

While she enjoyed the view of his broad shoulders and back—not to mention his ass—in his expensive and smart tailor-made business suit, Lana also took stock of her surroundings. Being so close to her office, it was possible to run into someone she knew—it would lead to bad press.

The elevator brought them to the 31st floor. Honda led them to a single door at the end of the hall. This wouldn't be a standard twin room. Once he had let her in, she discovered a suite, with a large king-size bed on the left, and a living area on the other right. As soon as the door closed behind him, Honda put away his jacket and grabbed her by the waist.

He pressed her against the wall, claiming her mouth with an unusual show of desire. Lana let him take the lead, her own arousal flaring up. With no warning, he pushed her hair away and bit her neck in one of his favorite spots, while almost ripping her dress off her back. Then she pushed him back, trying to put distance between them; it didn't have to be that easy.

"Anything goes?" Her voice was so low, it was almost a growl. Something heavy, hot, almost burning twisted below her chest. It swirled and demanded release. Odd and new, but then, nobody had ever affected her like this man who was now circling her, assessing her every move.

"Anything," Honda replied. His smile was calculating and knowing, sending shivers down her spine. "Now is the right time to tell me if there is anything you do not wish to do. You can also let me know later on."

Her guts twitched with anticipation, but also dawning understanding. There were constraints, yes; conditions, yes; rules, yes. But she had never felt so free. She had yet to figure out how fighting back and being self-servingly aggressive were compatible with obedient submission. But as long as this was what he ordered, she had *carte blanche.*

Hissing through her teeth, she stepped out of her crumpled dress and removed her bra; now in dark purple short pants, she moved to find herself behind him. She didn't even try to catch his arms; he knew dozens of ways to get rid of any grabbing from behind. Instead, she molded herself against his frame and embraced him.

With her teeth, Lana pulled on his white shirt. She didn't even try to be careful and left bite marks along the way. Blindly, her fingers searched for bare skin. He let her proceed until she pulled off his clothes, baring his broad back where supple muscles rolled under her lips.

Lana did a double-take. A large and ugly-looking light pink scar ran from his neck to between his shoulder blades. She bit back the question jumping to her lips when he unbuckled his belt and his pants fell on his ankles. Recovering from her surprise, she licked his spine and raked her nails from his neck to his lower back. His sharp intake of breath and growl made her smile against his skin; the next moment he had pivoted on his heels to face her.

Lana took a step back, but before she could slip away, Honda wrapped a powerful arm around her waist, and their bodies were once more in full contact.

He twisted a nipple hard and bit the other one, and by reflex, she dug her nails into his upper arms with the strong intent to hurt him. He purred and grabbed her hair.

"I want to see blood, sweat, marks, and hear your cries of passion and pain. Show me what you keep locked inside. What will make you beg for more and when you can no longer take it. Your deepest desires, the one thing you want so much but haven't asked of me yet."

His voice had an intensity she had never heard before. Arousal made her pant and become wetter by the minute. The last part caught her off guard, however. "I... I don't know what..." she stuttered, at a loss.

"Of course, you do," he growled. "And by the time this will be over, you will tell me, and I will give it to you. Now... show me what you hide inside you. Give me all of you." He plunged two fingers inside her pussy, making her cry out in surprise and pleasure. Following his example, Lana slipped inside his boxer shorts and grabbed him while biting his collarbone hard.

Honda groaned and curved his fingers to stretch her. With a jerk, she moaned and gasped, and pumped him with fervor, letting her thumbnail graze his head, making sure to make it hurt a bit.

"Yes, yes, yes... like this..." he whispered in her hair. His free hand was still working on her nipple, and it became quickly oversensitive.

Lana whimpered and clawed at his lower back while rolling his balls and pinching his soft skin with her other hand. He had brought them over to the bed. Emboldened, she switched her feet to the right position and managed to make him lose his balance with a sharp twist of her hips. He fell back on the bed.

Before he could react, she straddled him and pushed him on the mattress with a serious show of strength. She took the time to enjoy the power that coursed in her blood, the full view of his incredible body under her, and the tempestuous emotions flickering on his face. The next instant, his hands split her ass cheeks, and he brought her pussy over his pulsating shaft.

Lana leaned forward on her arms, her hair cascading around their faces like a dark-gold curtain. She brought her lips over his but stopped just before touching his mouth. She blew air on his face, then licked his lips ever so lightly, feeling like an awful tease. The narrowing of his eyes, the obvious tension in his jaw and his hands tightening on her hips were her rewards.

A coy smile on her lips, she positioned herself on his tip. He slowly pushed himself inside, and her breath left her in a long sigh. Pupils dilated by desire, their eyes locked, betraying their burning arousal. The contrast between the volatile tension humming between them and their slow and almost careful move was incredible. Both of them struggled to keep a semblance of self-control. She clenched her inner muscles.

"You are so tight and hot..." His voice was strained. Allowing her to continue her teasing cost him. Lana ran her tongue from his jaw up his ear and back along his neck until her forehead rested on his nape.

"Hm... *goshujin sama*... what are you doing to me..." she whimpered, drunk with his smell and taste. She nibbled at him, playing with his skin with her teeth. Her fingers grazed his chest, tantalizing, reminding him of what she could do but chose not to. Her hips pushed down hard until their bodies met and became locked together. She ground against him, and jolts spread from her stimulated clit. "You are so..."

A first unexpected orgasm crashed on her and cut her short. Straightening up, her head fell backward, as her body shook from head to toes. She let out a throaty scream. Honda sat up and took her in his arms while she still reeled. He squeezed her, so much, in fact, it was almost hard to breathe.

"You like playing games, don't you? My turn now," he growled against her jaw. He grabbed her neck. "One more time, what is our safe word?"

"Red," came her panting reply.

With a powerful hip move, Honda turned them over and brought her on her back. He pushed her legs up until her knees were on each side of her head. She winced; despite all of her training, her muscles were stiff. He knew it. He knew so well how her body worked and what it said, even when her mouth said otherwise.

Defenseless, she'd have to struggle hard to get out of his grasp. She found herself fully exposed to his gaze, fingers, tongue and of course his straining erection. He hovered above her, his chest pressing on her legs, increasing the muscular tension.

"I will not hold you, but I don't want you to move, is it clear?" he ordered. "Remain in this position until I say otherwise, regardless of what it costs you."

"Un... understood." Her legs would tire easily and would never remain in place on their own, so she grabbed her thighs and blocked out any discomfort. There would be soon plenty of other things to focus on that would make her burning muscles pale in comparison.

His mouth zeroed in on her pulsating and wet pussy. Oddly enough, it was a first for them. The fact that he was still waiting to get his own release, although she had already come, intensified her arousal. This jolt of pleasure soon turned into unbearable frustration.

Honda began by blowing hot air on her nether lips, mirroring her own action, and then licked all the areas around her most sensitive parts, slow and methodical. Careful, he avoided the most pleasurable spots. All of Lana's instincts screamed for her to grab his head and press him his face just there, to get him to touch her bundle of sensitive nerves.

The tension, the need to get release, was unbearable. Cursing him, begging – none were an option. This was yet another lesson of self-control and discipline. In any case, her pride refused to give in so quickly. Another effective demonstration that unsatisfied pleasure could be worse to handle than pain.

Lana whimpered and bit her lip until she tasted blood. Tears rolled on her cheeks, and her fingers dug hard into her own flesh, leaving red trails. For once, the pain was a welcome distraction from the highly skillful torture he inflicted upon her. But for all her iron will, she wailed when his hot and wet tongue dove inside her. The vision of his face buried inside her lit the right zones in her brain. To her dismay, he retreated and sat back on his heels just before his sucking and lapping brought her to release.

Lana roared as hot white anger engulfed her. It had to stop in one way or another, even if it meant to roll away from him and disobey him. She'd rather face his ire and punishment than call 'red' on what he was doing to her and admit weakness. Just as she considered breaking the rules, Honda moved up next to her head and caught her throat. His grasp was light, but this could change in a blink. She gritted her teeth and didn't bother hiding her unabashed aggravation.

"Yuki was right, you taste like honey," he said, overlooking her reaction.

His tongue cleaned up meticulously the droplets of blood on her lips. Then it slipped inside her mouth, offering her her own juice to taste. He took possession of it, like he had done with her pussy. She sighed and responded in turn, but his grasp on her throat intensified. She stopped moving her tongue, fresh tears of frustration burning her eyes.

Without releasing her mouth, Honda positioned himself again over her, let go of her throat and thrust his shaft inside her in one swift and powerful move. Lana's eyes rolled back, and she moaned her second, violent release. He put her right leg down, freeing her from her excruciating position, and she locked her heels on his lower back. Honda broke his smoldering kiss and caught her earlobe.

"Fight me back," he whispered in her ear. "Resist me and try to overcome me as much as you can. It's just you and me here. Don't hold back. I will not."

Lana growled, dug her fingers into his shoulders and pushed herself up to bite his chest. She would not be the only one bleeding today. Honda groaned in pleasure. He pulled her up until he was again standing by the side of the bed and carried her across the room.

He slammed her against the opposite wall with not much consideration and used the momentum to impale himself even deeper inside her. Relentless, he grunted his building pleasure in her ear, both hands on each side of her head. Her whimpers and his growls filled the room.

For a short while, rivulets of sweat trickling between her breasts, she was tempted to remain passive and ride his powerful rutting until completion; but then, she realized she had the opportunity—and above all the authorization—to do things differently.

Lana dropped her legs, and went with another powerful hip twist, combined with a push on his elbow and lock on his wrist. She slammed him against the wall, blocked his arm behind his back in a painful lock that left him powerless for a second. Honda was still buried inside her, but from their new angle, his shaft was now brushing against her clit.

Both moaned when she molded her body against his to bite his neck, drawing more blood. Honda grunted, grabbed her neck with his free hand, and pulled her head.

"Very well done, little *mudansha*," he uttered, trying to rein in his own frustration and control his pain. "Good inspiration and excellent execution. But where do you go from here?"

She licked her bloodied lips and twisted his locked wrist. He winced, but his erection throbbed inside her. A burst of dark joy and pleasure rocked her: he was as much a perfect match for her needs as she for his. Lana shifted positions until he slipped out of her. His eyes narrowed at the loss.

She quirked an eyebrow and fell on her knees, keeping her tight grip on his wrist. This was not the most comfortable position, but this allowed her to keep the upper hand-at least as long as he accepted it. She had no illusion about his ability to overcome her at any moment.

"Now it's my turn to you give you what you need... but at my pace," she promised in a hush.

Lana engulfed him, taking him in one gulp until he hit the back of her throat. It had not ended so well the last time they tried this, but she was determined to deep-throat him. She hummed her appreciation at having all his glorious size inside her mouth, but above all, her pussy twitched at the sight of raw pleasure that flashed across his face. He closed his eyes, and his body relaxed, like during practice when *uke* had to let *nage* take control.

Lana started bobbing her head, and his hand grabbed her hair again. But this time, she rebelled. She twisted his wrist again, his body jerked, and he let go of her, albeit reluctantly. To reward him, her free hand cupped his balls. Continuing to play with his nerves and patience, she let him go, rejoicing at the groan torn from his throat. Her tongue aimed at his puckered hole.

Increasing the pressure on his wrist, she offered him the perfect combination of acute pain and decadent pleasure with a sloppy and generous rimming. She pushed in with her tongue while making humming noises.

Honda began to grunt; he was getting close to release. Moving fast, she took him back in her mouth but didn't forget his hole. After dipping a finger in her pussy, she pushed it two-knuckle deep in one stroke, going in easily. To her great thrill, it worked beyond her expectations.

He moaned out loud and came in long, thick bursts. A lot spilled over her chin, but as she tried to swallow as much as possible, Honda showed how fast he could recover total control over the situation... and her.

Freeing his hand from her wrist lock, he grabbed her jaw and moved behind her.

"Don't swallow everything. Keep it in your mouth," he ordered, panting slightly. "Now stand up." Inhaling through her nose, Lana obeyed. An arm wrapped around her chest, he led her to the large couch in the lounge area, still maintaining her jaw shut.

He pushed on her shoulder blades, and she fell forward. Her hands and forearms landed on the headrest while she kneeled on the cushion, her ass now well up in the air. Honda collected his cum on her breasts and brought it to her asshole. He did it twice, taking his time until she relaxed fully under his touch, pushing his juices inside her with one, then two fingers, opening her wider and wider. Her mouth shut, Lana whimpered under an assault both painful and delicious. He placed his hand in front of her face.

"Now spit it."

A generous mouthful landed on his palm. The sheer filthiness of what they were doing made her head spin. Honda didn't waste time and brought his cargo to her back door. This time, three fingers went in.

"Oh, *goshujin sama*, this is... Please, this is too much... Ah..." Lana panted harder and harder.

"I will not stop until you come and beg for more, or you give me our safe word. No protestations, no amount of begging, no tears will move me. Do you understand?" He whispered while slipping in a fourth finger.

"Gn... yes... but... oh... *oh Dio mio*... oh, your hand is too big. I can't do this..." She tried to twist her upper body to face him, but his push on her shoulder blades only increased.

"Yes, you can."

Resistance was futile, and she was soon babbling and sobbing, biting her own arm so hard blood started to trickle. At no time did she think to use their safe word though. The more helpless she became, the further he pushed in, the more her body shook with tremors of pain. The more her rationality gave way to primal urges. The more the dark thing inside her rattling its cage came close to release.

She was furious and elated by his move, by his keen understanding of her buried desires, by his vicious needs only she could match. Honda pulled her back against him, wrapped his other arm around her waist and bit her shoulder hard while increasing the speed of his fisting.

"This is it, this is your precious gift. This pain, this delight. Take me in, serve me, feel me, feel my power over you; this is what we both want and need," he said, straining to keep himself in check. Lana wailed, all control over her body lost as it kept on shaking, drenched with perspiration.

"Yes... Uh... yes... Oh... oh please... Please..." she babbled. After long minutes of this extreme regimen, a powerful climax surged, and she welcomed it with relief and gratitude.

Honda slowed down, then took out his hand but didn't release her from his iron grasp. Humming with satisfaction, he lapped the perspiration streaming along her spine. Small tremors and silent sobs wracked Lana who relished being held in a tight embrace.

With a large smile tugging at her lips, she twisted her body to face him again, and caressed his powerful chest with a trembling hand. She enjoyed the sight of her bite and nail marks on his sweaty skin. Her tongue roamed on his chest, savoring his taste and smell, while his rapid heartbeat drummed under her fingers.

"What else can I do for you?" Lana whispered between two licks, throat sore from her moaning and shouting. "Please tell me what you need." He opened his mouth, but right then, the sound of an incoming Skype call on her smartphone shattered the relaxed mood.

Lila Mina

14

A Lesson in Discipline

"Oh, no... what time is it?" Lana attempted to get up, but he still held her tight.

"Much too soon for my liking," Honda growled. "Go ahead and take care of it." Lana jumped out of the sofa to run to her purse. All of her body hurt, but she had to set aside the discomfort. She picked up her smartphone, cleared her throat and sat on the bed, making sure not to push the camera button.

"Jeb! Good morning," she managed to say in her most business-like voice.

"Hi there, Lana, how are you doing?"

"Fine, fine, thank you. Sorry, I'm not in my office so I'm using my smartphone and have problems with my camera. Can we do this voice-only?"

"Sure, no problem. Christie is here with me."

"Hiya Christie, how have you been doing?"

"Hi Lana, just peachy. Before we begin, let me say you have our support. We totally disagree with Michelle's methods. It's really a new low for her."

Lana frowned as she grabbed a notepad and a pen from the nightstand. "Hmm, say that again? Are you referring to something in particular, following up the messy meeting my team had with her this week?"

The line went silent. "Ah no, Lana, I'm talking about the email she sent management-wide just two hours ago. Didn't you get it?"

Lana squeezed her eyes shut; rage engulfed her from head to toes. "No, I haven't seen it yet." It wasn't the time to rant. "I was in a meeting until now and haven't checked my emails for the past hours. My bad, but I've got a pretty good idea of what kind of nonsense she wrote. Anyway, thank you for your support. I'll deal with it after we are done here."

"Ah, well, sorry for being the one to break it to you. You should address that. Do you want to reschedule our call?"

"Not at all. It's a personal beef between Michelle and me, and it shouldn't get in the way of our work. She just showed how bad she is at handling that kind of stuff. Anyway, Jeb, tell me more about the new EU regulation you mentioned in your last email. How will it impact our Japanese clients operating in Europe?"

"Well, as I see it..."

Lana let Jeb go ahead, put the smartphone on speakerphone and wrote notes while laying, naked, on the king-size bed. Another part of her brain was busy coming up with the best way to shut down Michelle once and for all and reverse that shitstorm. Engrossed with her rambling and with keeping track of what Jeb explained, she shut out her environment, the mind-blowing sex she had just had, and the presence of Honda himself.

"So, what will be the timeline?" she asked at some point.

"Well, as you know, EU regulations are pretty much self-executing. As soon as it comes into force at the end of September, it will have the same rank and impact as any domestic statutes. I'd really recommend we start informing our non-EU clients right away."

"Yes, that would be sensible..." Lana's voice hitched, and she flipped on her back, looking down at her legs. To her horror and growing arousal, Honda was now licking and nibbling the inside of her thighs.

"Lana, are you okay?" She heard Christie from afar. Lana closed her eyes and fought to keep her voice steady despite the skills of the thrice-damned man between her legs.

"Yes, sorry Christie, it's just... the network acting up. Go ahead please, give me... give me more details about what your office plans to do on your side."

Furious and shaking her head, Lana threw a blazing look at Honda. She didn't need this! He had promised to let her take care of that call—with no time limitation! Honda's face remained expressionless while his mouth kept crawling higher until his tongue was so close to her traitorous pussy, he could lap her flowing juices at their source. Her body tensed, and it took all of her resolve not to moan out loud. This was delicious and naughty, but also a nightmare.

Her colleagues couldn't catch her climaxing on the phone, not right when her nemesis was unleashing hell on her reputation and would use every single opportunity to bring her down. Consequences be damned, Lana sat up and tried to crawl away from him, denying him the pleasure of eating her out. He had none of it and dug his hands into her legs, keeping her in place. She hissed at him, furious.

"So, Lana, what do you think?"

"Hm, very interesting, Christie..." Lana lied through her teeth; she hadn't listened to one word her colleague had said. "Any chance you'd be okay to send me a short memo to share with my team?"

While she said this, she threw caution out of the window and grabbed Honda's hair to keep him from touching her crotch. She needed to finish her call at once and couldn't care less for his controlling behavior. Looking up, he slapped her hand away, pushed himself up and overcame her, hovering above her. Obviously, he didn't care much for her attitude either. He pursed his lips, and a low growl rose from his chest.

"You'll have it by Tuesday," said Christie's disembodied voice.

"Great, thanks!" It got increasingly difficult to hide the urgency in her voice. "I'll prepare something along those lines for my team and get back to you ASAP for coordinating the details. Please excuse me now. I'd better address that crisis with Michelle..."

"Oh yeah, go ahead! Nice talking with you Lana, good luck! Once again, you have our support."

"Thank you, guys, have a great weekend!" Lana uttered, breathless, just as Honda plunged with his once-again hard shaft inside her with an angry thrust.

"You, too Lana! Bye." And to her immense relief, they ended the call. Lana moaned out loud, another climax shattering her.

Eyes hard, Honda grabbed her hands and held them fast above her head while pounding inside her. "Let's be clear," he uttered. "You should have let me finish it. This is a typical situation where your self-control is key, and I expect you to handle your reaction!" He quickened his speed, and she shook like a rag doll under his assault.

"Understood... ahhhh... nnnnhhhh..." Right then, a thought struck her. She bit her lip. "Ahh... *goshujin sama*... uhnnnnn... forgive me... I... you should discipline me..."

Her words made Honda stop in his tracks; he brought his face just over hers, pinning her down with his gaze and his erection, asserting his dominance over her body and mind.

"Yes... discipline is in order. What do you have in mind? Another, longer session in frustration management or in self-control?" His voice almost a purr, he seemed to enjoy that prospect.

Lana growled. She should have been checking her phone, making calls to her boss, answering her emails, and addressing her professional emergency. Instead, there she was, negotiating with her master the best way to be disciplined. This situation, this request was brand new, and she didn't know how to express her growing, aching need. Maybe this was the hidden desire he had mentioned. *Maybe he meant to bring me to this point all along.*

"I..." Lana closed her eyes, ashamed, feeling like a virgin on her first night. Embarrassment made her blush red, rousing strong waves of anger inside her; she hated being like this, so unsure and ambivalent about her own emotions.

"Open your eyes, and don't look away," Honda ordered while grinding against her even further. She moaned and failed at meeting his gaze. "Shame has no place between us, little *mudansha*. Express yourself, express what is coiled inside you."

Lana squeezed her eyes and raised her hips to meet his, relishing how their bodies joined, taking comfort and strength in it. She let the whirlpool of confusing feelings inside her grow and bloom, like a balloon, until she was able to name them and give them substance. Inhaling deeply, she looked at him square in the eye.

"Please spank me, *goshujin sama*," she answered with a low voice. "Spank me until you come again. My lack of respect was terrible, and I need to learn a lesson."

His pupils dilated, his jaw tightened, and his entire body tensed between her legs. Now, whose self-control was being tested?

"Careful, little *mudansha*," he growled, "for this could last longer than what you find manageable. I will not stop before I find my release... whatever you tell me."

Defiant, Lana quirked an eyebrow. "Well, that's why we call it a punishment, right? Let me prove I am strong enough to endure it, and that I do have some self-control even if it's still lacking. Please."

The more she talked, the more she knew it would be an important test for this unusual relationship of theirs, and the better she felt with her decision. And deep down, regardless of his warning, she also trusted him to stop everything if she found herself in too much distress. Honda brought his mouth over hers.

"You are remarkable, Lana san," he whispered between two licks of her swollen lips. "I have chosen well. Giving you this much-needed punishment will be... enlightening for both of us, and I am confident you can take it." His words sent butterflies to her belly. His confidence in her abilities was staggering. Honda sat on his heels and pulled her toward him. "Lay over my knees. You need not keep silent, but don't move away."

Just as she positioned herself on him, raising her ass and putting her head on her folded arms, her discarded phone buzzed and flashed next to her hand. Richard. Lana tensed but didn't dare move. His grip on her hips increased.

"Do not answer it. Do not think about this. Focus only on me, on yourself, on us. Your mind needs to be centered now; it needs to support your body. As long as your mind remains strong, your body can endure a lot. Do you understand?"

Lana nodded and closed her eyes. "Yes, *goshujin sama*."

"Good," he replied and the next second, his palm connected with her ass cheek. The pain was stringent and more acute than expected. Lana hissed and bit her lip. Fueled by revenge, she wanted to hold on as long as possible; it would be her cries of pain that would bring satisfaction to Honda.

Soon, there were only slapping sounds filling the air. Her cheeks began to burn, covered with angry red marks. He wasn't gentle yet wanted it to last. Tears ran down her cheeks, but still, she kept silent, focusing on the sparkles of pleasure ignited with each slap. His erection jutted against her belly. Now and then, a finger grazed her engorged lips and collected her dripping juices. Lana sobbed, muttering curses under her breath.

Her brain registered what was going on: the fact she turned him on so much, that she was strong enough to give him this, that she had such power over him. It transformed her suffering into a new source of dark pleasure.

Her whimpers of pain became moans of arousal, and renewed energy coursed through her body until a powerful climax washed through her, from head to toes. To her great satisfaction, her release pushed him over the edge. He didn't shout: he roared. Gripping her hips, he spent himself all over her cheeks and lower back. Her abused skin was so hot that it felt cool to the touch and was a blessing.

With heavy pants, Honda collected her in his arms, scooping her from behind. Body shaking, she wept in silence, not only because of the pain and pleasure but also because of her powerful emotional release. Falling asleep on the spot, nice and safe in his arms, sounded perfect. *Wake up now! If you don't tackle Michelle right now, you're as good as dead and can pack your stuff come Monday.*

"*Goshujin sama...*" she whispered, "I... need to make phone calls before I lose the upper hand at my office."

Honda grunted in her hair and removed his arm with no comment. He rolled away from her, in dire need of a break.

Grimacing, Lana got up from the bed, grabbed her smartphone and purse and limped to the huge and luxurious bathroom. With the gorgeous view of Tokyo skyline in front of her, the deep and large bathtub was awfully tempting. *Get a grip, girl. A shower will serve you much better.*

A glance at the mirror and the red and blue finger marks on her ass confirmed that sitting down would test her resilience over the coming days. She had to get her hands on some cream. Turning on the ceiling shower, she sighed in pleasure when warm water cascaded on her head. The various parts of her body that had been roughly handled protested. She focused on the deep-set feelings of satisfaction inhabiting her, channeling them to address the nuclear attack the bitch had unleashed on her.

With a sigh, Lana dried herself and put on a fluffy bathrobe. She sat down carefully on the vanity chair and opened her mailbox. There were twenty-three unread emails, half of them from her senior management. *Brace for impact.*

The email from Michelle was vitriolic, unprofessional, but far from stupid. She knew which buttons to push. After twisting the entire situation to Lana's disadvantage, she made her sound like a megalomaniac, arrogant, incompetent SOB.

Lana swore and cursed aloud in three languages. Her management and colleagues were not stupid or blind, but still, this was getting out of hand and would leave a stain on her record. On top of it, there was the limited, yet real risk that after hearing about this, those two idiots Jonas and Frank would add their two cents just for spite. She didn't even read the other emails. She speed-dialed her boss Richard, vowing to sound composed and unaffected. He picked up right away.

"Lana, where the fuck are you? And what kind of fresh hell have you stirred up again with Michelle?"

"Good evening Richard," she replied, ignoring his rude language and anger. "My apologies for not getting back earlier. I had no chance to do it before now, but you'll soon understand why."

"Really? It'd better be good, because this thing is taking up like wildfire and I don't know how long I can have your back. But first, where have you been all afternoon? How come you went AWOL?"

"I didn't!" Lana lied through her teeth, her hands squeezing her bathrobe out of sheer exasperation. "The other evening, Gabriella and I ran into high-level people from Nakazawa Holdings at a party."

"Nakazawa?! Are you kidding me?"

"Anyway, I ran again into the same people today at lunch and... well, we had a non-stop conversation for two or three hours straight. Extremely intense," she added, grateful her boss couldn't see her blush. "And then, we took a break, I had my Skype call with Jeb and Christie who broke the news about Michelle. I've just finished talking with the Nakazawa people, and now I'm calling you. Do you see now why I didn't drop everything? Nakazawa, Richard! Can you imagine?"

"That... that would be the contract of the decade..." His dreamy voice told her everything she had to know. If his team landed something like this, his annual review would be off the charts; he would get any transfer he'd ask for. "Okay, okay, I'll let it pass this time," he continued, regally. "But please, next time, drop me a line before getting out of touch like this. Now about Michelle..."

"Richard, she is crazy. We can't just allow her to go bonkers like that, CFO or no CFO. She's terrorizing everyone, it's pure power harassment. I'm her target because I'm the threat. We can discuss this on Monday, but don't listen to her mad ramblings."

"Hm, well, she's well-connected and holds many people by the balls, which is why she can continue like this. But I hear you. She's a harpy. Okay, let's talk about this on Monday with Yukiko and Toshiro. We need to come up with a strategy to stop making this sound like it's just about you."

"Thanks, Richard, I appreciate it. Have a nice weekend, then."

"You too! And... good job with Nakazawa. I want to hear more about this soon."

"Yeah, of course!" Lana grimaced; she would have to come up with a plan to wriggle herself out of her lie. After hanging up, she stretched her arms.

Gabriella had sent her a couple of frantic IMs over the previous hours. She decided against a phone call as this would lead her to a delicate conversation she was not ready to have. Besides, who knew who would be right next to Gabriella? Lana sent her friend an upbeat message, telling her everything was under control and that she was meeting her 'main contact' at Nakazawa Holdings. Gabriella wouldn't have to lie to anyone else.

Lana wasn't surprised when she got an instant reply under the form of a string of emojis that said 'you naughty and lucky girl, enjoy your ride, I want all dirty details ASAP'. She snorted in an unladylike fashion. No way she'd give Gabrielle the whole picture. The M-rated version would be enough.

Back in the room, Honda still lay on the bed, flat on his stomach, with a simple white sheet that had fallen off him. She lay down next to him and seized this chance to take a good look at her companion. There were many details on his smooth, heavy-set body that had gone unnoticed when she had been otherwise busy handling him.

While his unlined face and smooth hands were tanned, he was otherwise pale brown. His large and robust back revealed taut muscles. Her nail and teeth marks, some made a couple of hours earlier, others inflicted over a week before, were obvious. But there was also older, paler scar tissue on his lower back that she had missed until now. Other pale pink marks crisscrossed the back of his biceps.

The long scar she had spotted earlier, almost invisible, made her frown. It had too many jagged edges and ridges for a blade or knife to cause it. An accident, most certainly. She couldn't fathom how the wound had looked. Would he ever tell her about it? Asking him seemed impossible.

His thick waist and shapely ass gave way to sturdy legs powerful enough to carry her weight effortlessly. Like his wrists, his ankles betrayed the fact that he was an aikidoka: decades of practice had thickened them to a point where they were next to non-existent.

Lana had always found sleeping men endearing; it was hard not to reach out and caress him. But he was not one to cuddle, so she turned her back to him and closed her eyes for a short nap.

Lana woke up surprised by the lack of a warm body at her side. The sound of running water came from the bathroom. Already 8 pm. On a whim, she got up to knock at the bathroom door but heard nothing. After a second of hesitation, she went in anyway and was greeted by the breathtaking view of Tokyo's skyline and, most importantly, the sight of Honda sliding in the hot tub.

"*Goshujin sama*, forgive the intrusion…"

Honda waved his hand. "It's fine. Join me, but first, please order room service for dinner. A rare steak with vegetables for me; order whatever you wish."

"Very well. Would you care for red wine or anything else?"

Honda smirked at her. "Red wine is fine, but I am no expert. You are Italian, so choose something suitable."

Lana made the call. Back in the bathroom, she took off her bathrobe before stepping in, opposite to him. She hissed at the scalding hot water's touch.

"Too hot for you? You never go to *onsen*? I thought your skin to be thicker than this." Honda chuckled.

Lana threw him a wry look. "I love hot springs, but usually I'm not so bruised when I go there."

His eyes narrowed, and he extended a hand. "Come closer. Let me see." She glided toward him, ending up between his arms. "Stand up and turn around." Lana rose out of the water and faced the windows, spreading her legs. The sight of her purple buttocks where his fingerprints lingered ripped a growl from him.

"We will not do this too often. It will affect your aikido practice, and I will have none of that. Hopefully, this will relieve you a little?" he whispered before ducking lower to press and slide his tongue from her pussy lips to her puckered hole. Lana gasped; only his firm grip on her hips kept her from crumbling down. The combination of stinging pain and sensual pleasure was delightful, and both knew they enjoyed giving and receiving it.

"Yes... Thank you..." she replied under her breath. Honda grunted, face buried in her, and showed his thorough appreciation for her bruised ass. It was outrageous to have such a skillful tongue. Being the object of his devotion made her juices flow anew, and it didn't take long for her to climax.

She had long lost track of the number of times she had come over the past hours. Whatever happened next, it would be a challenge to find a partner who could top him. As domineering and downright annoying—or rather, infuriating—as he was, giving her pleasure was as important to him as taking his, even if under his terms. When Lana recovered, Honda directed her to sit on the border of the tub and then moved to the opposite side.

"So, what is the situation at your office?" he asked.

Such a quick change of topics. She blinked and tried to switch to a more business mode, despite their current situation. "It's far from perfect but seems under control. A meeting with my senior managers on Monday will sort it out once and for all." *High time I get rid of this pressure. I'm tired being Richard's human shield when it comes to handling Michelle.*

Honda quirked an eyebrow. "They didn't demand to see you at once?"

"Was this even an option for me?" she inquired with a mix of defiance and humor. She didn't wait for a reply. "Actually, they did, but thanks to you, I could justify my ill-timed absence."

To her deep satisfaction, Honda seemed puzzled. For once, she was the one surprising him. She shrugged and threw him a coy look. "I told them I was meeting someone associated with Nakazawa Holdings. Funny how dropping that name makes a boss much more understanding and stops them from breathing down your neck."

He pinched his lips in annoyance; maybe he didn't appreciate her use of that name for her own benefits. But he didn't comment on it, merely uttering a grunt.

The doorbell rang. With a sigh of relief, Lana stepped out of the tub, put on her fluffy bathrobe and let in the hotel staff delivering their room service. He set up the table in front of the sofa. Honda came out of the bathroom just as the door closed behind the hotel employee's back, wearing a simple *yukata* provided by the hotel. Lana groaned but kept her composure. There was no helping it: she was way too much appreciative of his body wrapped in traditional attire.

They ate in comfortable silence. After the eventful lunch they had shared earlier, it was nice to enjoy dinner without having to navigate the delicate waters of cross-cultural dominant-submissive and three-way power dynamics. Not to mention the stormy situation at her workplace. It also proved they could be alone in the same room without ending up naked, with body parts probing each other. For the sake of any future interaction in public, it was crucial.

After emptying her second glass of Primitivo, Lana stifled a yawn. The day had been long and demanding at all levels even if beyond satisfying. She would welcome more shut-eye but didn't dare assume this was what her partner had in mind. Her longing look at the bed didn't go unnoticed though, and Honda chuckled.

"Oh, have I exhausted your stamina? This is yet another thing we should work on." Such an insufferable show of typical male cockiness had her throw him a glance that was anything but respectful. This turned his amused smile into a more predatory one, and his eyes took on a warning gleam. "I am almost of the mind to start that part of your training now and remind you of basic rules in matters of etiquette and respect," he purred. "For the sake of your bruised assets, and because I intend to keep you busy tomorrow, let's get some rest now."

Before joining him in the bed, Lana put back on her pants and swapped her bathrobe for a lighter *yukata*. Her eyes closed on what she would later remember as the day before her life was thrown upside down.

15

On Shaky Legs

The room is dark. Empty. Broken furniture and glass clutter the floor. A sickening tangy smell fills my nose. The world is pain. Red, black pain. My body is in pieces, soaked by rivers of blood, but the hole in my heart hurts even more. I can't move. Can't lift a finger. My eyes are open, but everything around me is blurry. Fear rises to new levels when two legs come to stand in front of me.

So. They came back to finish it. Finish me. I choke on the hatred and rage swelling in my chest. They crouch, and a face fills my field of vision. I whimper, the need to scream is overwhelming, but I can't even draw a proper breath.

Slanted yellow eyes stare at me. Lips pull into an ugly smile to reveal long, inhuman teeth. A long red tongue darts out.

With a gasp, Lana sat on the bed, clutching her sheets. The disgusting remnants of her nightmare dissipated like smoke, and already, she couldn't remember all details. Yet fear gripped her, and her heart drummed wildly in her chest.

Danger. We're in danger!

Her trembling hand shook Honda's sleeping form. "Wake up... please, wake up!" She switched on her bedside lamp and glanced at the time. 3:32 am.

Her companion opened a bleary eye. "What is it?"

"*Jishin desu! Jishin desu!*"

Their phones came to life, blaring the shrill alarm and the flat recorded voice warning of an impending large earthquake. Wide awake, the couple jumped out of bed. Lana grabbed her smartphone and started counting seconds. On average, the alarm—which picked up a tremor's P waves, that traveled faster than its destructive S waves—could offer between three and fourteen seconds of heads-up.

"Jishin desu! Jishin desu!"

Four, five, six...

"I have the flashlight, take the bed cover, go to the bathroom!"

Seven, eight, nine...

Honda had barely pushed open the room door when the building began to move, slowly at first, and then with increasing speed. By the time he reached Lana in the shower area of the bathroom, he couldn't keep his balance. She caught him when he fell, saving him from hitting his head against the bathtub wall. She covered their heads with the thick and fluffy duvet to protect them from anything heavy enough to split their skulls.

"Shouldn't we go into the tub?" Lana had to shout to be heard over the frightening rumbling noise.

Honda shook his head. "No! So close to the windows, it would be too risky!"

"Oh, *Dio mio...*" Lana whispered, trying to suppress her exploding fear.

"So long... It's a strong one..." Honda acknowledged, knuckles white as he held on the edge of the tub.

Their building was now oscillating awfully. Lana squeezed her eyes shut; the ground at their feet was not made of hard rock, but sand and porous clay. Adjacent to the bayside, their hotel had been built on man-made land, regained over the sea. Even worse, being on the 31st floor amplified the quaking.

Peeking outside, Lana beheld an impossible, out-of-this-world spectacle. Lana's stomach flip-flopped. "*Dio mio!*" she exclaimed again, this time not bothering to hide her terror.

Steel and glass skyscrapers screeched and undulated like bamboo trees in a storm, lights flickering against the heavy blackness of the night. Mother Earth heaved and shrugged, indifferent to the transient world of men and their understanding of reality.

Honda put a hand on her arm. "Listen to me." The fact that he didn't bother with the formal register betrayed his tension. "The building's doing what it's supposed to do. It's good it's moving like this, as it's new and follows the strictest standards. The epicenter isn't under us, so we'll be fine!"

Lana let his words sink in. He was right; it was terribly impressive and frightening, but they would be all right as long as they didn't get hurt by debris on the floor or falling on them.

After two long minutes, the rumbling and shaking subsided. They shared a knowing glance. Many strong aftershocks could be expected, and they needed to get to the ground floor. Her smartphone was already feeding detailed data.

"It was a M8.4! And here in Minato-ku, it registered as *shindo* 5+." The Japanese earthquake scale went up to a maximum of 7. It provided a precise indication of how strongly the surface shook and the level of destruction caused at a specific point.

"The epicenter was in Gunma prefecture," Lana pointed out, relieved. This was deep in the mountains, north of Tokyo metropolitan area. "No tsunami alert for now."

Honda nodded, but his next words didn't brighten her spirits. "Remember what happened in 2011. Strong earthquakes like this one can be either pre-shocks announcing larger ones or trigger other faults. We should expect bad surprises in the coming days, weeks or even months. For now, let's put on our shoes and head for the staircases."

Back in the main room, Lana grabbed her purse and didn't bother changing back into her dress. Her *yukata* would have to do. She threw a disgusted look at her black pumps and their 7 cm-tall heels.

"I won't get far with those..."

Honda took one shoe and snapped the heel at its base. Before she could protest, he did the same with the other one and handed her the 'reformed' pair without any further comment.

"Th... thank you," Lana managed to utter, outraged. "I'll write that on my insurance claim..." she added under her breath. Of course, her shoes were far from being flat, but she had to concede it was a little easier to walk fast now.

The corridor was dark, only illuminated by emergency lights and the flashlights of guests coming out of their rooms, some more frightened than others. Everyone was heading for the emergency exits. Small aftershocks rocked the ground, but after the main tremor, they were manageable.

Right when Honda and Lana were about to push the heavy emergency door, a commotion behind them caught Lana's attention. An obviously pregnant Western woman in nightwear stood on the threshold of her room, skin too pale and eyes wide with fright. She held the hand of a sobbing boy in pajamas, not older than three or four. Blood from a nasty gash on his brow smeared his face.

"Help! Help us, oh please... someone help us!" She pressed her distended belly and had difficulty standing upright. Lana grabbed Honda's elbow and pointed wordlessly at the distraught family. They wouldn't make the trip down 31 floors on their own.

"You carry the child while I support the mother," he said. "Explain this to her."

"Understood." Lana ran up to them and kneeled in front of the boy. The gash needed medical attention but didn't seem life-threatening. "Hey hey there, shhh, don't be scared, everything will be fine," she tried with the kindest voice she could muster. Comforting children wasn't something she was used to. She glanced up at the mother who grimaced in pain and clutched her lower belly. "Ma'am, we'll help you evacuate. Can you walk?"

The woman groaned and supported herself against the wall. "Thank you. I'm due in six weeks, it's really hard..."

Lana translated, and Honda frowned. "We have to go now, but we will be as careful as possible. Also, they need to put on shoes."

After Lana relayed his concern, the woman pointed inside the room. "Our shoes are in the closet." Lana went inside to pick them and saw various pairs of sneakers, including one close to her size. She took a pair and joined their group in the hall.

"Do you mind if I borrow one of your pairs? It will be much safer to carry your son if I can walk properly." Embarrassed, she showed her dismantled Louboutin.

"Yes, of course! Help yourself."

Relieved, Lana put on a black and white pair. "I will take care of your son. What's his name?" They were taking too much time, but she tried her best to rein in her impatience. It became urgent to reach the ground floor.

"Leo, but he doesn't speak English, only Dutch. I'm Maya."

"I can't speak Dutch," Lana said with a smile, "but we will make do. I'm Lana, and this is Honda san. Are you traveling alone?" They headed to the staircase.

"No, but my husband is in Kyoto for a two-day business trip. We were supposed to wait for him here before flying back home…"

Right then, dozens of phone alarms went off. "*Jishin desu! Jishin desu!*" The recorded voice blared from everywhere, turning even more frightening.

People screamed, and everyone dropped to their knees. Lana covered Leo's head as best as she could. The building shook again, and she tried to calm the boy with shushing sounds. The poor kid shivered and whimpered. She gritted her teeth. It was going to be a hard trip down the stairs, with sensitive buttocks on top of it.

The stairways were packed with guests heading for the lobby floor. Most were Japanese and knew how to behave and what to do, to Lana's great relief.

"Lana san, don't wait for us. Go as fast as you can with the boy; we will be behind," Honda ordered.

Over his cries of protestation, Lana moved the boy to her back and winced as his small legs dug into her bruised buttocks. "Okay, let's do this together, big boy." Not looking back, she started their long trek. "I'm sorry, coming through... please step aside... this is a medical emergency... please let me through... thank you... so sorry, we can't wait... this boy needs help...". On and on, Lana blurted out apologies as she scrambled down the stairs, trying to keep it civil.

Soon, this became one the most harrowing experiences in her life. After six or seven flights of stairs, her legs started to protest and couldn't stop shaking. It was now next to impossible for her to stop without crumbling to the ground. After ten floors, her lungs screamed for more oxygen.

Admit it, girl: he was right. You've got to work on this lousy stamina of yours...

Her back and arm muscles burned under Leo's weight, and her bruises acted up. She lost count of how many times she cursed Honda, while at the same time praying nothing serious would happen to him. She had to focus on each step in front of her.

Phone alarms kept blaring as aftershocks rocked the building, eliciting more and more shouts of fear from the hundreds of people in the darkened stairs around them. Leo couldn't stop crying and moaning in her ear, making the whole ordeal even more strenuous. 17th floor... 13th floor...

On the 4th floor, a door was open, and hotel staff were calling out to the guests with flashlights. "Come here! This is the lobby! Please be careful and follow us!"

With a big sigh of relief, Lana stepped out and limped to the nearest staff member. "Please! Help me! This boy has a nasty wound!"

"Go over there—we have a small first-aid zone set up over there."

Lana cried out in pain and relief when she put Leo on the floor. Her trembling legs gave way, and she fell on the floor, unable to move anymore and panting hard. Reclining against the wall, she extended her limbs with a grimace, keeping an eye on the boy as the staff cleaned his wound and put a bandage on his head. Her muscles were twitching on their own. Guests kept coming out from the emergency exit, but Honda and Maya were still nowhere to be seen. Anxiety and exhaustion made her nauseous. *Hurry up already!*

While the 4G network was out of service, the hotel's Wi-Fi was still accessible. Facebook had wasted no time activating its emergency location service, and like other friends and colleagues, she was identified as being affected. She checked the box confirming she was fine. To her dismay, Gabriella hadn't been online since the previous evening. Tim, Yukari, Naomi... her closest dojo friends were still unaccounted for, too.

Lana switched to Line, a Japanese IM app also used for placing calls. The company had also reacted right away and made their phone service free of charge in the affected zones. *Come on, Gabriella, come on! Pick up!*

Her friend didn't answer. Lana rubbed her eyes as tears threatened to spill. She sent messages on her accounts, asking her to poke her back as soon as possible. Her thoughts snapped back to Honda, and then to Yuki. She had no way to contact her. *How can I even face her if her husband dies on my watch? What can I tell her if–*

Her spiraling train of thoughts screeched to a halt when Honda and Maya came out the door. Lana tried to get up, but her legs didn't obey. "Leo, see? Here comes your Mamma!" His head wound now patched, the little boy rested at her side in shock.

"Oh, Leo!" Maya walked the final meters on her own and sat next to her son. "Thank you, thank you both so much" She squeezed Lana's hand with tears in her eyes.

Lana smiled, eyes blurry with her own tears of relief. "I'm so happy everyone is safe. It was scary," she added, looking at Honda who had plopped down on her other side.

He nodded in agreement, eyes closed. His breathing was shallower than usual. "Are you all right, Lana san?"

"Yes. My legs and other places are killing me, but it's okay. You?"

"I need to work on my endurance as well. I am unharmed, however."

"Have... have you heard from Yuki sama?"

Honda opened his eyes and took out his old-fashioned mobile phone. "Nothing for now, networks are out."

"Is she on any social network?"

"No, we have *keitai* phones and don't use those."

"Ah, too bad." Lana hesitated. "I can't reach Gabriella, either..."

"I imagine she is as connected as you?"

"Yes, precisely. I mean, she could be outside Wifi range or something..."

"Yes, it is too soon to draw any conclusion." His head rested against the wall. "Try to sleep for a while. We will leave at dawn, about one hour from now."

"Leave?"

"Yes, we will walk back to my home. We will collect water bottles and depart as soon as possible before it gets too hot."

"But I should try to get home..."

Honda shook his head, his face set in his now familiar stern mask. "We will first go to my home and when the traffic conditions allow it, we will take my car and drive to your place. But if you think for one second that I will let you walk home on your own, you are mistaken. As for me, I need to get back to check on Yuki."

"I... It's true I can't see myself trekking to Mitaka on my own, but... where do you live?"

"South of Mitaka in Setagaya ward, twenty minutes by car from our dojo and near Soshigaya park—about fifteen kilometers from here. In normal conditions, it would take us about three hours. But we are tired, it will be hot and humid, and there is no guessing the road conditions. So it will take us twice the time, a little less if we make good speed. Mitaka is even farther from here."

Lana sighed. "All right then, let's go back to your house. But do you have any idea of the way? We can check on my smartphone and make some kind of rough itinerary."

"This will not be necessary. It is almost on a straight line westward if we take Tokyo Tower as the starting point. After Roppongi, we will aim at Shibuya and then advise. Have some rest now." Lana didn't argue. One more check of her various apps told her Gabriella was still offline. She turned off her phone and closed her eyes, hoping she wouldn't slump against him and drool on his shoulder.

It seemed like she had only slept five minutes when a solid grip shook her shoulder. "Wake up, Lana san. The sun is up. We should be on our way." At that time of the year, sun rose before 5 am. Honda handed her two PET bottles of water. "They are rationing water, and I could only get one for each of us. Put them in your bag. Can you stand?"

Lana tried to hide a yawn and pushed herself up, grimacing. "Hm, it's going to be tough, but we don't have a choice, do we?" She turned toward Maya who was half asleep, holding Leo tight. "Maya, we are leaving now. Please stay here where it's safe. I'm sure your husband will soon be with you. Try to get in touch with your embassy, okay?"

"Thank you so much again, Lana." Maya struggled not to cry. "Please be careful. God bless you."

Lana gave her an encouraging smile and patted Leo's head. It was tough leaving them alone, but they were in no condition to travel with them. A glance at her phone informed her Gabriella had checked in on Facebook, and the other members of their dojo had done the same. That was enough for now. Lana shared the good news with Honda who nodded in satisfaction.

They stepped outside the hotel. Lana stopped in her tracks, stunned by the scene around them. Glass and debris littered the empty road, but overall the damage wasn't as severe as she would have expected. No car drove around. The noise level was deafening though: firetruck and ambulance sirens blared in the distance and helicopters hovered in the sky. In this business neighborhood, with new skyscrapers all around, it didn't surprise her that every building still stood.

Many people were already walking home. As the day advanced, the streets would be packed. From what Lana remembered of the footages from 2011, it would turn the city into a low-key remake of a zombie movie.

"Lana san!" Lana spotted Honda on the other side of the street. "Come on now, let's keep together!" Lana jogged to join him. "Let's head this way," he added, pointing west.

Lila Mina

16

Burnt Bridges

After walking a few hundred meters, Lana shook her head in relief. *Thank goodness I'm not alone in this.*

The crowds around them were subdued and for now kept their wits. On such a large scale as this, catastrophes brought out the worst in people, not to mention the worst people out.

Stopping now and then to sip water, they walked slowly but steadily. Her body hurt everywhere, so she focused on putting one foot in front of the other. When they reached Shibuya crossing, they had gone a meager five kilometers in more than an hour and half.

As they moved to a smaller street, away from the main lanes, Lana grabbed Honda's arm and pointed at a convenience store. "The *conbini* over there is open. Can we stop to buy something to eat?"

"Good idea. If we are lucky, they have a few *onigiri* left."

The store was designated as a safe place for those walking home during an emergency. A dozen people stood around, drinking water and eating plain onigiri rice balls handed out by staff. They could also use the Wi-Fi access point or queue for the green NTT phone outside the shop. The ISSN line made it possible to leave and listen to safety confirmation messages on landline numbers through the national disaster emergency number. They were lucky; as this was a side street, fewer than ten people waited in line.

"I'll buy a couple of things, enough to give us energy," Lana said.

Honda glanced at the line of people with a sigh resignation. "Go ahead. I will call Yuki in the meantime. Do you have cash? Take no free products if we can pay for them. These should be for people in need."

There wasn't much left on the shelves, but Lana grabbed three *onigiri* filled with dried salmon, two bottles of orange juice and two chocolate and cereal bars. She also picked up hand soap sheets, two pairs of socks and the last pack of band-aids. Without socks, bloody blisters already covered her feet; her borrowed sneakers were a bit too tight and rubbed on her naked feet. The shop's restrooms were out of order, but a sign said the staff had installed chemical toilets outside.

Outside, Honda was already fourth in line. "Could you please hold everything for me for a moment? I need to use the toilets set up over there."

A glance at the narrow street along the shop made Honda frown. "Hm, all right, but hurry."

Lana hastened toward the designated area. Her business done, she found herself alone in the dark alley. Her spine tingled as she headed back to the main street, and goosebumps covered her arms. Glancing over her shoulder, she inhaled sharply. *Oh shit, way to go. Did you forget all you learned back in Italy?*

She was no longer alone. Three men with bleached hair and leather clothes were creeping up on her. *Yakuza.* On normal days, she would never care about those criminals. Messing with foreigners meant more trouble than it was worth for the organized crime. Thugs left them alone as the police would be hard pressed not to do a serious inquest with a foreign embassy breathing down their neck. Still, her relative immunity didn't mean much in a time of crisis. Police were busy and had no time for the fate of a lone businesswoman.

"So, pretty blond, where're you goin'?"

"Come and say hello to my big friend down here!"

"Come on, don't be shy, let's have fun! I'll make you forget all those puny Western boys…"

Lana kept moving and quirked an eyebrow. "What's the matter, boys? Are you lost or what? Looking for your mamma?" she sneered, staring straight ahead of her. Playing the hapless victim wasn't in her habits. Her unexpected language proficiency and aggressive behavior stopped the men in their tracks. It gave Lana the opportunity to continue, so she quickened her pace.

She was almost out of the backstreet when one of them grabbed her arm from behind. "Bitch, look at me when I'm talking to you," he snarled, furious.

Recoiling in disgust at the animalistic lust distorting his face, Lana didn't stop in her tracks. Her training kicked in and she went with *shiho nage*. Using his momentum, she caught his wrist and led him away, made a cutting movement across his hips, twisted on herself and brought him on his back. She pulled hard enough on his hand to hurt his shoulder. To her dark satisfaction, he crumbled at her feet with a scream of pain. Right when she was about to dart, the second guy blocked her path, and put a blade under her nose.

"Oh, feisty, aren't we? Even better! You'll pay for that, cunt!"

Determined, Lana reached out to seize the hand holding the knife. Right then, the man flew back and crashed against the opposite wall.

In front of her stood Honda, his face a mask of cold fury. He disposed of the third guy who thought it was a good idea to jump him. Thanks to a version of *kotegaeshi* where Honda didn't hold back, the thug collapsed, in tears, his hand and wrist broken in two different places and his shoulder and elbow dislocated.

Honda's pure killer look, total control over his body and fluid moves were a gloriously arousing sight. Lana understood why he had chosen aikido over other kinds of *budo*. Even though aikidoka could maim and kill, any martial arts not giving priority to self-defense would have made him a mortal danger for anyone else. Looking at the three men on the ground, cradling their limbs, she couldn't help a satisfied grin. *What a great team we make!*

Adrenaline pumped through her system, mixing with an unexpected rush of arousal. They were in public, so it was a bad idea. Still, she took two steps toward him, and before he could even ask her if she was unharmed, molded herself against his frame. A hard kiss landed on his lips.

Then, just as quickly, she stepped back. "That's how you say thank you in French," she whispered, her voice a little too rough.

Honda snatched her chin in a tight grip. Lana held her ground and didn't blink, delighted by the dark energy flowing from him, pressing against her. His eyes were heavy, lust for blood battled with lust for her; to her surprise, her reaction was stronger than expected. Blood rushing to her head, the sound that passed her lips was more a groan than a gasp.

"I would love to teach you a lesson on self-control in public, but we have no time for playing games," Honda grumbled. "We need to be on our way."

Lana remained in his grasp for two more breaths, enjoying the moment in all its danger and promises. Then she lowered her eyes and submitted; she still couldn't believe how easy it was to do with him. What kind of spell had he cast on her?

"Of course, *goshujin sama*." Honda waited a few more seconds before releasing her, his own temper once again under control.

He handed her the bags; incredibly enough, he had kept them in his hand during the short-lived fight. "Have a *onigiri* and something to drink."

Lana marveled at how easily they switched back to a normal conversation; with any luck, she was getting the hang of the compartmentalization thing. "Could you let Yuki sama know about our situation?" She took the pair of socks and band-aids out, followed by the food and drink.

"Yes, and she also left a message. She is unharmed, our house suffered no clear damage, and thanks to our well, we are not experiencing any water shortage. Electricity is still out in our neighborhood, but we are not affected thanks to our generator."

"You're well prepared."

"It is a large estate," Honda explained, "and we have enough space to store what we need. Let's go now."

Lana gulped down her rice ball and her orange juice but stopped in her tracks. "Oh, before we leave, please give me five minutes to use the *conbini's* Wi-Fi. Let me try to contact Gabriella."

This time, her friend picked up right away. "Oh, Lana! It's such a relief to hear you, are you okay, *cara mia*?"

"Yes, don't worry! And you?"

"Scared like hell. A few glasses fell over and crashed on the floor, but nothing serious. Electricity was out for a few hours, but now it's back on. I've got bad news though. You'll want to sit down, darling"

"What? What is it?"

"I passed in front your building on my way to the supermarket to stock up basic goods... A fire broke out in your condo wing. Most of it is gone and still smoking. I've got pics, I'll send them to you in a sec."

Lana leaned against the CVS wall and slouched down to the ground, stunned. Of course, it was replaceable stuff, and she was not invested in the unit itself. *But what about...?*

Squeezing her eyes shut, she pushed the thought back, bile rising in her throat. Then she took a deep breath. If that was lost as well, there wasn't nothing she could do, and perhaps it was even for the best.

"Ahhh... shit... oh my... that's tough. Well, I'm glad I wasn't there..."

"Yeah, I wept in relief knowing you were out last night!" Gabriella sighed. "All right, I sent you the pics. It's bad, but you know I have a copy of all your papers."

"Yes, thank goodness we planned for it." Lana grunted.

The pics made her ill. Gabriella hadn't exaggerated: soot blackened four or five floors of her nine-story high condo block, right in the section hosting her unit. Talk about no luck. Even if by some miracle her apartment wasn't burned to crisp, moving back in right away would be impossible. She'd have to throw out everything.

"Well, you can crash at my place. Where are you now, and where are you going?"

"Outside Shibuya, on our way to Honda sensei's house in Setagaya. Do you have steady access to the network now?"

"Yeah, more or less. I forgot my portable Wi-Fi unit at work, but my neighbor opened her network to everyone, bless her soul. The good news is, Michelle is no longer a major priority, right? The bitch..." Both women chuckled ruefully before Gabriella continued, serious again. "Lana, about him. Is everything okay? I know it sounds stupid to ask this now, and you're a big girl having a great time. I told you to have fun, but I shouldn't worry, right? You've got this under control and can handle him?"

Lana smiled. Her friend was such a mother hen. "Everything is fine; we're not doing anything I don't like or don't want, and right now, we're focused on more pressing issues anyway. Let's discuss this next time we meet, because we have to get moving now. I'll call you later today, okay?"

"All right, good luck out there. I guess you're in for a long walk, right? Be careful."

"Thank you, you too!" Lana hung up and pressed her palms to her eyes. *Can this stop now? I wanna sleep...*

"What happened? What did she tell you?"

She glanced up and winced against the harsh sunlight behind Honda's hovering frame. It was still early, yet too bright and hot for comfort. "I'm homeless. My apartment was at best damaged, at worst destroyed in a fire that took out most of my building."

Silent, Honda cocked his head and stared at her. Time came to a standstill; Lana grew aware of the gravel scratching the skin of her knees through the thin cotton of her *yukata*, adding to her throbbing thighs and buttocks. A part of her embraced this tolerable pain—a welcome distraction from the chaos around them and the uncertainty swelling inside her.

Then, with surprising softness, Honda seized her elbow to pull her up. "This is extremely unfortunate, and I am glad you were with me last night. But no, you are not homeless. You will stay with us."

Only his firm grip prevented her from taking a step back. "What? It's impossible, too much too soon. And what about Yuki sama? She can't agree to this. Can you imagine the unbearable tensions? I'll go to Gabriella's."

"Oh, the news will delight Yuki to no end." Honda smirked. "She will make the same proposal immediately. As for the rest, we have plenty of room. You will continue to lead your life as you please and move out whenever you wish. This is an easy and practical solution, with more space and flexibility than at your friend's place."

It was her turn to scrutinize him in silence. *We've bared ourselves to each other, and yet, I know almost nothing about him, even less her. Where are we going with this? It's not a game, is it? Am I so important to him?*

She suckled her bottom lip and jumped to the next level. "Well, her apartment has only two rooms, so yes, I guess it would be convenient. But only as a temporary solution until I find something else, or my company provides me with a furnished unit," she hastened to add. "Thank you very much for your generous offer. I'll pay a rent and cover my share of expenses."

Honda snorted. "Out of question, you will be our guest. Your continuous presence will already be ample compensation."

A smirk and quirked eyebrow told him what she thought of his thinking. She fixed her clothes, re-tied her hair and put back her half-empty bottle in her bag. "This time, I'm ready to go."

Lila Mina

17

Creepy Encounters

They took off, still going westward but moving up north, avoiding the larger avenues and narrower streets where aftershocks would expose them more easily to falling tiles and debris. During the first stretch, they joined an endless line of people drifting in the same direction.

The crowd followed the tracks of the Keio-Inokashira train line as it was the easiest way to not get lost. The first goal was Shimokitazawa station, and then it would be a straight line for eight kilometers.

At Shimokitazawa, Honda led them back to quieter streets, away from the throngs of walkers. Despite her best efforts, Lana lagged behind him. With each step, the day grew hotter and her legs heavier. The weather was cloudy, the humidity levels high, and she perspired profusely; for now, they weren't burning under a scorching sun. Still, her fair skin was doomed to get sunburned. Honda would turn a darker shade of tan, lucky him.

She wasn't the only one to notice. "Let's take a short break," Honda said. "Your face is red. Go sit in the shade on that bench over there."

"I'll be fine. We don't have time to waste."

With an aggravate sigh, Honda grabbed her elbow, and led her to the bench. "Sit. Five minutes will not make a big difference anyway. Let me check to see if I can find anything else to drink around here. Wait for me."

Lana sighed, not even trying to argue with his unnecessary bossiness. *Boy, I must be exhausted. Let's be honest, it'll be good to stop for a minute.*

She took a long sip at her now lukewarm water and grimaced. Her last bottle was almost empty.

Honda had just turned around the corner when someone tugged at her elbow. Lana couldn't help a yelp when she recognized the granny who had taunted her in front of the love hotel in February. *What is she doing around here?*

"*Obaa san*," Lana said softly. The disaster had to be especially daunting and stressful for older people. "I'd never thought we'd meet again. Are you all right? Do you need anything?"

"Do you have *amazake* with you?" This time, her voice was frail and high-pitched. What an odd request. Sweet sake wasn't something anyone carried with them, even less in those circumstances.

Lana frowned and shook her head. "No, I'm sorry. How about water instead?" She showed her almost empty PET bottle. Quick as lightning, the old woman grabbed the proffered bottle and emptied it. Lana blinked in surprise.

The woman offered a slight bow of gratitude as deep as her hunched back allowed. Lana returned the move by reflex. "Thank you for your kindness, little one. Let me give you something in return." She foraged in a large bag hanging on her back and took out two worn-out long towels. "Put one on your head."

"Oh, thank you so much *obaa chan*, but I cannot accept. You'll need this more than I do."

"Don't be stupid, now. Take it and use it as a hat before you burn to a crisp. Why, with light hair like this, you might go up in flames!" she cackled, and Lana shivered despite the heat, remembering their unsettling first meeting. "This one is for your husband. Glad to see he made you an honest woman," the old woman added with a wink.

Lana blushed and shook her head, embarrassed and once again annoyed at the woman's mingling in her business. "Ah, he is not my husband."

The old one snickered. "Is that so? You called him as such, and he does seem to order you around, as he would his wife. Those men. Always so bossy, aren't they?"

"Errr... yes... well, it's... a bit complicated, I'm afraid..."

The same odd gleam in the granny's hooded eyes that had rattled Lana in February was back. Her face shifted to wear a knowing, unsettling look. "Oh, I see. Then he is your *master*. Hm... *Nogitsune* will find this very informative."

"Wait... what? What did you—"

"Lana san, here is some water, drink this bottle in full before we move on."

Lana jumped on her seat and turned toward Honda, who had come back on her left. "What? Oh, thank you, but listen, I don't understand what's going on. This old woman here..."

Honda frowned and glanced around. "What old woman?"

"Well, this one, of course. This small—"

To her dismay, they were alone the narrow street. "I... Where did she go? I had a full conversation with an old granny while you were gone... She... she even gave me those towels to protect our heads."

Honda shrugged. "Well, these old people walk faster than we often expect. This is a nice gift though. We can use it."

The encounter left Lana confused, but she kept it to herself. The heat and exhaustion had certainly made her oversensitive. Finishing her new bottle of water, she wrapped the not-so-clean towel on her head, following his example. In the end, she couldn't help herself. "*Goshujin sama*, what is '*nogitsune*'?"

Honda rounded on her. The intensity on his face startled her and she took a step back. "Why are you asking me this?"

"Errr... it's just something that *obaa chan* said."

His face darkened, and he gave a hard glance at their surroundings. "Hm, there is no reason for her to use this word. You must have misunderstood. Let's go now," he ordered, taking off without a back glance.

Lana blinked at his rebuke. Looking up the word sounded like a good idea because she was convinced she had not misunderstood the creepy woman. Shaking her head, she jogged to catch up with him; they had more pressing things on their plates, anyway.

They made two more pit-stops at a CVS, but food and drinks had become scarce. Disrupted supply routes wouldn't get back to normal for several days. The need for water became urgent. Finally, they came across a Buddhist temple nestled in a park. Bordered by a long, white and grey wall, its imposing eight-meter tall gate marking the entrance. The tall and elegant pagoda, standing in a large courtyard right in front of the entrance, seemed intact.

"Sorry, but can we stop again? I need a short break. How about sitting under that *karamon*?"

A quick glance at her face was enough to convince Honda. "Yes, go ahead and enjoy the shade. Sometimes temples have vending machines in the back, I will check it out."

Lana sat on the large and flat stones paving the main gate of the temple. Her back against the heavy and bronze-ornamented wooden doors, she contemplated her surroundings.

A mix of new and older houses, a couple of apartment condos, but mostly private homes with tiny gardens: this was a typical Tokyo neighborhood. Many older buildings had suffered from the previous night's strong shakes, but none had burnt down or been reduced to dust. A stroke of luck, but also good preparation and experience. *People and buildings sway, but at the end they resist and overcome. Resilience is the blood of this country.*

Honda came back and handed her a bottle of water. "Drink this and pour this one on your face and neck to cool down. Keep some to wet your towel. You are again too red to my liking."

Lana gulped the precious liquid. "It can't be worse than when we train in August, can it?"

"You are almost as purple and much more exhausted and dehydrated than after a simple one-hour training session. Let me help you. Bend back," he said before pouring water on her reclined head and hair with a careful gesture. Relief was instantaneous. Too bad everything would dry in a blink.

"Don't you need water as well?"

"A wet towel is enough. Don't worry about me." His voice had softened. Water trickling down her face, she opened her eyes and caught him watching her with a new intensity.

She arched an eyebrow. "I'll stop worrying when you do," she retorted matter-of-factly while re-tying her wet and messy hair in a low bun. *A shower. My kingdom for a nice, cool shower...*

Honda grunted; any softness that had crept in disappeared. "I am not your responsibility."

"Ah, that's what you say! While this is heavily tilting in your favor, our agreement goes both ways in my book. What will I tell Yuki sama if you end up with a heat stroke, hm? 'My apologies, we walked for more than six hours under relentless heat, he drank less than me, but he told me everything was fine, and it wasn't my job to ask, and you know men, when it comes to their health, they're always spot on, so I trusted his word...'" She smirked. "I'm sure she would understand and not be mad at me."

She wasn't surprised when Honda stepped inside her personal sphere and towered over her, but the smile tugging at his lips was unexpected. "I wonder if inviting you to stay in my home is such a good idea. Two strong-headed women with quick wits... I can already see you conspiring against me. Maybe I should sleep with a blade under my pillow from now on?"

Lana stifled her own smile and lowered her eyes with a falsely demure attitude. "Oh no, you shouldn't be afraid. After all, I'm the poster girl for obedient respect..."

Something a little dark and dangerous clouded his face, and he cupped her cheek. "Yes, I will have your obedience, particularly in more private settings."

Lana shivered, their memorable moments together flashing in her mind. "You have it. I promised, didn't I?" she replied in a whisper.

His grip tightened on her jaw. "You did, and I am grateful for it," Honda said in kind. They stared at each other for a few heartbeats, but a moderate aftershock interrupted whatever brewed again between them. Wary, they watched their surroundings, checking if anything threatened to fall on their heads.

"Let's hurry now," Honda urged after the tremors ceased. "Those clouds over there? A thunderstorm is coming our way. It will help with the sun and heat, but our trek will become more unpleasant."

Thirty minutes later, the skies opened over the battered megalopolis. In a blink, those walking home got drenched to the bone. At first, Lana was relieved to feel so much water on her, but after a while, her spirits became as dampened as her body. Her legs and lower back were a thick mass of hurting muscles; it was hard to keep herself from sitting by the road and crying her eyes out. Only her pride kept her from breaking down in front of Honda, giving her the motivation to keep on walking.

Two broken and discarded umbrellas laying on the ground saved them from complete misery. Still, with their *yukata*, the rain slowed them—or rather Lana—down, and it took them two more hours to arrive in an upscale neighborhood. The street signs around them told her that they had reached Setagaya ward. By then, not many people walked with them anymore. The properties surrounding them were larger than usual for Japan. Money was no issue for the residents.

"I only see fallen tiles here and there, no sign of significant damage," Lana pointed out.

"Residents around here take good care of their houses, with frequent repairs and maintenance work. It is expensive but necessary."

They were alone in the street now, and it wasn't surprising given the downpour falling on their heads. Movement caught her eye, and she tapped her companion's arm.

"What is this kid doing on his own, playing in the rain today of all days? Do you know him?" Ahead of them, a child jumped in muddy puddles under a yellow umbrella.

"Hm... no, but then, many new families have moved in recently. Oi!" he shouted at the child. "Go home! You shouldn't be outside now!"

The child didn't stop playing, and the couple heard him laugh. "Ah, come on." Lana sighed. "Let's not waste more time. He is well equipped to play in the rain, anyway."

Honda grunted, and they turned a corner. He came to a brusque halt. "Oh. This is Nakazawa sama's car in front of my house." He didn't even bother to hide his annoyance.

"He must have wanted to check on Yuki sama," Lana mused aloud, tired, soaked, miserable and dreaming of dry clothes and a bed. "Wait, how are we going to explain me being with you?"

"Leave it to me. Whatever happens, speak only if asked a direct question. Stay behind me and be quiet."

"I get the picture. Can we go in now?" she replied tartly.

Honda pivoted on his heels, lips pinched with aggravation. "This. This is what you need to keep in check: your attitude. You may be tired but behaving like this around him is the last thing you should do. I have a low tolerance for it in general, but this could be disastrous right now. Do you understand?"

Lana's blood began to boil. *My attitude? Give me a break! What about yours? Can we not just relax a little bit here?*

By some miracle, she managed not to lash out. Both were at their limits, and it was neither the time nor the place to argue; Nakazawa's abrasive reputation preceded him. "Yes..." she hissed between her teeth. "My apologies, *goshujin sama*. I will keep quiet."

Honda stared at her for a few more heartbeats like he was prone to do when they clashed. It reminded her of *zanshin*, the necessity to keep an eye on your opponent after taking them down to make sure they were neutralized. It summed up their relationship pretty well. Their wordless confrontation came to an end when they heard the same laugh as before. Both glanced around, expecting to see the kid, but he was nowhere to be seen.

"Oh... how beautiful. Would you look at that?" Lana grabbed Honda's arm, forgetting the mischievous child. A bright and colorful sun shower lightened up the western side of the horizon.

To her surprise, his muscles stiffened under her fingers. "*Kitsune no yomeiri!*" he muttered. "Here and now? But then... was this *amefurikozo*?"

Lana frowned; his words didn't make sense. "What does a fox's... 'wedding' have to do with this? And what is *amefurikozo*?"

Honda gave her a blank stare, but then regained his usual composure. "*Kitsune no yomeiri* means indeed just this-the wedding of a fox-and this is what we call this phenomenon. *Amefurikozo* is the name of... a sort of... spirit who can adjust rainfall to help foxes who need it for their wedding."

"What a nice story!" Lana exclaimed with a smile. "In Italy, we say it means that two cats are... well, doing it." She chuckled. "I love this kind of lore. I don't know much about *yokai* and other Japanese ghosts, however."

Honda's face turned dark again, and his eyes narrowed. "Those are not–" He stopped, shaking his head. "Anyway, we are standing here in the rain when my home is right there. This is ridiculous. Let's go now, and remember, let me handle this."

Lila Mina

18

Master and Mistress of the House

HONDA STROLLED TOWARD his home and typed in the entrance code to the side door of a larger gate. Once inside, Lana caught herself before she whistled in admiration.

The property included a huge one-story, traditional house with a blue-tiled roof; a spacious garden surrounded it. A snow-white wall ran around the estate and provided privacy from prying eyes.

An engraved family crest decorated the extremities of dark grey roof tiles on top of the wall, similar to the one Honda had worn on his formal kimono during the wedding. Behind the eastern side of the wall, she caught a glimpse of a middle-sized Shinto shrine. It was tucked among tall pine trees planted across the grounds that offered cool shade during summer.

Crossing a small courtyard, Honda pushed aside the sliding doors of the house, and they stepped inside the *genkan*. They took off their shoes, to Lana's great relief.

"Yuki san, I am back. Are you here?" He grabbed a couple of hand towels hanging on a rack and gave her one. After scrubbing his face and legs, he removed the soaked upper layer of his clothes and walked up to the raised wooden floor of the house. In silence, he signaled to Lana to wait on the lower stone floor of the entrance.

Too tired to remain on her feet, Lana stopped fighting gravity. She slumped onto the highest step before attempting to dry herself as best as she could. Inhaling the air made her smile despite her exhaustion. Everything looked and smelled like cedar, her favorite scent, with the unmistakable grassy aroma of *tatami* mingling with it. Daylight poured into the elegant hall from a series of small windows under the ceiling, adding to the warm and welcoming atmosphere of the house.

"Oh, *goshujin sama*, finally! Welcome back!" called Yuki's voice; the second after, she was in the hall with them. She wore simple jeans and a large white shirt under a green apron; a matching kerchief covered her head. She had been busy cleaning up, and soot smeared her brow. To Lana's eyes, she was as composed and beautiful as in her memory. Lana didn't even want to guess what she looked like herself, but her sweaty smell was an assault on her own nose.

"Are you all right? Are you unhurt?" Yuki's eyes roamed over her husband's body, searching for injuries. Honda's arms engulfed her to give her a brief hug; his lips brushed her hair for a quick peck. Such open display of tender affection coming from him took Lana aback.

"I am tired, but I am fine, thank you. You seem well, too."

"Yes, I am, and everything is more or less in order here. Nothing significant broke—only bookshelves that were not properly fixed, and bottles and cups that crashed down. We are still checking all rooms and the roof for structural integrity though. When the worst is over, we will call in a specialist."

"I agree. Now, I wanted to tell you—" Honda fell silent when an older man showed up behind Yuki. The level of tension in the air jumped. Lana tried to make herself as small as possible.

"Son. Here you are. How... unfortunate you weren't home last night," the newcomer said in a droning voice.

Suddenly, Honda's earlier trepidation and the rumors flying around the man in business circles made perfect sense to Lana. Almost bald and with deep-set eyes, Nakazawa Toshiro was rather short and well into his seventies. Still, he was intimidating as his natural authority and cunningness could not be denied despite his apparent physical frailty. His unforgiving stare probed at people's weaknesses.

Honda and Yuki kneeled on the floor to greet their elder, but he kept his head to the ground longer than usual. Lana did her best to keep a straight face. She could bet that there weren't many people who got such humble deference from Honda, never mind ones who threw such poorly disguised accusations at him. She straightened her wet clothes and hair. Even if she smelled like one, there was no need to look like a stray dog.

"*Otoh sama*," Honda addressed his father-in-law with a level voice. "Good morning. I am relieved to see you in good health. There is no excuse for the concern I caused. I did my best to come home as soon as possible, but it still took me six hours to walk from Minato-ku area due to the road and weather conditions."

"And perhaps because you were not alone? Who is this?" Nakazawa asked with a snarl, suspicion marring his voice. Lana followed Honda's example. She bowed her head to the floor and didn't dare to raise it again.

"This is Lana Martin san, *otoh sama*," Honda replied, with unwavering poise. "She is one of my aikido students. I met her and offered her to come with me when she told me her apartment unit was destroyed in a fire." How smartly put. No lie, but a careful edition of reality.

"Oh no! My poor Lana san!" Yuki exclaimed, horrified. She ran to Lana, kneeled next to her and put a comforting arm around her shoulders. "So awful! You will of course stay here with us for as long as needed!"

Lana glanced at Yuki, then at the two men. "I am so grateful, Honda sama," she said with a bow, using the highest degree of formal register she knew. "But, I cannot accept your offer. It is too much of a bother and inconvenience for you. My company will provide me with a furnished apartment until my unit is repaired—"

"Oh, nonsense! You will not end up in a gloomy 1K flat somewhere in Shinagawa. No, no, I insist, you will be our guest. We have plenty of room. I am sure you agree, *goshujin sama*?"

Honda nodded once, his face unreadable. "This is acceptable."

"It is settled, then. Come with me; I'll get you new clothes."

"Wait!" Nakazawa's voice boomed in the narrow hall, freezing everyone in place. "Daughter, you know her as well?"

"Yes, *otoh sama*, she is a friend of mine," Yuki replied without batting an eye. "Also, I have told you about her last week. She was one of the two Italian ladies who helped us with the incident at our event, and who suggested that we check and increase the level of our information security."

"I see." Nakazawa remained silent; everyone held their breath, waiting for the verdict. "Well, I guess both of you wish to clean up and get some rest. It must have been quite a trek, with this heat and now the rain."

"Thank you for your consideration, *otoh sama*," Honda said with another respectful bow. "Yes, it was... harrowing. From what we could see, while there is damage all around town, it is not overly extensive. The timing was fortunate as well."

"Indeed. I have to leave to oversee our emergency response team from our headquarters. If I can, I will come back later tonight or tomorrow."

"Of course. Please be careful and let us know how we can be of assistance."

Nakazawa grunted and headed toward the door. Honda, Yuki, and Lana bowed until he was out of sight. A shaky hiss escaped Lana. *Crisis averted.*

Temper: Deference

As soon as they were alone, Yuki sighed in relief and turned again to Lana. "I am so, so glad that you are here with us, sweetling. Losing your home, your belongings... this is devastating. But look at you! You got too much sun on your face, yet your lips are white. You must be run out. Are you injured?"

"Nothing serious, Yuki sama. Only blisters, cuts, and wooden legs. Actually..." Lana chuckled. "I don't think I can stand anymore. I'll just lay down here and sleep for a while if you don't mind."

"Don't be ridiculous," Yuki huffed and puffed. "Both of you need a hot bath for your cramped legs, and an invigorating meal afterward, before a long nap. I will prepare you a bath in the guest bathroom, cook a miso soup and rice, and set up a bedroom. *Goshujin sama*...?"

"Yes, this sounds good."

To Lana's relief, everyone seemed to agree on giving her time and space. "Ah, may I ask if you have any Wi-Fi access? I have to get back in touch with Gabriella, and check in with my colleagues and company, as per our SOP. Phone lines must still be overloaded, but social networks are working fine."

"Yes, we do, and I'll give you the access codes later," Yuki said. "All right, can you go to the kitchen over there? Give me ten minutes to run your bath."

Lana tried to get up but failed when her legs didn't respond. "Woah! Ah... no, I can't." She laughed at herself, grimacing in pain at the same time.

Honda was by her side in a blink. "Put your arms around my neck," he instructed.

Lana frowned. "But you are exhausted..."

Honda didn't bother with a reply and merely stared back at her with an arched eyebrow. She gulped down her pride, and he brought her to a high chair in a spacious and surprisingly modern American-style kitchen. A counter bar ran on the other side of a central unit and a large wooden table with six designer chairs stood at the center. The window panels showed a beautiful garden outside.

Lana grimaced at the pain shooting through her butt, but compared to the state of her legs, it was manageable. After bringing two glasses and a full pitcher of chilled barley tea, Honda sat opposite her and couldn't hide his own wince. Exhaustion made her head spin. Drenched and covered with dirt, she felt out of place in this beautiful setting.

Sipping her drink, trying to find something safe to say, she looked around her. "Your house is remarkable. How old is it?"

"It has been in my family for more than two centuries, although the property itself used to be much larger. After we got married, it became mine. We did extensive renovation works to modernize it, reinforce it and insulate it while keeping the original spirit and intent intact. It has eight *tatami* rooms; two bathrooms, each with a *rotenburo*; one dojo and two different kinds of gardens outside: a Zen stone garden and another used for growing flowers and vegetables."

"Amazing," Lana whispered, impressed. She loved traditional Japanese houses, and this one was the perfect blend of modernity and tradition.

"What kind of home did you grow up in?"

Lana hid a grimace. She fidgeted and emptied her glass before answering. "My parents are well off. On my mother's side, it is old money. Her family owns houses all around Italy. I spent my childhood in one of them, in a coastal town by the Mediterranean Sea where we have our roots. It was... huge, with a swimming pool outside, overlooking the sea. I guess it was beautiful and breathtaking, but I never liked it. It was for showing off, not for living in. Anyway..." Lana gave him a wry smile. "It's far from here and happened a long time ago."

"You never go back there?" Honda blinked, and she understood his surprise. Turning your back on your hometown, where your ancestors were buried, was anathema in Japan.

"No, I don't," she replied curtly.

Yuki came back in the kitchen. "Your bath is almost ready. Let's bring you to the bathroom, Lana san."

"Thank you so much. I'm so sorry for the inconvenience..."

"Stop this nonsense. Come, I will help you out once you are there."

Honda picked her up again. It took Lana a lot not to bury her nose in his neck and smell the bare skin showing above his collar.

The bath section opened on a miniature enclosed garden with an artificial stream and small pond. The water had yet to fill the *rotenburo*—a large tub in cedar similar to those found in hot spring resorts—but she had to clean up thoroughly before stepping in anyway. Honda helped her sit on a wooden stool and took his leave.

"Take it slow," Yuki said. "I'll come back with a fresh *yukata* and a first aid kit once our lunch is on its way. I'll also prepare the *tatami* room down this hall. It will be your bedroom."

"Thank you very much." Lana didn't waste time; she took off her dirty *yukata* and underwear and threw them on the floor of the powder room. She grabbed the shower head and turned on the water, choosing scalding hot. After a vigorous scrubbing that turned her skin red, she was clean enough to crawl into the tub. A sigh of relief escaped her; her head came to rest on her folded arms on the edge.

"Lana, Lana san, please wake up!" Lana opened an eye and found Yuki hovering above her, worried. "You shouldn't fall asleep in a tub! It's dangerous!"

"I'm sorry, I couldn't help it," Lana replied and groaned. "Ah, my body hurts everywhere."

"Your muscles are cramped, so you could use a massage," Yuki said, roaming a critical eye over Lana. She was a mess of bruises and small cuts. Some had nothing to do with her trek. "The meal is ready, but maybe you need more time here." She proceeded with removing her clothes and putting them away in the powder room. "Let me help you."

"Oh, you don't need to! Perhaps *goshujin sama* needs to be attended...?"

Yuki chuckled while cleaning herself up in the shower section of the bathroom. "He can take care of himself for now. I want to make you feel better after this taxing ordeal."

Lana's thoughts evaporated when a naked and slender Yuki stepped into the tub, large enough for four adults. "Let me massage your legs first, and then your back."

Yuki's voice carried a stern undertone. It reminded Lana of her talk with Honda the day before–it seemed like a lifetime ago. She had to come to a decision regarding her relationship with his wife, and fast. Not breaking eye contact, she extended her legs. Yuki's touch was utterly professional and lacked any sexual innuendo. Her companion wanted to help her get better. A wave of emotions rocked her, and unshed tears burned her eyes.

"Does it help? Is it your calves or thighs? Those blisters on your feet are ugly and must be so painful; you should put a lot of antiseptic cream on them. We have efficient lotions to help skin heal faster, don't worry."

"Thank you," Lana said, subdued. A part of her wished Yuki's fingers would trail a bit further up, but she kept it to herself.

Then Yuki moved against the tub's wall. "Please sit in front of me and let me have a look at your shoulders and back."

Lana moved and caught Yuki's hiss of surprise at the sight of her buttocks.

"Hm... *goshujin sama* was... harsh yesterday." It wasn't a question, but a prudent statement of fact.

Lana sighed, and her core tingled at the memory of the spanking. It had been one of many highlights of the previous evening. "Well, I deserved it and asked for it. Of course, I wasn't expecting a six-hour trek a few hours later, and it didn't help." It was still odd to speak about this with his wife.

"Let me put lotion there, too." And even odder that said wife took it in stride.

Except for the occasional hiss and moan of pain, both remained silent as Yuki dug her expert fingers into Lana's knotted back.

Maybe it was the peaceful setting, the feeling of relaxation, or simply because Lana was tired to the bone and didn't want to struggle anymore. She broke the comfortable silence after a time, going with a delicate and submissive turn of phrase. "*Oku sama*, may I ask you a question? May I be direct, even blunt?"

"Anything, sweetling." Yuki's voice was a low purr; Lana reacted at once. There was something liberating and soothing in putting herself in the other woman's sensual care, similar to slipping under a fluffy and warm blanket on a cool autumn night.

"Why do you submit to him? I don't believe in your 'traditions and customs' argument. Besides, you prefer women, right? It seems you are like me, a dominant in your other relations. Why do you give him such power over you? I'm sure you could have come to another arrangement after your wedding. Other couples do."

Yuki stopped massaging and embraced her from behind, bringing Lana against her. She cupped a breast and fondled it tenderly, adding to the whirlpool of relaxing sensations.

"Well... He is who he is. Whatever your personal orientation or tastes, there is no denying his natural authority. From the beginning, he made it clear that he would let me lead my intimate life as I wished, as long as I showed him the deference he was due as my husband. And from the first day, he has always shown me the most gracious respect and attention, even care. And should I describe in detail the whole range of his... talents?"

Both chuckled in common appreciation and understanding, their bodies scooping against each other. "Yes, I love women, and until my marriage, my limited experience with men had been disappointing and frustrating at all levels. My wedding night showed me men could have merits in the bedroom, and perhaps outside as well. His practical and no-nonsense approach to our daily life convinced me it wouldn't be hard to do what duty required of me."

Yuki sighed and grew silent for a short while. When she spoke again, her voice was low. "Ours is not a love story, sweetling. It's a pact, the renewal of a long-standing yet fragile alliance between two clans with historical and established roots. Where tensions and rancor run deep. But against all odds, and more often than not the heads of our families, our... personal agreement works. Even with you stepping into the picture."

Yuki shifted her body to stare at Lana, and Lana was reminded of Nakazawa in the intensity of her glare and the natural confidence she projected. This was no ordinary housewife; she was as much of samurai stock as her husband.

"But you, Lana san. You. Will you really accept him, his demands and his place in your life? And me? Do you wish to challenge my role in our dynamic?" There was no denying the steel behind the other woman's words.

Lana stared back, letting the jasmine perfume of Yuki's hair register deep within her; Yuki's soft curves brushing against her own; her kind yet piercing eyes. She acknowledged what shifted inside her and the longing it created. Tears blurring her sight, she realized she had lost, but to her surprise, it didn't feel so bad. Quite the opposite. Relief bloomed inside her belly.

"He gave me the right, you know?" Lana whispered, needing to come out clear. "Yesterday he told me he'd accept it if I challenged your position. But..." Lana frowned. "You're the mistress of this house, *oku sama*. I will not come here, live under your roof, eat your food, serve your husband, and then challenge your place. He believes this is irrelevant and completely different, but

I disagree. I... Hm..." She faltered and looked away. "It was and is still hard for me to concede the upper hand in a relationship and to let you lead ours. But I'll work on it. On top of it, it's so nice and relaxing to be in your care. So different from being with him, but also different compared with my everyday life and past relationships."

Yuki left a trail of kisses on her neck, from her shoulder up to her hairline. "Then, no challenge, *neko chan*?" she whispered in her companion's ear, softly dipping two fingers into her pussy and turning Lana's face toward hers. Lana closed her eyes and sighed. "Little cat' would be her other pet name.

"No, *oku sama*," she replied with certainty. Yuki groaned and tightened her embrace, before claiming Lana's mouth in a searing kiss.

"I am so happy to hear it, and you know why?" Yuki went on after letting go of Lana's lips. "Because all of this will work. I'll take care of you and give you the chance to rest. The velvet glove on your skin after the burn of the scorching rope. Simply follow my lead. You find freedom, a matching release of your own blazing temper in his arms, a sort of... echo chamber in him. But you also require something else. Let me try, at least, to give you a little bit of this."

While she spoke, Yuki never stopped working her fingers inside Lana's pussy, increasing her speed. Lana fumbled and found Yuki's, mirroring her gestures. As Yuki's voice got rougher and rougher, Lana plunged her tongue in her lover's mouth and aggressively dug in three fingers, while her thumb brushed her clit. She came hard, her scream muted by Yuki's lips. Her companion shuddered, swept away by her own orgasm.

"You and me, we can be tender and sweet to each other, or naughty and dirty, or even a combination of both, as you prefer," Yuki whispered afterward while Lana panted and licked her lips.

"The combination suits me well, *oku sama*. You know how much I love being naughty."

Yuki chuckled and twisted a nipple, hard, eliciting a strangled gasp from Lana. "Oh yes, I do. How is your back now, *neko chan*?"

"Much better, and so are my legs. Thank you."

"Then, let's get out and tend your other wounds."

Later on, they stepped out of the bathroom together. Lana's legs were stiff, but she could limp and walk by herself again. They found Honda in the kitchen, eating his late lunch and watching live reports of the earthquake on a flat-screen 4K TV mounted on the opposite wall. He looked at the two women and quirked an eyebrow.

"It is done then? Everything is sorted out? Lana san?"

Lana bowed while Yuki picked a couple of dishes and set them up for herself and Lana. "It is, *goshujin sama. Oku sama* and I had a productive discussion."

Honda leaned forward and searched her face. "You did more than talk about it." His voice was flat, unreadable, free from either irony or leering. He didn't even sound disappointed at her capitulation.

Yuki chuckled while Lana tried not turn into a blushing teenager. "Indeed," Yuki piped in. "There was a brilliant demonstration along with it, *goshujin sama*. The matter is settled." Yuki seemed eager to move forward.

"Good. Lana san, given your situation, what do you need right away? It would be useful to sort out your priorities."

Lana welcomed the change of topic and used it to compose herself. Sitting at the table, she accepted the rice and miso soup Yuki gave her, before stating the traditional expression of gratitude at the beginning of a meal.

"*Itadakimasu*. Well, Gabriella has copies of all my essential papers. I have my foreigner ID and bank cards with me, so I'm not an undocumented alien without any resources."

Right then, the house shook as another moderate aftershock rattled the city. The trio glanced up at the ceiling and kitchen shelves; nothing fell off, so they continued as if it hadn't happened. This would be their new normal for the coming days and weeks. After a while, people would start feeling 'phantom shakes' out of sheer anxiety. Lana figured that as long as her phone didn't blare any alarm, she'd be fine. She had set it at a high level to avoid being warned about non-threatening tremors.

"As for what I need... Clothes, mostly. My office will be closed on Monday if the trains don't run. Still, I'll have to go there next week to meet with management to figure out the next steps. I want to grab a laptop if they ask us to work from home."

"Let's wait until tomorrow to see if anything opens around Kichijoji. In the meantime, we'll make do with what I have, even though we don't wear the same size," Yuki said, finishing up her meal.

"Especially when it comes to shoes." Lana chuckled. "I can get by with my borrowed sneakers for now. I'll ask Gabriella to help me out, and I've got clothes in a storage container in the parking lot of my condo."

"We will see what the traffic and road conditions look like tomorrow morning," Honda said. "Come with me. Let me show you our home office and give you the Wifi access codes."

Lana followed him to a room lined up with filled bookshelves and two large workstations. Five minutes later, she was back on the phone with her friend who was safe at home. Lana's phone battery was too low to make it a long call, so Gabriella offered to get in touch with their office's emergency unit on her behalf.

Afterward, Yuki showed her a bedroom, a spacious 15-*tatami* room with sliding panel windows opening on the Zen side of the garden. To Lana's satisfaction, it had next to no furniture, in the traditional Japanese way.

Finally, Yuki led her to the private dojo of the estate, a 30-*tatami* room. As tradition requested, a *kamidana*, a portrait of O'Sensei and an impressive work of calligraphy that Lana couldn't decipher hung on the main wall facing the entrance. A large collection of *bokken* and other various staffs were stacked along the left wall. It was much more than necessary for practicing the aikido techniques using weapons.

Yuki noticed Lana staring. "Like my father and two brothers, I practice iaido and kendo, so these are my training weapons. My blunt edged sword and my *katana* are not on display here but in my room. Of course, *goshujin sama* also uses those now and then."

Lana quirked an eyebrow. "Yes, I was wondering what kind of martial arts you do."

"I am a third *dan* in both those *budo*, but I have been a little remiss in my practice."

"If you ever have time, would you mind introducing me to iaido?" Lana asked, hopeful.

"Certainly, but I am no instructor, so I can show you only basic moves. My father teaches both arts. He used to be *goshujin sama's* kendo sensei when he was still training in that art before he decided to focus on aikido. About twenty-five years ago."

"Ah, so... both have known each other for a long time," Lana said prudently. She didn't want to sound like she was prying, but something about the relationship between the two men disturbed her. The way Nakazawa had almost snarled at Honda had been unsettling.

"Oh yes, they do. Our families' relations go back to the Edo period. We used to be samurai clans, direct vassals of the Tokugawa family. My family's domain is located in Shizuoka area, while *goshujin sama*'s ancestral land is near Nikko. This used to be their townhouse in Edo, and the property was much larger in the past, as it included the shrine grounds next to us. Our families have shared close ties for centuries at personal and political levels. But when we got married, it had been well over forty years since there had been a wedding between our families. The general political context had changed, of course. It was the object of careful and detailed negotiations."

Yuki didn't offer more information, and Lana didn't dare show too much curiosity. The other woman sensed her hesitation though. "You may ask me questions, but I might not answer all of them, Lana san. Some things aren't mine to tell."

"I understand. My apologies for being so nosy," Lana said, bowing her head.

"You're not," Yuki chuckled. "Let's agree we don't have to share everything today, right? We have time to get to know each other better." Lana nodded, there wasn't much to add. "Come now, you must be exhausted, we'll finish the tour another time. This has been a challenging day for everyone."

19

Memories Buried under Ashes

THE NEXT MORNING, Lana found herself sitting in the passenger seat of Honda's car, moving in a long line toward the district of Mitaka, Gabriella, and what was left of her apartment.

Staring at the various levels of damage along the road, the trio remained silent until they arrived in the outskirts of Mikata. Lana guided Honda until she could see her building down the street.

"Oh... it's even worse than I thought," she whispered, shocked, as they came to a halt. The entire apartment complex was built in four wings, each of them counting nine floors. The walls and outside corridors of the south wing, where her unit was, were blackened by soot, from the third floor up to the sixth.

"Where is your apartment?"

"On the fourth floor. Right above where the fire started..." Lana said, a lump in her throat. "Can you imagine what would have happened if..." Her voice trailed off.

"Units in condos as modern as these have good fire and smoke alarms. I'm certain you would have been able to escape," Yuki tried to reassure her.

"The police and fire brigade haven't left yet. With any luck, we'll get answers. Ah, Gabriella's over there, near the bicycle parking." Leaving the car, Lana jogged across the street. Both friends fell into a warm and emotional hug.

"Oh, *cara mia*, I can't believe it. What a mess..." Gabriella sobbed in relief in Lana's hair. In tears, her friend could only nod, her own well of emotions overflowing.

After a long while, Lana sighed and tried to compose herself. "It's so good to see you. I'm so happy you didn't get hurt."

"I was lucky. Here, take this. It's not much but should be enough for a few days." Gabriella handed Lana a large duffel bag. "Copies of your papers, smartphone charger, underwear, a pair of sandals, sweatpants, two skirts and a few shirts... I know we don't have the same style, but I swear I picked up the blandest stuff in my closet. In other words, you can keep it!" They shared a laugh, feeling much better.

"Lana san," a grim Honda interrupted them. "I talked with the police officer over there. It is highly disturbing, but according to the fire brigade, the timing does not match with the earthquake. They are considering all scenarios, including arson."

"What?" Lana exclaimed, turning pale. "But... how? Who? Any casualties?"

"They would not give me details, obviously, but two bodies were found in the unit on the third floor where the fire started. Unit 312."

Hand flying to her mouth, Lana gasped. "The Kurozawa's! A family of four. The kid is five or six and always stays home with his grandma because the parents work irregular shifts at the hospital nearby. Oh gosh, do you think the kid...?"

Honda shook his head and handed her several sheets of paper. "I cannot say. Anyway, the police officer told me you can fill those forms to start the insurance process. You are allowed to go to your unit if you want to shoot pictures of the damage. I will come with you."

"Use my phone. I'll forward them to you later. Arson? What a nightmare..." Gabriella whispered, subdued. "I'll stay here with Yuki san and see what else we can learn."

After Lana had shown her ID confirming her place of residence, Honda and Lana headed for the building entrance, accompanied by a firefighter and another police officer. In the staircase, the smell of smoke and burned materials overwhelmed her. She gagged and her eyes watered. She gratefully accepted the cotton mask offered by the policeman. By the time they reached her floor, her legs reminded her of their trek, and she was panting while cramps crippled her calves.

They arrived in front of the remnants of her door; it had been demolished by the fire brigade. "The fire started in the kitchen in the unit below, so you will see that your kitchen and your living room were the most affected by the flames. Unfortunately smoke and fire repellant destroyed everything else," the fireman explained.

"How come there was so much damage? Why was the blaze allowed to grow so large?" Honda asked behind Lana, who was busy shooting the first round of pictures from the entrance.

"The closest fire respondents couldn't make it in time because they were victims of vandalism: they found all their tires slashed thirty minutes before the call came in and were still replacing them by then," the police officer answered. "It took another unit much longer to arrive, and then things became hard to control when the earthquake struck. It's a series of unfortunate coincidences... although now that we're considering the arson lead, I don't know if this is the right word."

"Martin san, the room in the front and the one in the back can be accessed, but don't step on the floor of the rooms on the left, as the structural integrity of the flooring is not guaranteed," the fireman advised, seeing her hesitation to step inside.

Heart beating wildly, Lana stopped listening to Honda's conversation and walked inside, aiming at the first room on her right: her bedroom. *Maybe the safe was resistant enough... maybe everything is intact...*

She started coughing right away, the smell and thick, heavy air making her eyes water. She took a couple of pictures of her room. Everything was covered with soot and drenched by water, beyond repair or use, but the flames had spared it. Crouching on the floor, she grabbed the small safe she had put under her bed when she had moved in. It had been years since she had opened it, close to a decade.

With trembling hands, Lana entered the combination code. To her enormous relief, the inside of the safe was in perfect condition. She took out a lucky charm bracelet, a pair of fantasy earrings and a small photo album. There were two pictures in it. One of herself and her father, when she was seven, on their yearly ski trip to the French Alps. The last one they would ever take. *Uh. Why do I even bother keeping it, anyway?*

With a shaky breath, she dared take a look at the second one. *Hi there. Long time no see.*

Two smiling faces greeted her, forever stuck in a beautiful moment she could not forget. She chuckled at the goofy grin her younger self wore but couldn't bring herself to stare much longer at the other person. She shut the album closed and bit her cheek hard. This was a dangerous memory lane, and there were good reasons why her safe had remained locked all this time. But she was grateful the flames hadn't eaten everything away.

Lost in thought, Lana straightened up and turned back toward the door only to stumble on Honda. "Oh!" She caught his arm to avoid falling on her butt, and the album clattered on the floor.

Before she could move, he picked it up. The second picture was hanging loose; there was no way he could miss it. Their eyes met, and something soft sparkled in his. "You look very young in this one."

Lana chuckled to hide her emotional turmoil, but her burning cheeks betrayed her. "Hm, yes, seventeen... and definitely acting like it!" More forcefully than warranted, she snatched the album from his hands and tucked it into her handbag.

For a few heartbeats, they remained standing in the semi-obscurity of what was left of her bedroom and of her past. He stepped aside when she didn't provide any further detail, especially about the young man biting her younger self's bare neck. *Sorry, access to this part of my life is a strict no-no for you.*

"Is there any other belonging you can salvage and bring along? I took the liberty to shoot other pictures down the hall. To my regret, the smoke and soot damage is total. No need to linger here with those toxic fumes."

"Yeah, the smell is pretty awful and makes me nauseous. Let's go. I found nothing else worth taking with me. Do you mind coming with me to the storage containers behind the parking lot? I'll ask a moving company to handle most of all the contents, but I can take a few things with me today."

Honda nodded, and they stepped outside the apartment. She gave her companion's back a quizzical look. Grasping what their agreement implied was still hard, in particular now that they would share more than a hotel room every blue moon or so. None of them had expected such a turn of events, and his behavior blurred the lines in her book.

But then, in his mind, perhaps he's simply doing what he promised he'd do.

Her hand gripped the staircase ramp as she took careful steps. "For the record, you will not make me do any *suwari waza* anytime soon, and even less walk around in *shikko*," she groaned. The mere thought of roaming around the mats on her knees made her legs ache.

"Have no fear, I would not be able to make any demonstration on my end," he replied over his shoulder. His pace was more prudent than usual, and his hand rested against the wall for support. The twenty-six flights of stairs of the previous day had left their imprint on both of them.

Yuki and Gabriella were waiting for them outside the main entrance, agitated and worried. "It's even more terrible than we thought," a pale Yuki told them. "The police officer just informed us the father is now the prime suspect. The mother was found yesterday morning, wailing and wandering barefoot in the streets. It's only now they could identify her, and she's mumbling accusations against her husband."

"But then, it means... the bodies..." Lana whispered, heart in her throat.

"Yes, the grandmother and the son," a grim Gabriella confirmed.

"I can't... can't believe it!" Lana recoiled in shock, blood draining from her face.

Yuki laid a soft hand on her arm. "Let's go home, now. We shouldn't stay here; it's too sad and terrible."

"Yes... yes, you're right, but give me five minutes to check my container over there. I'll be right back."

Lost in thought, eyes blurred by tears of sadness at the tragedy that had struck her neighbors, Lana hurried to the rows of storage units. After unlocking hers, she stepped inside the small space, going for the boxes where she kept old and winter clothes. As she rummaged through them, the sound of footsteps resonated behind her back.

"*Goshujin sama*, would you mind–" She stopped mid-sentence. Honda didn't have such heavy and raspy breathing. Even at the end of a strenuous practice session. Or in bed.

"You! It's your fault! Your fault!"

Lana screamed and stumbled against the piles of boxes behind her. Twisting on her feet, she faced the intruder while her hand searched frantically for something useful to grab.

"Kurozawa san!" she exclaimed, icy threads of fear clutching her heart.

Disheveled, hands and face smeared with soot and dirt, her neighbor pointed an iron bar at her head. "It's your fault!" he repeated with a hoarse cry. "He made me do it because of you! It's all because of you! He made me do it!"

Blood rushed to her ears and drowned out all noises while she ran through her options. He was a burly man, blocking her way out, and she had limited movement capacity. The only solution was to incapacitate him.

Kurozawa stepped inside the container, and she inhaled deeply, attempting to focus on his attack, and on what she would have to do. She would get only one chance.

When he struck, his speed caught her by surprise: she barely saw the iron bar coming straight at her head, at a perfect and precise angle.

He knows how to hold a sword!

Acting more on instinct than anything else, she managed to parry the bar by pivoting on her heels, moving out of its way, then slapped his hand away with the edge of hers, before catching his wrist.

After unbalancing him, she brought him face to the ground. But before she had time to apply enough pressure on his wrist to disarm him, she lost her footing. Her left hip and leg caught the sharp angle of a metallic bookshelf. Acute pain shot from her limb and ripped a cry from her; her grip slackened and to her dismay, it was enough for Kurozawa to scramble on his feet.

He seized his weapon and with a horrendous snarl, raised it to above his head again. The feral look distorted his face so much that Lana froze, bile rising in her throat; it reminded her oddly of the awful nightmare that had woken her up during the night of the earthquake.

Right when the enraged man rose his arm to strike, Honda appeared from behind and grabbed him. The iron bar clattered on the ground, but rage and despair fueled the man's energy, and he pushed back against Honda.

"Ahhhh! Lemme go! Let go of me, she has to pay! It's her fault!"

"Silence!" Honda roared and slammed the man's back against the container's wall. When Kurozawa faced Honda, his face twisted with renewed hate.

"You! It's your fault! It's because of you! He made me do it because of you!"

Jumping at Honda's throat, he attempted to strangle him, but his opponent controlled him and submitted him with the same wrist and elbow lock Lana had begun but failed to finish. Mouth frothing, their aggressor continued shouting and babbling the same incoherent accusations.

Right then, hurried footsteps and shouts could be heard outside the container; the two police officers and the firefighter had caught up with them. After a couple of minutes of confusion and shouts, Kurozawa was handcuffed and taken away to the police car, still screaming his rage at the top of his lungs.

In a daze, Lana walked outside the container on shaky legs. Shock and other emotions caught up with her. Head throbbing, a wave of nausea had her empty her stomach onto the parking lot. A warm hand rested on her neck and held her hair away from her face.

"You're fine, you're fine, it's over Lana san..." Yuki's voice wasn't so steady.

Lana took two steps away from her mess before slumping heavily onto the ground, face buried in her hands. She lost her nerves and couldn't keep a lid on the sobs wracking her. Yuki sat beside her and wrapped her up in a tight embrace, rocking her softly; Gabriella crouched on Lana's other side, rubbing her back.

"Shhh, breathe, relax, you've been through a lot," Yuki continued, kissing Lana's hair. "Sweetling, this man is clearly mad; he can't face the horror of what he's done... It's awful, so sad! Don't listen to him. He has to blame someone, and both of you were in his path."

"Lana san, he did not have time to hurt you, did he?"

Lana wiped her face and looked up at Honda. His face was a blank mask, but she recoiled slightly at the dark flame burning in his eyes. "No, he didn't. I was taken by surprise, hit an obstacle and lost control of the situation."

"A mad and angry man with a weapon and nothing left to lose is a true threat. You were indeed in grave danger and did what you could. You should not feel bad for not taking him down yourself. And do not take his words to heart. He is now locked in his own personal hell."

Gabriella got on her feet and gave Lana her hand, followed by her handbag. "Come on now, *cara mia*. Enough fun for one day. Leave this place and get some rest. Someone else will come and handle this blasted container."

"Thank you very much, all of you," Lana said, her mouth dry. "I'm sorry for losing it."

Gabriella smacked the back of her head, half serious, half playful. "Stop your bullshit now," she said in Italian, pointing a finger at her friend with barely restrained aggravation. "Have you seen what you've gone through over the past two days? It always kills me me when you apologize for acting like a mere human being. I realize he's a tough-ass model, and you've got this martial kink going on together, but please! Drop this 'stronger-than-thou' game. She seems more balanced, thank goodness. It looks like you're going to live with them for a while, so do me a favor and let her work her magic."

Lana gave her friend a small smile and a quick peck on the cheek, accepting the rebuke. It was true affection and worry that motivated Gabriella to react so strongly. This was only the thousandth time they had had this discussion.

As she was about to follow her companions back to the car, she winced and doubled down; shooting from below her rib cage, acute pain made it hard to straighten properly. To her relief, nobody noticed. They had fretted over her enough for one day. On top of it, there was nothing they could do; heartburn had been a constant companion all her adult life.

Damn it. It's supposed to be under control, but it keeps flaring up these days, stronger than ever... I should ask Dr. Stein for a different, stronger subscription. What he's giving me isn't working anymore.

Deep and steady breaths helped her regulate her pain long enough to walk to the car; this time, she sat in the back. Throwing a final glance at her building was above her strength, but when they took off for Setagaya, Lana offered silent prayers to the victims of such senseless, horrific tragedy. The burnt stench stuck to her clothes and hair, a terrible reminder of the horrors she had escaped.

As they drove back to the Honda estate, her eyes fell on the photo album in her open handbag. She resisted the urge to give the twenty-year-old picture another look; despite her sadness and despondency, a wistful smile tugged at her lips.

What would you say if you saw me with them today, huh? You'd laugh. You'd tease me so hard... Don't say you saw this one coming, 'cause I sure didn't. And now I'm going to live there. Another new chapter for little ol' me. Don't know how long this one will be though. I feel like those characters of yours going through incredible adventures, who went from being librarians to space pirates, or jet pilots.

Nobody had rotten hearts, or twisted souls—nobody died in your stories. All those magical worlds you built for me, and I can't even remember the sound of your voice.

Only the warmth of your skin. And the taste of your blood.

Lila Mina

20

A Ladies' Night

"Lana san, do you have any plans for Friday night?" Yuki's head peaked through Lana's bedroom door as she was finishing her hairdo.

"This Friday? No, my agenda is empty for now. I don't know yet when I'll be home though. We're still deep in post-crisis mode." Lana glanced at her watch and winced. Her company held their first all-department meeting after the earthquake at 9 o'clock sharp. Not the best day for running late.

"Oh, it's fine, what I have in mind is done later at night. I know you're in a rush, but a quick question: do you like going out?"

Lana stopped fighting with her rebellious morning hair. "Going out… as in, to a club? For dancing?"

"Exactly. I've got VIP access to the best places in town and I want to take you to my favorite spot. I thought you'd enjoy some downtime after these past two weeks, and they're back in business."

Lana wet her dry lips; her brain struggled to process the image of this composed and refined lady participating in serious partying. At the same time, it was difficult to imagine her doing the naughty stuff they shared together.

"Er… yes, I guess I could use it, but then it would be a sort of date?" Her voice wasn't so steady anymore. She had never been out with a woman before and feared being too self-conscious.

Yuki grinned and gave her a conspiratorial wink. "Why, yes! A ladies' night if you wish."

Her eyebrows lost in her hairline, Lana nodded. "I would be… delighted." She didn't know how to ask the question burning her lips, but Yuki seemed to read her mind.

"Don't worry about him. *Goshujin sama* isn't much into this in any case." Lana tried to imagine Honda on a dance floor, and indeed, things didn't add up.

"All right then! It's a date. I'll try to get my hands on something suitable by then, because finding new party dresses has not been on my priority shopping list so far."

"Excellent! Go for something classy; a little black dress will do. We'll go to a more underground place I love next time." Lana's eyes bulged out, and Yuki burst out laughing. "My my, sweetling, I think shocking you will be my new favorite pastime. For your information, one of the reasons my father couldn't wait to marry me off was my intense passion for clubbing. He didn't know my husband would be fine with letting me go out, all by myself. I don't go out so often now, but it's high time we hang out together. Off you go, don't be late because of me!"

Friday night was upon them, and Lana stood in front of her vanity mirror, grimacing at her reflection. They were supposed to leave in thirty minutes, but doubt gnawed at her. *This dress is too slutty... showing waaay too much cleavage, what was I thinking? This isn't Torino, and I'm not twenty anymore! And how about I let my hair down? But up is better for dancing. And I have too much foundation.*

"Ack!" She threw her brush on her *futon*, frustrated at herself and annoyed at the butterflies making her stomach queasy. This was a date, all right, but with someone she was already in an established relationship with! And since when did she care so much about that stuff, anyway?

With a heavy sigh, she picked up her brush. The truth was, it was the first serious thing Yuki and she were doing together, on top of it as a real couple— something out of the question with Honda. Lana rolled her eyes at herself. She was the only one who struggled with how to handle it. Honda hadn't made any comment when informed of their plans.

A soft knock at the door jolted her from her moody train of thoughts. "Yes, please come in!" Yuki stepped inside, and Lana's breath left her in a rush. "Oh, Yuki sama, you are... amazing, so beautiful!" she stammered, blood rushing to her cheeks.

Her mistress was stunning: her high collar, dark green dress, slit on each side from her knees to mid-thighs, left nothing to the imagination. She wore gold jewelry, which managed to be discreet, yet highlighted her perfect skin. Her hair was held in place by a clip and was wavy for a change.

Lana gulped hard. She was falling head over heels.

"Thank you sweetling," Yuki replied with a warm smile. "May I say, you are absolutely delicious yourself. This dress fits you so well, and it's a sweet pleasure to be able to enjoy your wonderful assets like this." She grabbed Lana's hips and pulled her closer for a searing kiss. "We shouldn't wait much longer. Otherwise I'll lose all interest in going out and I'll lock you in for the whole weekend instead."

Lana moaned and leaned to steal another kiss from those ruby-red lips that knew so well how to turn her into a weak puddle.

"Come on, now. The taxi is waiting. Are you ready?"

Lana nodded, happy. Her doubts and anxiety had vanished, replaced by excitement and pure pleasure at spending quality time with her lover.

Yuki stopped by the reading room on their way out. "*Goshujin sama*, we are leaving. We will be at *Chicago's Soul*, have a nice evening."

Lana was already in the *genkan* and didn't hear his reply. "Will there be a band tonight?" she asked as they climbed into the taxi.

"There are always several live acts. At this hour, we might still catch a couple. Afterward, DJs take over the place." Yuki took Lana's hand and squeezed it. "Now, let's make good use of tonight to get to know each other better. I intend to make you drink enough champagne to have you spill out your life story, sweetling," she chuckled.

Lana's smile turned forced. She would have to control her intake because she wasn't ready for this. "Hm, I'll make sure you don't spike my drink, then. Who knows what would happen to me? I could wake up in your bed, and not remember anything, or something just as terrible," she smirked.

Yuki's laugh sent new butterflies to Lana's stomach, but nice one this time. *Honda sama, you idiot, why can't you be content with such a queen at your side...*

Yuki leaned toward her ear, warm breath sending shivers along her spine. "Now I regret not having ordered a limousine with a privacy screen. It would be bad press to give this grandpa a good show; and we wouldn't hear the end of it."

Lana closed her eyes and stifled a moan. "Let's wait a bit longer," she whispered.

"Don't worry, *neko chan*, our VIP lounge is a separate room with full privacy." Both women shared a steamy look filled with promise before falling back into a comfortable silence while their taxi brought them to Shibuya district.

The exclusive nightclub Chicago's Soul occupied a four-stories high building. Hundreds of patrons waited in line, but without hesitating Yuki brought them to the VIP entrance. She didn't even have to show her membership card for the doors to open wide. Two hostesses brought them straight to their lounge. Lana discovered a spacious room, all in burgundy, red, and black tones, with large sofas. A bay window offered a perfect view of the dance-floor and scene, two floors below.

"Champagne?" Yuki asked, offering Lana a flute.

After a toast, Lana pointed at the jazz band performing. "Do you mind if we go downstairs to listen? It's been ages since I had the chance to enjoy live jazz and I'd love to be closer than this."

"Of course! There's a table booked for us. This band is so good, they come back from Chicago every year, and the crowds love them. Come on, let's go." Yuki grabbed Lana's hand and led them to the flight of stairs.

As soon as they sat at the table, only a few meters away from the scene, Lana found herself lost in the amazing performance of the band. The saxophonist was gifted, and his music stirred a whirlpool of emotions flushing her cheeks and making her hands shake. Warm fingers squeezed her wrist.

"I wish you could see the look on your face and those sparkles in your eyes, sweetling. I am so happy we came here tonight. It was high time you enjoyed something pleasurable and easy," Yuki said in her ear.

Tears blurred Lana's sight, and she pressed her companion's hand back. "I didn't think I needed it, but it seems like I truly did. Thank you, Yuki sama."

They remained at their table for about an hour, savoring a fresh bottle of champagne until the concert came to an end. Like everyone else, they jumped on their feet for a standing ovation.

"Dancing time!" Yuki exclaimed. "Do you want to go back to our lounge, or shall we stay here and join the crowd when there is some movement going on?"

"Why don't we remain here for a while? I'm dying to hear how, you, the eldest daughter of a fearsome industry tycoon, get to open the doors of the most exclusive nightclubs in stride?"

With a deep laugh that made Lana shiver, Yuki massaged her companion's thigh under the table; her fingers crawled up, sending electric shocks to her lover's core. "Well, you see, while my father has given me the same education as my brothers, to his eternal frustration, he's never been able to curb my endless search for personal freedom. My desire to explore my drives and be truthful to myself. My mother understood it and helped me, enabling many of my wildest choices—including my love for partying. My father was mad at us, but he never knew how to hold a grudge against her for long." She caressed Lana's cheek and took a shaky breath. "You would have loved her, and she would have definitely loved you." Emotions thickened her voice.

Not caring about the crowd surrounding them, Lana leaned forward to kiss Yuki's neck. Her lover cupped her cheek, pressed her lips and swept her tongue against hers, demanding entrance. Their deep kiss left them panting.

"Come on, let's dance," Yuki said huskily. "Show me what all this extra harsh training is about, sweetling."

Lana gave her a dazzling smile and led her by the hand to the center of the dance floor. Soon, they were lost to the outside world, letting the fast beat and loud music take over their bodies, sweat drenching their backs. Lana's desire for her companion built up fast, and she had to remind herself that they weren't alone. The fire in Yuki's eyes told her a similar story when she grabbed Lana's waist for a highly charged sensual dance.

"So *neko chan*, do you see anyone here who catches your eyes, whom you find... interesting?" Yuki purred in Lana's ear.

Lana squeezed Yuki's arm around her waist. "Yes, indeed. Lucky me, I'm in her arms," she replied, beaming.

"So smooth and sweet." Yuki replied with a large smile. "Now, don't forget, you're allowed to look... and more."

"As if I could have the energy or even the need to search for someone else with the two of you in my life," Lana chuckled. "Right now, I am quite complete and content, *oku sama*."

Yuki remained silent for a while, continuing her complex dance moves and leading Lana through them.

"Intimacy is such a serious thing for you. Why not try the fun side of it? How about finding out if any of those beautiful young ladies wants to come upstairs with us?"

Cradling her lover's cheek softly, Lana smiled against her smooth and damp skin. "I envy you so much for knowing who you are and for this freedom you've found. Please *oku sama*. Go ahead, ask one of them out, don't mind me, you don't need my blessing. Maybe one day I'll get there, but right now, this is impossible."

Yuki's eyes flashed. They stopped dancing and found themselves in a bubble, surrounded by hundreds of dancers. Lana didn't blink under the searching gaze of her companion.

"Of course not, I'm not ditching you! Hm... don't take me wrong, but the two of you are so similar. All these years, *goshujin sama* gave me complete leeway, but when he met you, only then did he grant himself some self-indulgence. He chose you."

Lana winced. "Ah, this must be hard for you—" A slender finger on her lips cut her off.

"No, it's not. I've already told you why. And it's such a blessing it's you, and that I find myself drowning in your personality, care and your other delicious skills. He couldn't have chosen better," Yuki added with a warm smile before resuming dancing.

Lana followed suit but had to look away to hide her trouble. *Chosen... always this word.*

She exhaled to let go of her tension; her eyes found the VIP area on the second floor and fell on the last man she'd expected to see. Honda.

"Oh!" She came again to a stop, shocked. "I can't believe it. He's here, just outside the VIP room, by the stairs!"

Yuki didn't even glance up or lose a beat. "Yes, he's been there for fifteen minutes or so, watching us."

"Did you expect him?"

"No, it's the second or third time in the past ten years he's come here. He dislikes the noise and such crowds. Maybe the picture of you in this amazing dress I sent him earlier did the trick," Yuki teased.

Lana burst out laughing, her unease evaporating and replaced by the wicked pleasure to make jokes at his expense with the only other person who would get it.

"Oh my, this and the video of your incredible hip move *I* sent him!" Both women whooped in laughter. "All right, it's nasty of us to give him such a nosebleed."

"A nosebleed and something else, which must be bothering him a lot right now," Yuki said with an unladylike snort. "We can always blame it on the alcohol, and if he complains, the door of my bedroom will be locked next week."

"This is your prerogative," Lana chuckled.

Something serious flickered again in Yuki's eyes, and the older woman grabbed both hands of her companion. "Lana san, it's yours as well. Let me be clear here. If you don't want to join him when he asks you to, you don't have to. You're in his service, yes, but not at his service. Whatever role we play, whatever pledge of obedience you made. Your limits aren't only there for when you're already in action. They also apply before starting anything. If you want to give him the cold shoulder for one week or one month, it's fine, as long as you are clear and forthcoming."

Lana inhaled deeply. "My problem is not having to go to him when I don't want to. Rather, the issue is, I *always* want to. Even now, even though we're together, and I want you and would like to do so many naughty things to you on the spot..." They shared a knowing smile. "Knowing he's here, I..." She blushed and looked away.

"You want to climb the stairs and join him," Yuki purred in her ear, once again against Lana's hip and chest.

"Yes!" Lana exclaimed, exasperated. "I'm mad at myself for being so weak when it comes to him, in particular when this is supposed to be our night."

Yuki grabbed her neck and pulled her in for another deep kiss. "It is, sweetling. But this is also supposed to be a fun and relaxing time. The choice is yours: you can go up to him, stay with me, take me up with you, or leave us here and get back home."

Tugged by too many contradictions, Lana groaned and threw another look at the VIP space. What she saw made her frown and burst her self-pity bubble. "Yuki sama, there are several women around *goshujin sama*, vying for his attention."

Yuki gave her a voracious smile but still, didn't glance upstairs. "Oh, I'm sure there are, glittering moths drawn to a dark, brooding flame leaving them panting and all kinds of bothered. Don't fret. He's not going to spare them one glance."

"Really? They're so beautiful. It would be hard not to react, at least a little bit."

Yuki went behind Lana and molded herself against her back. "Oh yes, they're so lovely they make my eyes hurt and my mouth water, but he doesn't work like this. These women could be Miss Japan and jump him while completely naked, but he wouldn't touch them. None of them would last even a minute with him, and he can't even be bothered. Even I can't always follow. Only you seem able to manage him at his highest degree. But perhaps it's because this is not about fun but fight for the two of you, isn't it?"

Once again, Lana turned silent and squeezed Yuki's hand. Her words hit their mark with frightening accuracy, but it was also a relief to hear this truth expressed so plainly. Yuki nibbled her lover's sweaty neck. "Come on now, let's go upstairs, and rescue him from such unbearable harassment."

21

Snarls and Teeth

A BORED AND SOUR look painted on his face, Honda leaned on the metallic handrail running all along the VIP floor. As soon as his companions moved in his direction, his wandering gaze locked on them.

Lana couldn't tear her eyes off his dashing frame as they climbed up the flight of stairs. In a black business suit and no tie, with the two top buttons of his light-blue shirt undone, his bulky body was even more attractive. He was the only one motionless in the crowd of jet setters, and it was impossible to miss him.

No wonder all these panties are getting drenched.

The rising tension flowing between the trio became almost tangible. The group of young ladies who gravitated around Honda gawked at the two newcomers with badly hidden hostility.

Baring teeth, Lana let her repressed alpha self pierce through. For Yuki, it was a second skin.

All except one moved out of the way. In her twenties, wearing a cream and lace dress barely covering her butt, a little minx with waist-long hair and an hourglass body stared straight at Lana with an ugly smile that was almost a snarl. She licked blood-red full lips; teeth flashed, black eyes burning with something else than mere lust.

A sudden and powerful impulse to smash her beautiful face on the nearest table made Lana shudder.

Nerves tingled. Goosebumps erupted all over her skin despite the heat inside the club and an iron taste filled her mouth. Her vision tunneled as all of her senses, all of her being, seemed to zoom on the girl.

Deep in the corners of her mind, an alarm bell rang. *Wow, what's going here?*

A more primitive, instinctive need seized her and swept aside the warning blaring in her head.

Lana gave the *slutbitchwhoreenemy* her blandest, deadest stare. Taking two steps closer, a low growl escaped her. Blood pulsed in her temples, a perfect match for the speed of the rapid techno beat filling the club.

The girl's eyes narrowed, and her stance shifted.

Right then, Honda's large frame filled Lana's field of vision, and she had to crane her neck to lock eyes with him. He wasn't happy.

"Stand. Down."

Lana worked her jaw before replying. "This one is no doll," she hissed. "She is dangerous and has an agenda. She should be put down!" The violence of her own words took her aback. *Where did this come from? What am I even doing?*

"Enough!" Honda barked. "It is not your call to answer her challenge. Do not waste my time over this kind of futility. Follow me. I did not come to this infernal place to remind you of our basic rules."

Reminded once again she had no claim over him, Lana obeyed. Still, it took her a tremendous amount of willpower to ignore the snarling girl and focus instead on her two companions. To her chagrin, Honda didn't spare the intruder a second look despite the unsettling vibes pouring from her.

Yuki was waiting for them by the entrance of their VIP lounge, a beaming smile on her lips. Seeing her so relaxed and composed threw water on Lana's raging fire.

Looks like I'm really overreacting. I need to learn how to deal with the kind of attraction he draws. If she isn't even twitching an eyebrow, there's no reason why I should. And like he said... it's not my place. It's hers. Another reminder of our terms. My rules of engagement.

"*Goshujin sama*, what a pleasant surprise to have you here with us. May I help you with your jacket?" Yuki asked, always so smooth, once the door closed behind them.

Lana welcomed the relative silence and strolled to the low table to fill three flutes of champagne; the sparkling drink would soothe her rattled nerves.

"Thank you," Honda nodded to his wife and handed her his vest. He rolled his sleeves up to his elbows, revealing his trunk-like forearms. "The noise outside is unbearable, I don't understand how you can enjoy spending more than five minutes in such a hellish environment." Accepting the flute Lana offered him, he signaled her to sit on his right, while Yuki sat on his left. "My wife is a hopeless cause, but do you also often partake in this kind of activity, Lana san?"

Lana smiled and emptied her glass. "Never in such high-end establishments. And to be honest, I've had only a handful of opportunities to do it since I moved to Tokyo. Back in my undergrad days, yes, I was a regular; Gabriella and I had several memorable nights.

The techno scene in Europe was crazy. In Spain, there's a whole island dedicated to partying and beach clubbing. In my twenties, I went there twice, or maybe three times? I have to admit, it was a bit wild… almost too wild!" she chuckled. *Hm, yep, those two guys knew how to move… when was that… 2000? 2001?*

Her faraway look wasn't lost on Honda who didn't seem so pleased. He put his glass on the table and leaned forward, a predatory sparkle in the eye. "With you, I cannot imagine what 'too wild' can mean," he grunted. "And did you wear many impossible and outrageous dresses like this one? Or was it something my scheming wife came up with to nab me, to test my patience?"

Yuki laughed and made a humming noise, which could be interpreted either way. Lana quirked an eyebrow. "Well, we weren't really expecting you tonight. I only hoped to match Yuki sama's extraordinary style. A poor attempt at meeting her impossibly high level of class if you wish. Anything else would have reflected poorly on her and we all agree this would be unacceptable, wouldn't it?"

Honda's eyes narrowed at this not-so-subtle reminder he was crashing their party. Before she could blink, he pounced on her; his teeth caught her neck, she found herself pushed back on the sofa.

With his usual skills, and not bothering with kindness, his teeth were all over her. Soon her gasps and soft moans filled the room. There would be no way to hide those marks, and everyone outside would know what had transpired inside the lounge. The thought made her head spin, and she grabbed his shoulder to encourage him.

With a smooth move, Yuki knelt by Lana's side to push her hair back and expose her neck. Her tongue found her lover's ear and her fingers pushed her dress to reveal her left breast, topped by a taut and sensitive nipple. Never leaving their sub's throat, Honda made room to give his wife better access to their companion's body.

Yuki's mouth moved away from her earlobe to launch a relentless attack on her nipples. Alternating licks and hard bites, she didn't stop until Lana, driven delirious, wriggled under her, sobbing, begging. Her masters weren't done playing with her though. Two very different hands slipped under her garments, each of them gripping a leg with enough strength to leave fingerprints and pushed them wide open. Dress trussed on her hips, she was exposed.

She wasn't fighting back, quite the opposite. Combined with the effects of alcohol, her feeling of utter helplessness fed her arousal as she let her doms feast on her. Too many fingers to count found her slick pussy and worked in tandem, probing, pinching, twisting, stretching and teasing until she couldn't remember her name.

She came long and hard, with a scream swallowed by Yuki's hungry mouth that was once again on hers. Her body jerked but was kept in place by Honda's powerful grip. The frenzy subsided, and Yuki broke off her maddening kiss.

The couple seemed pleased with the decadent picture she offered, sprawled on the sofa, thoroughly spent, and clothes in complete disarray. They brought their moist fingers to her lips; temples wet with tears, she licked them clean, humming in appreciation and gratitude.

"Now, this is what I call a party," Yuki chuckled. She turned to Honda. "What can I do for you, *goshujin sama*?" she asked amiably while caressing her husband's apparent bulge.

His hand glided along her shoulder and neck to her shiny and silky hair to pull her closer. Yuki freed him, grasped his base and gulped him in one smooth move until her lips were buried in his crotch, with an ease betraying long-time practice. He pounded her skull with fast strokes.

Disheveled, Lana was still sprawled on the sofa, pussy throbbing. She slid down to the floor to kneel next to Yuki and watch them with rapt attention.

Honda's shaft distorted Yuki's mouth, and she made delighted sounds each time he hit the back of her throat.

It would have been a shame to forget Yuki's pleasure. Lana molded herself against her back. One hand found a nipple through the shimmering tissue of her dress, the other moved along her thighs, inside her pants and caught her dom's clit. She chose frantic and hard stimulation, a retaliation of a sort, but also aiming at making her mistress cum right at the same time as her husband. It worked like a charm and soon the lounge was filled with Yuki's muffled moans, and Honda's grunts.

Both spouses reached their peak together, Yuki doing her best to swallow as much as possible. She ended up cradling Lana's cheek, and her lover responded without missing a beat; both women shared another heated and passionate kiss, before sitting again on the sofa, glowing with satisfaction. Hands on hips, Honda remained standing and stared them down.

"Now, let's address your little show on the dance floor. Did you think I would let it pass? Yuki san, you were aware of my presence during your dancing, if I can even call those vulgar jerking moves as such. You did it on purpose." Dark clouds gathered on his face. "While this was your night, I am not pleased both of you went on full display in front of such a large audience."

Lana bit her cheek to refrain from smirking at where this was going. She was pretty sure he had enjoyed it. He wouldn't have waited upstairs otherwise.

"My sincere apologies, *goshujin sama*," Yuki replied with a demure tone. "I found it impossible to resist Lana san's raw and unleashed sensuality."

"So, little *mudansha*, your lack of discipline is causing trouble again?" her master challenged her with a dark purr.

Lana inhaled deeply and attempted to demonstrate appropriate contrition. "Unfortunately, it is. I have no excuse."

"Do you, now?" Honda growled. "I am not so sure of your sincerity. But you might indeed regret it painfully after I am done with you. Yuki san, I am not pleased by your behavior either, you will not escape punishment."

Lana wet her lips; her cheeks turned crimson in anticipation. Memories of his harsh spanking at the hotel flooded her. *Oh yes, just like that time, it would be so good...*

She kneeled again on the plush rug. "*Goshujin sama*, please, I would hate to see *oku sama*'s beautiful and smooth skin damaged in any way because of my serious lapse and appalling failings. Whatever you had in mind for her, I beg you to allow me to bear it." She bowed her head to her folded hands.

"*Neko chan...*" Yuki whispered, blinking in surprise.

Honda grabbed Lana's hair and pulled back her head. "Good, you remember your duty and role. Back on the sofa then, on your knees, and raise your hips."

A mindless yet pleasant buzz ringing in her head, Lana hastened to comply. With her new position, her state of arousal was plain for her masters to see.

Honda sat on her right side so Yuki wouldn't miss one second of what was about to take place. Lana shuddered when his large, hot and calloused hand swept along her thighs then over her cheeks, up to her lower back and then again down on the inside of her legs, moist from her recent orgasm. He made sure to avoid touching her most sensitive areas even though they craved for his touch.

"You still bear faint marks from our previous session, little *mudansha*," he pointed out. "We will not push it as far as that night."

From velvet caress, his hand turned into burning iron in a blink. He wasn't holding back much. Each slap was harsher than the last one, and all sent her reeling against the sofa. She grabbed the cushions and closed her eyes shut, focusing on her breathing.

"Yes... *goshujin sama*..." she moaned, filled with gratitude. *It feels so right! I need this so much! Everything makes more sense now!*

Perspiration broke out all over her quivering body and tears began to flow.

"Yuki san, no! Do not touch her yet," Honda's harsh order resonated in the room. Systematic, relentless, he turned Lana's cheeks and upper thighs bright red.

"Ah please... more... ah... forgive me... I'm so sorry..." Lana babbled.

Whether the noises passing her lips were of pleasure or pain didn't matter. It made no difference.

There was only complete surrender, loss of control, and total trust. Only his hand on her burning skin, reminding her of her choices and deepest longings.

She buried her face in the cushions and let out a long and high-pitched scream as a glorious climax overcame her, born out of pure pain. Millions of stars danced behind her eyelids. Strengthless, boneless, she slouched on the sofa, shaken by small tremors and a smile of intense satisfaction on her lips.

Powerful arms embraced her and collected her against the large chest she had come to cherish, way too much for her own good. No soothing words, but simple physical comfort, and assurance she wasn't alone, as well as silent recognition of her achievement.

"Let me put ice here," Yuki whispered, her voice shaky. "My apologies, *neko chan*, this might be quite uncomfortable." She pressed a pack of dripping cubes wrapped in a towel on the most vivid areas before landing soft kisses on the untouched skin.

Lana hissed but didn't move away, welcoming the cold numbing of her heated flesh and the delicate feather touch of her mistress' lips.

"Do you need some for your hand, *goshujin sama*?" Yuki asked pointedly. The tightening of his arm around her told Lana he didn't appreciate his wife's sassiness.

"No, I do not," he growled. "Focus on her."

Yuki rested her head on Lana's lap. The trio remained entangled in a careful heap for almost half an hour until Lana stirred, convinced she had recovered enough sense to stand up again and walk without assistance.

Honda let her go and rose on his feet. "Come now, it is time to go home."

After Lana had put back some order into her dress, makeup and hair, they stepped out of the room. Yuki and Lana walked side by side behind Honda who strolled ahead, not caring for the club patrons who parted before him. There was a congestion near the doors though, and they couldn't get back on the streets immediately.

Lana's aching body still hummed with pleasure at their intense session. While they waited in line, her teasing fingers roamed along her mistress' arm and lower back. To her delight, Yuki closed her eyes and a large smile bloomed on her lips.

But the delicious mood was shattered when Lana's spine tingled. and her stomach began to burn. A bolt of tension jolted her.

Danger!

Out of reflex, not knowing what she was even looking for, her eyes scanned the dense crowd of merry partygoers; she came to a halt and a long hiss passed her clenched teeth.

What the...

The young woman in the cream dress stood a few meters from them, staring in their direction with the same hateful snarl and dangerous stance as before.

Another rush of pain in the pit of her sternum made Lana wince. Anger flooded her system once again, mingled with a low-burning anxiety; her bruised buttocks forgotten, Lana was in front of her in three strides and invaded her personal space.

"What do you want?" she spat in the plainest and rudest language register she knew. "Leave us the fuck alone, or I'll wipe this ugly smile off your face."

The woman smacked her blood-red lips and chuckled. "My my, such violence, why am I not surprised he picked you as his fucktoy... but if you think for one second you can help him, you're dead wrong, tramp. There's no way out, and he will–"

A sudden wave of rage suffocated Lana and the need to strike overwhelmed her. A large hand grabbed her wrist just as she raised her arm.

"Go to the taxi line with Yuki and wait for me there. I will take care of this." Honda's low voice left no room for arguing. Those two had met in the past, but nothing good had come out of it given the stormy look on his face. Her words were so strange though. She didn't sound like a disgruntled lover.

Lana was tempted to watch what would happen next, but his orders had been clear. After a last hateful glance at the troublemaker, she walked back to Yuki, put an arm around her mistress' waist and led her outside. With each step, she felt better, and her heart finally calmed down.

"Where did *goshujin sama* go? Did he forget anything inside?" Yuki asked as they hailed a taxi at the bottom of the stairs.

"Ah, I think he wanted to drill some sense in that sl... errr... young woman's head. You know, the one from before, with the lacy white dress? She was so aggressive, I almost slapped her. She was near the exit right now."

Yuki frowned and shook her head. "Really? I remember three or four, but none with a white dress."

"Uh, perhaps you couldn't see her from where you stood, but her behavior struck me. As if she had been onto something serious and we had... ruined her plans when we joined *goshujin sama*."

"And he went back to talk with her? They... know each other?"

"Looks like it, but I don't see how she could be any threat to him and trust me, there was no love between them. He looked downright livid, and she was full of... spite and hatred."

Right then, Honda jogged down the long flight of stairs of the nightclub and caught up with them. Face a blank, his left hand was in his pocket, something he never did. "Let's get in the taxi," he told them with a curt nod.

They climbed inside the car, Yuki first, followed by Lana and Honda. Swallowing back a wince of pain, Lana shot a careful glance at her companion, aware of his body tension and the fact he still had not taken his hand from his pocket. The three of them were squeezed together on the back seats, and she dared brush his sleeve.

"Did she—"

"The problem is solved," he uttered. Then he threw Lana a side look. "If you ever see her again, wherever it may be, let me know at once, but do not approach her or talk with her. She is... unstable."

Overhearing despite his whispering, Yuki leaned forward to look at her husband. "What is the matter here? Is this woman threatening you... or Lana san? Should we call the police? Did you..." Her quirked eyebrow and inquiring glance asked quite plainly the question she wouldn't say aloud given their audience.

Marble-stiff, Honda let out a long hiss. "No, Yuki san. Never. And no need to call the police. Please do not worry about this... person. She will never bother you. She is an unbalanced nuisance, that's all."

Lana frowned. *Uh. 'Bother you'? Why not 'us'?*

She locked eyes with Honda; he was unreadable. A heavy sigh escaped her; sometimes, too much got lost in translation. When he switched to such a clamped-down mode, it was useless to attempt to pry open his jaws for more details.

The late hour and the excitement of the night caught up with her. As she dozed off, her head fell on his shoulder. With Yuki's fingers enlaced with hers, a new sense of peace and contentment bloomed inside her heart and mind.

22

Strange Neighbors

Sunday practice was over. Lana stepped under the dojo porch and glanced upward, aggravated. It was well into the rainy season, the only time of the year when she longed to be back in Montreal. Heavy rains drenched the city and all its inhabitants at least twice a day. Even when it didn't rain, humidity levels skyrocketed, and everything felt damp all the time.

"Oh my, it wasn't raining so hard two hours ago... but look at this now, it's a downpour!"

Tim and his wife put their shoes on and joined her, umbrellas already open. "Well, this is when I'm happy to have a car," he said. "Do you want us to drive you home? You're welcome to tag along."

With a headshake, Lana put her bag on the stairs leading to the dojo. "No, no, it's fine, this will be just like a long shower!"

"At this late hour, it's a bit dangerous, don't you think?" Tim insisted. "The visibility is so poor..."

Lana waved her hand in a dismissive gesture. "Don't worry, my lights are powerful. See you on Tuesday!"

"As you wish Lana, you and your stubborn head... Take care! Don't rush..."

Lana stuffed her blouson in her duffel bag, readjusted her baseball cap, and wearing nothing but a sports bra and a tank top over knee-length running pants, she walked into the open. She was a wet dog in seconds. The rain and air were warm, however, so she didn't mind.

"Oh rats," she muttered under her breath when she saw her bicycle. One of her tires was flat. She grabbed her pump, kneeled in the muddy sand and got to work. When the rain stopped, she looked up, surprised. Honda was behind her, protecting her with his umbrella.

"What is the matter?" Honda asked, making sure to not play any familiar card while many of their fellow aikidoka were around.

"Just a flat tire, Sensei, luckily it's not punctured. I'll be done in a minute, thank you," she added with a smile.

"You should go home with me," he said a few minutes later in a low voice. Lana shook her head, still pumping air.

"Thank you, but I don't want to leave my bicycle here overnight. And I'm already soaked, so I'll be fine and won't ruin the leather of your front seat." She stopped and glanced behind him. There was nobody around. "If you could take my bag though, I'd be grateful."

They hadn't disclosed that she lived with him and Yuki; it would kick off the gossip mill, and for once, people would be right. Even if he was harder with her than with anyone else, it wouldn't be good for the morale in the dojo, despite the valid excuse of her burnt flat, and that he wasn't in charge of grading her.

"Of course."

Lana was done and straightened up. They stood close to each other under his umbrella, now so familiar with the other's body, none of them felt the need to step away.

After a few heartbeats, Lana handed him her bag. "Here it is, thank you very much. I will see you... later," she whispered before bowing and stepping back under the rain.

Her bicycle led her south toward Setagaya ward using the back streets. With this weather and the traffic, Lana would be home before him. A change of clothes and something to eat were at the top of her list.

She arrived at the gate of the Honda estate in less than fifteen minutes. Ever since the episode at the club, she had been growing at ease with her two companions and their new domestic life. The right words to describe their complex three-way relationship still failed her but even though the three of them were keeping a low profile for obvious reasons, there was no embarrassment.

She typed in the entrance code and pushed her bicycle inside before coming to an abrupt stop. The house was dark. Lana swore aloud: it was Yuki's night out. Her keys, along with her wallet and smartphone, were in her jacket pockets, inside her bag, in Honda's car. There was nothing to do except wait. Sitting under the porch, she stared, morose, at the water gushing down the gutter and the darkened walls running around the house.

Her head shot up, startled by an incongruous noise coming from the east wall of the property. The side connected to the Shinto shrine. Lana frowned. The sound repeated itself, and her eyes widened. *It's a child laughing! But at this hour? With this weather? Could it be the same kid?*

Lana jumped to her feet, went back on the road, and then stepped on the shrine's gravelly grounds. Something made her pause under the tall vermilion *torii* gate marking the entrance.

Except for street lights behind her, there was not a single source of light to pierce through the damp darkness ahead. The pine trees planted around the grounds cut off any light from the neighboring houses and deepened the pitch-black obscurity surrounding the small shrine. Even its shape was swallowed by the night; for all that she knew, there was nothing in front of her except for a black abyss.

Out of sheer curiosity, she had visited the shrine two weeks before. There was nothing special about it: it was small, yet the neighbors did a great job with its upkeep. According to Yuki, after the war, the Honda clan had donated a part of their land to the local community. The shrine had been established in honor of a minor deity, *Kagu-tushi*, the *kami* of fire, for protection against fires threatening to wipe out entire neighborhoods.

Lana shuffled on her feet, annoyed at herself. Dark places didn't scare her. On the one hand, she felt a pressing urge to go and check out what was going on there. On the other hand, something undefined held her back from stepping any further inside. Instincts or irrational fear, it was impossible to say.

Out of sheer curiosity, she had visited the shrine two weeks before. There was nothing special about it: it was small, yet the neighbors did a great job with its upkeep. According to Yuki, after the war, the Honda clan had donated a part of their land to the local community. The shrine had been established in honor of a minor deity, *Kagu-tushi*, the *kami* of fire, for protection against fires threatening to wipe out entire neighborhoods.

Lana shuffled on her feet, annoyed at herself. Dark places didn't scare her. On the one hand, she felt a pressing urge to go and check out what was going on there. On the other hand, something undefined held her back from stepping any further inside. Instincts or irrational fear, impossible to say.

She was about to return to the house when the kid laughed again. Goosebumps covered her arms. This time, sharp and brief, the laugh had sounded like glass shattering.

With a head shake, she planted her feet in the wet sand and put her hands on her hips. "Hello! Anyone out there? Hey kid! What are you doing, you should be home!" It was ridiculous to shout at dark trees, under the rain. Summoning all her courage, she took a step forward.

The hell? "Ah!" Lana exclaimed in fright and anger.

In a blink, she found herself on all fours, face a few centimeters away from a pool of mud and gravel. Her aikido training had been the only thing allowing her to break her fall. Something had rubbed her shins and pulled at her legs, making her trip. To her surprise, a small and roundish dog with odd long hair that covered its face watched her, expectant. She had never seen one like this.

"Hey, watch out, you idiot!" she protested, half-amused, half-exasperated. She got on her feet; to her chagrin, her jogging pants were torn at her knees. Better than her skin, but still...

The dog wasn't deterred by her reaction. "Ah stop! Go away now, hushhh!"

There was nothing to do. It wasn't aggressive or even barking, but Lana couldn't walk past it unless she wanted to land again nose first in the wet ground. Every time she took a step toward the shrine, the animal kept coming back to slalom between her legs. Wary, she chuckled at its odd behavior and gave up.

After a last glance at the trees, she walked back to the house, rubbing her muddy hands on her ruined pants. To her relief, the small animal didn't follow her. Right when she moved to sit again in front of the house, the main gate opened. Honda's car drove in, going straight inside the garage.

He didn't bother hiding his smirk when he joined her by the door. "Forgot something?" It wasn't frequent for him to be anything less than strict around her. After the creepy moment she had gone through, she welcomed the change of mood.

"Don't get me started, the list is endless, starting with my brain," she replied with a grin of her own. "It wasn't smart of me to give you everything, including my wallet."

"Indeed not, make sure this does not happen again." The ground was still shaking now and then. It wasn't a good idea to be outside on her own, at night, without any ID, money or communication device. "What happened to your clothes? Were you in an accident?"

"No, just a… late encounter with a too friendly dog while I waited for you."

In the *genkan*, the cool and dry A/C flow welcomed them. Even though it was a pain for her sinuses, there was no other choice to keep control on the humidity levels inside the house.

"Wait!" Honda barked as she was about to remove her shoes and step on the wooden stairs. "You will flood the hall. Let me fetch a bath towel."

Lana sighed and crossed her arms, watching his retreating back while small pools of water accumulated at her feet. Then she quirked an eyebrow, feeling like a tease. She got rid of her wet clothes and waited for him, where he had left her, but this time completely naked. Honda came back with several towels and stopped in his tracks, eyebrows lost in his hairline.

She struggled to keep a smooth face; She struggled to keep a smooth face; it was always satisfying when his composure crumbled because of her, even for a split second. However, he demonstrated once again he could easily keep control over the situation.

Face again a blank, he handed her towels. "Dry yourself, and go put something on your back, we haven't eaten yet."

Lana gulped down her disappointment and wrapped the towel around her chest. "Would you like me to prepare dinner?"

"It depends, do you plan to cook *washoku*?"

"Well, except for instant miso soup, cups of ramen and putting rice in a cooker, there isn't much I know about Japanese recipes. I thought I'd fix a basic dish, spaghetti with a simple tomato sauce... you know, garlic, basil, olive oil... topped with parmesan cheese..."

Honda grimaced. "Then no, thank you. I will reheat the noodle soup Yuki prepared yesterday."

Lana rolled her eyes at his back. *Why this fixation on Japanese cooking?* "Is there any chance you might one day try what I cook?" she inquired with a soft smile to avoid sounding like she was whining. "I assure you, Italian recipes are popular here... tomato and parmesan are known for their umami taste. What I make is not spicy at all... well, at least not in general."

Honda scoffed as he entered the kitchen and went to the fridge. "Spicy is not the issue. I prefer *washoku*. Eat whatever pleases you."

By the time Lana came back to the kitchen, fully clothed, Honda was reheating a handmade soup as well as a mix of vegetables and pork slices topped with *teriyaki* sauce. Lana fixed what she needed for her own dish and heated her tomatoes while she waited for the water to boil. The combination of smells was interesting. Famished, she prepared an easy appetizer of toasted bread dipped in olive oil.

"With the June testing session behind us, it is time for you to get serious about preparing for first *kyu* in September," Honda remarked while tossing his vegetables.

Lana quirked an eyebrow. "Serious, as opposed to the relaxed and easy training you have put me through since January?"

His pointed glare transfixed her. "Serious in the sense that you need to be clear on the test requirements and prepare specific combinations for the *jiyu waza* parts. Inoue *shihan* will oversee this testing session and if you believe I have high expectations, then think again. He treats candidates for the first *kyu* as severely as those going for *shodan*. You know by now that he has a keen eye and will see every little flaw. As many of your *kohai* will also undergo testing, I should focus on them. I count on your own discipline to make sure you forget nothing, understood?"

Swallowing a spike of stress, Lana nodded. It would be her first test since they had begun their relationship. The level of expectation had soared.

"Of course, we will also train here now and then, to fix details together," Honda added. It did nothing to appease her; one-on-one sessions with him were exhausting, tense and challenging. If there was one place where her temper and smart mouth had no room, it was on the mats.

"Ah, thank you. I... look forward to tackling this new challenge."

Her pasta was ready. They sat on each side of the counter table, eating in comfortable silence. That they could share easy moments like this was also something she appreciated, as she needed her own space, physically and mentally.

Their peaceful moment came to a brusque end when her phone flared to life from the depths of her duffel bag in the hall. "My apologies," she muttered before darting out of the kitchen.

Lila Mina

23

Two Sides of the Same Coin

Lana's eyebrows shot up at the caller's ID. "Ikeda san, good evening. What's the matter?" she asked her colleague while going back to the kitchen.

"Martin san, I am so sorry to disturb you at this time of the day. It's about the Daihanko-Dos Santos meeting tomorrow, we have a problem…" Ikeda sounded embarrassed, almost scared.

Lana frowned and sat back on her seat. "What kind of problem? We've been on this at length over the past weeks with Castillo on my end, Hayashi san on yours.

I spent the weekend at the office to set up everything. Tomorrow is a mere formality."

"Ah well... I just received a call from Hayashi san. They... want to rescind their commitment to the five-year embargo on parallel imports."

Lana blanched, her dismay quickly turning into downright fury. "What? Are they out of their mind? This is the most sensitive condition for the Spaniards! You know it, Hayashi san and above all, Goshima san know it! There will be no deal without this!"

"I know! I am so, so sorry Martin san," Ikeda replied, desperate. "Hayashi san... exploded on the phone when I pointed it out and hung up on me..."

Lana pinched the bridge of her nose. *Damn this sneaky COO.* "Listen, Hayashi san was never happy with this distribution agreement. But we can't just sit back and wait until the shit hits the fan in our boardroom tomorrow morning."

"Let's meet up at 7 am, discuss it with the rest of team..."

"It will be too late! We need to act now! Castillo and his people are on the plane, and if they are welcomed with this news, everything will go up in flames. Our collective asses will be whipped. It's our job to make sure such things don't happen." She took a deep breath. "I'll call Hayashi san."

"Martin san, it's too risky... if we lose this account..."

Temper: Deference

"Well, what's the alternative, hm? If we keep our mouths shut, our reputation is toast, here and in Europe, too. Not to mention the penalties, which will make M&F go bankrupt before the end of the year. You can bet your last dirty sock the Spaniards will turn on us like rabid hyenas and strip us naked."

"Please understand, this kind of global-level negotiations is new to them..."

"No. I'm sorry Ikeda san, I don't want to be rude, but there are rules. Things like reasonable expectations and trust, and if they want to play with the big boys, they need to stop acting as if they were still an *aracha* producer in the countryside."

"Okay... all right... I'll let you call him," Ikeda replied, defeated and uncertain.

Disgusted and exasperated, Lana terminated the call and stared at her phone on the table. What a pitiful way to end an otherwise nice evening. *I need a working angle. That double-face asshole is shrewd and won't listen to anything if his own interests aren't threatened.*

"Watching you handle a crisis at work is always fascinating and quite instructive," Honda's deep voice interrupted her thinking. She looked up, startled. *Instructive? What does he mean?* "But whatever you do next, get a grip on your temper first."

She grimaced. "Oh, I will be a model of composure when I talk to this backstabbing traitor. I should have seen this coming. I didn't expect him to pull this off the night before the meeting though. Too bad I'm not the one in charge of the Japanese side of this deal. I would have made sure he didn't think he could try something so cute. Well, I better get this done."

Hayashi picked up his phone after letting it ring for a long while. "Who is this?"

"Good evening, Hayashi sama," she began with her most neutral voice. "This is Lana Martin from M&F. My deepest apologies for calling you at such a late hour, but there is an urgent issue to discuss, which cannot wait until tomorrow."

"Martin? Ah yes, the sassy girl," he snarled, and she had to bite her tongue not to lash out at his condescending tone. "What is it? I've already talked with Ikeda, and the matter is closed. We want no embargo clause. Make it work."

"Indeed, it is crystal clear, Hayashi sama, but this will not be possible," Lana replied, her voice turning icy cold.

Hayashi huffed, not bothering to hide his anger. "Who are you to dictate what your client wants or doesn't want? This clause was a mistake from the beginning, but our President now understands it. Be careful, or I'll guarantee your company will pay if you don't support us... and that you'll lose your job, insolent woman. Go back to making coffee."

Lana made a fist; it took all her willpower not to hurl back a string of creative insults at the douchebag. "Hayashi sama, this has nothing to do with what my company prefers, and at this stage, it's not even about what yours wants. Dos Santos will have all leeway to make you pay for it, and all your attempts to set foot in Europe and South America will crumble. They will not hide their furor or find a way for everybody to keep face. Think whatever you want of me, but there are certain rules when you do international business. And my job is to guarantee that they are respected for everyone involved."

"Silence! How rude and arrogant of you! You're supposed to defend our interests, but you have no problem making us lose huge amounts of money with a one-sided deal!"

"If you think your company will lose money with this five-year embargo, I look forward to your explanations to your shareholders about why the doors to the two biggest overseas markets of your sector are now locked down. Have a good night," Lana said with a pleasant tone and ended the call.

"The phone will ring again, twenty or thirty minutes from now. It will be my boss." Her hands shook, but not out of anxiety; rage made her see stars.

Face unreadable, Honda scrutinized her as if she were an insect under a microscope. She flung a blank stare back at him and hid her hands under the table.

"You checked your temper, yet your words were rude," Honda commented.

Lana's eyes narrowed, and she pinched her lips. "I won't apologize for telling him the naked truth. Our client is the company he works for, not him. He's not protecting his company's interests, only pushing his own agenda."

"You want to hurt him, your body shakes with the need to punch him, to break something," Honda continued with his observations.

She hissed and looked away. *Are you done dissecting me?* "And what if I do," she spat. "It's natural when confronted by an imbecile like him. What do you expect me to do? Roll over, smile and be grateful while he ruins my work and reputation?"

Swift as lightning, Honda was by her side. "I am not telling you to *enjoy* it. I am saying, you should not allow him to affect you so powerfully. You will make deadly mistakes if you let people like him get under your skin."

Exasperated at his constant meddling in her professional life, Lana growled. She opened her mouth to give him a piece of her mind when her phone rang again. The name "Richard M." flashed on the screen.

"My boss. Ten minutes. He was quick," Lana commented wryly. Honda grunted but remained so close, his body heat pressed against her skin. To her chagrin, it was distracting.

"Richard. Good evening," she said with a cool voice.

"Lana, why do I have to handle an angry and unhinged Hayashi on a Sunday night? What did you do this time, for God's sake? He wants you out of the deal and is this close to cutting us loose!"

"Are you aware of the situation? Do you know what he plans to do?"

"Yeah, yeah, yeah. Ikeda called me. It's a mess— okay, it's a real shitstorm, but why did you have to antagonize the man so much? He was rabid on the phone!"

"Well, do what you have to do, but you know what's at stake and what will happen if we let him go ahead."

"Of course I do, and I told him so. The good news is, what you said must have gone through his thick skull, as they won't go back on the written agreement and the current clause. But you're out of the picture. Once and for all. We'll tell Castillo you're sick and then come up with something else. I'm sorry, but maybe you should stop playing the goddamned school teacher and acting as if the senior management of our VIP clients need a good spanking. Understood?"

Lana gritted her teeth and closed her eyes. "Yes," she spat, before inhaling deeply instead of giving her boss a mouthful. "But Richard, please, keep Hayashi on a tight leash. Who knows what kind of other stupid stuff he can come up with before tomorrow."

Richard sighed. "Of course. Take a few days off, don't show up until the Spaniards have gone home. We'll do a proper debriefing at the end of the week. Good night!"

Lana rubbed her face to hide the tears of rage blurring her sight. Eighteen months of hard work, of countless hours, spent writing and checking every single detail of a 340-page agreement, of smoothing things out... *Look at me, thrown out of the loop like a garbage bag.*

She cleared her throat before grabbing a glass of water. "Well, I guess that's what they call taking one for the team..." she muttered. "Looks like I'm off until Thursday. So much free time, what am I going to do with myself? This was a rhetorical question by the way."

Honda put one hand next to hers on the table. "You knew the risks and still did what you thought was in the best interests of your team... and client. I disagree with how you did it, but you showed a remarkable sense of duty. Focus on this and don't allow the rest to bother you. But you should reflect on what went wrong."

Lana let out a shaky hiss and got on her feet. She needed space. To do something with her hands, she started cleaning up the dishes and pans.

"I did the right thing... but at the end, the bastard wins—he removed me from the game. I can guarantee that if I had been a man, he wouldn't have acted like this, so... condescending and insulting. I confronted him with the consequences of his bad decision, and he couldn't handle it because I'm a woman." She slammed her hands on the sink and pivoted to face Honda.

"Even you call me rude when I am being direct. Oh yes, I know it's cultural, but it's more than that. Do you think I should make things more pleasant and easier for everybody else? If I had been kinder, he wouldn't have listened. So, yes, I shouldn't be fuming, wishing I could... throttle him and break his jaw. It's a problem. But I won't sweeten things because you all would rather have me smile and nod like a doll!"

Lana stopped, panting hard. She had managed not to shout, and he wasn't barking back. Yet. He had moved closer to her again, not getting the hint she preferred him to stay away... or not caring about it. He wasn't threatening, but it was hard to think straight with him so close.

"You... you can't understand my perspective, *goshujin sama*," she added, this time with less vehemence. "You are at the top of... the food chain.

Your gender, your age, your social status... all your privileges make it so that you don't have to fight against almost half the world to validate your position or even your existence."

Honda closed in and caught her chin between two fingers. She wasn't so small, and he wasn't so tall, but still, he had a good head on her. "Not half the world, indeed not, but even I must bow sometimes. Including to some who have no sense of duty or honor. Duty requires accepting such things. I am glad to see you can go to great lengths to do what is right, even when it means self-sacrifice. This is the core, the essence of *budo*."

He stepped even closer; this time his body pressed hers against the sink. "It is one thing to decide you cannot and will not change how you act. But if you have any ounce of self-preservation, you must work on how the consequences affect you." His hand snatched her throat. "One last thing: I am not pleased at all that this deplorable man makes you react so. This dark urge... this desire to hit him, to draw his blood... it is only toward *me* you should feel it."

Lana's eyes widened in shock; she tried to recoil, but his grip of steel made it impossible. "What?... No, no... it's... totally different! I... don't want to do this to you! And... I don't want this repulsive man! How can you think that?" she spat, disgusted.

"And this is what you still do not understand. Those are the two sides of the same coin. We have been playing along this thin line long enough now. All those drives of yours, when they overwhelm you and make you see red, make your body shake, when those images dance in front of you, I demand to be the one and only answer to them. Your mind should not get... cluttered by powerful urges toward others, even less other men."

Lana was trembling again, but this time for other reasons. Licking her lips, she grabbed his shirt so hard her biceps bulged. She pulled herself up to be the one towering over him for once.

"But then... if I get to be... so aggressive with you... it means... you allow me to take the lead, now and then?" she growled, staring at him in the eye, her repressed alpha self sniffing an opportunity.

His thick thigh slid between her legs, and his free hand slipped inside her panties to cup her pussy. "No, absolutely not," he retorted, crushing her attempt at rebellion. "You will fight me back, defend yourself, draw my blood, carve my flesh, but I am in command."

To test her level of readiness, he pushed two fingers inside her. Lana shuddered and buried her head in his nape, biting him hard in frustrated retaliation. He brought down her pants and panties, seized her hips and made her sit on the sink. His hands grabbed her knees to push her legs wide open and keep her in place. They would leave fingerprints.

She was trapped, exposed.

"We will fight this destructive desire to hurt and maim with fire, but of another kind," he finished as his shaft slipped inside her with an unforgiving thrust.

Honda began to pound her, showing no mercy. Her body shook like a leaf, she was helpless against his assault, but that was the whole point. *He's making me as powerless as I am against Hayashi! No way... no way I can escape his grip! I need to... to take the fight to him!*

With a rageful shout, Lana wrapped her arms around his neck and slammed her upper body against his chest. Hands on each side of his face, she set off to devour his lips with a fierce and invasive kiss. Her sudden move and passion threw him off balance long enough for his grasp on her legs to ease. She managed to lock her ankles behind his back and grind her pelvis against his. Both moaned in each other's mouth as he found himself balls-deep inside her.

He couldn't fight inertia; he stumbled a couple of steps back. Before he could regain a footing solid enough to make him in effect unmovable, her feet dropped down, and with a hip twist she brought them on the floor, making sure to protect his neck and head.

The landing was rough and painful for both of them, but nobody cared.

He was still buried in her, and she clamped her inner muscles to keep him that way. Her fingers moved under his shirt and clawed at his flanks, just as she bit his shoulder. He roared, his rock-hard member twitching inside her. Blood oozed, and she licked his shoulder before giving him a vicious rough kiss.

Unfortunately for her, she wasn't so good yet, not skilled enough and above all not strong enough for handling him like that for very long–even less when struck by a powerful orgasm. After a few more violent shakes, her body turned limp. One moment she was grinding his shaft and twisting his nipples, the next she was on her back, her wrists caught in an iron grip above her head.

Everything stopped. The sound of their heavy pants filled the kitchen. They were covered in sweat, his body pinning hers against the floor.

"Yes, this... this is exactly what I meant... There is much room for progress, but you understand now, don't you?"

"Y... yes, I do..." she replied in a throaty whisper, unable to free her wrists.

"Good." He claimed her mouth and came hard inside her before disentangling himself. He stood up in one fluid motion, seizing her elbow to bring her up along. Her legs were shaky, but she kept her balance.

"Think about tonight's events. Prepare yourself for more situations like this in the future. I will not be as helpful next time."

Lana quirked an eyebrow. Helpful? He was pushing it. But she bit her tongue and nodded. "I will go to my room now, good night."

She picked up her clothes and left the kitchen, lost in thought. To her surprise, she could think about all her work drama without reacting so violently anymore, as if looking at it on a screen, and not going through every discussion and clash herself.

Maybe there was something to say about Honda's unorthodox therapeutic methods.

24

Fighting Ghosts

THREE NIGHTS LATER, Lana and Yuki sat at the kitchen counter for dinner. It was a relaxed moment both women enjoyed, but also a welcome distraction for Lana who didn't want to delve too much into her upcoming debriefing with Richard the next morning.

"Even after all this time in Japan, I still can't convince my brain that rain doesn't mean cooler weather..." Lana mused aloud, listening to the heavy downpour outside. It was hard to dismiss the drops of perspiration sliding along her neck and drenching her back. "Also, figuring out how to dress for work is a nightmare. The only good shoes are plastic sandals, and I wish I could wear one-pieces all day long, but no! I swear, by the time I arrive at my office, I need to change blouses. Same when I get home."

Yuki laughed in sympathy. "Yes, I hate this season, everything gets covered with mold if we don't keep the A/C on, my hair keeps curling, and I have to spend extra time straightening it every morning. Even if actual summer is so much hotter, it is better than this constant humidity. Well, three more weeks to go! More of this incredible wine?"

Handing out her empty glass was Lana's silent answer. Yuki refilled it with the delicious *primitivo* Lana had found at a nearby imported liquor shop. By far, red wine was her poison of choice, and she was more than happy to introduce Yuki to lesser known cultivars and labels from Southern Italy. To her secret satisfaction, even Honda had taken a liking to them.

"How do you like this *lasagna alle verdure*?"

"It's exquisite! I wish you cooked more often," Yuki replied with a wink.

Lana shook her head, a wide smile on her lips. "So do I... I tried the other day, I cajoled, pouted, but I can't make him have a single bite of my cooking... and I know nothing of Japanese recipes, except for the instant stuff."

"*Goshujin sama* swears only by *washoku*, I'm afraid. But fear not, one day his taste in food will become as cosmopolitan as his appreciation for fine wines... or women." Both chuckled. "As for me, I love what you do, so let me toast to it. And for once, I almost wish he could go to *nomikai* more often!"

After-work drinking parties were a big part of corporate life in Japan, but they made little sense to Lana. Everyone turned half comatose after a few drinks. Come the next day, they'd pretend nothing had ever happened after spending the night complaining about their boss who sat with them.

"Me too, I confess because as much as I like *washoku*, my taste buds just long for cheese, raw ham, spicy sauce, pasta and so on. You can't take home out of your stomach, can you?"

Yuki chuckled. "I guess not." She sipped her wine, then her smile turned dreamy. "Hm... I'm so excited about watching tonight's new episode, what a terrible cliffhanger last week!"

"You mean, you can't wait to see Viola back on the screen, right?" Lana winked, a large grin on her lips. Ever since she had introduced her to it, Yuki had become a huge fan of *How To Get Away With Murder*.

For sure, Viola Davis' powerful acting and her stunning looks were to thank for it.

Before her companion could reply, the sliding door of the main entrance slammed with a loud noise, shattering the peaceful mood. Lana and Yuki jumped on their seats and shared a puzzled glance. It was much too early for Honda to be home, and what could make him act like that? They hurried to the *genkan*.

"*Goshujin sama*, welcome back, is everything all right?" Yuki asked. Her husband had taken his shoes off and was removing his tie with brusque and angry gestures, completely out of character.

"Never!" he exclaimed, talking to himself. "Never has anyone shown me so much disrespect, has insulted me like this!" His hands shook. "This is unforgivable!"

Without any further explanation, he strode right past the two women, not sparing them a glance. But just as he stepped inside his office, he stopped and turned on his heels. He pointed at Lana. "You! Attend me!"

Startled, Lana froze at first but then jumped on her feet, responding to his barking as if they were in the dojo and he called her as his *uke*. In a way, this was exactly what was about to happen: she'd be the recipient of a violent technique, and she'd have to make sure to take a proper fall to avoid being hurt. She tried to hide her trepidation. This round would be more than a little dangerous given his abysmal level of self-control. Yuki reached the same conclusion.

"Please, she doesn't have to... maybe I can..." she began, trying to calm her husband.

"Silence, wife!" Honda shouted in a plain and downright disrespectful register. Both women tensed and gasped in surprise. He never spoke so rudely, and above all not with Yuki. "Stay out of this. You do not have the requested... skills. It is not your role. Come now," Honda grunted, grabbing Lana's wrist and leading them to his bedroom.

"Yes, *goshujin sama*," Lana tried to sound much more unaffected than she was. As soon as they were inside his room, he used their momentum to slam her against the wall.

"Do not resist me. Do not challenge me. Do not make one sound, or gesture, of opposition. Do you understand?" Honda rasped in her ear while tearing apart her dress and panties.

Lana couldn't deny a part of her was aroused by his extreme show of dominance and rough handling. Still, she was downright pissed at his gross attitude with Yuki. She regulated her breathing to keep her emotions under a tight lid. For someone who had lectured her on not letting anyone get under her skin, his seemed quite thin and fragile today.

She analyzed the situation with a critical, analytical eye. Whatever had happened at his dinner party must have been bad to push him so far that he couldn't handle it on his own. This looked like a distorted image of what they have gone through just a few days earlier. This time, there seemed to be no room for her own aggression as he spiraled out of control; she had to be calm waters and no oil on his fire.

He was so tense under her hands, a block of marble pressing on her, ready to crush her. No flexibility. No softness. *He's right. No way Yuki can do it. He didn't have to be so insulting though!*

"Yes, *goshujin sama*, of course. Please... let me serve you." It was going to be a one-way game, at least in the beginning. Perhaps she would have the chance to bring back some balance later on.

"Good. Now be silent. I only want to hear your moans and cries, or your answers to my questions." Honda got rid of his pants, flipped her against the wall and slid into her in one move. His grip on her hips was like steel claws. "Where is your loyalty? Where is your allegiance? Is your entire body ready for me?" His voice was pressing but cold.

Lana was rattled by his odd line of questioning but lost the ability to think straight as he began to thrust inside her. "Yes... *Go... shujin... sama*... Always..."

"Let's see that. Open your cheeks! Wide open!" Lana stretched her legs and opened her cheeks to offer a perfect view of her ass.

She gasped when he slapped her hard three times, and she stifled back a first moan of pleasure, trying to let go of unnecessary tension. For once, she didn't feel as safe as usual. *He's so volatile and unhinged! What's going on here? Did he have too much to drink? But there's no smell on his breath...*

"Better now." He resumed his pounding, then pinched her nipples. He bit her right shoulder so hard that blood started to drip. Lana moaned even louder, and her legs buckled under her.

"Don't be weak, be strong, be stronger than this, you can take it, you can take anything," he grunted in her ear. "I ask for your loyalty and total submission, not weakness and passivity." Then he slipped out of her, clasped her shoulders and pushed her to his *futon*. "On your back. Open your mouth."

Honda straddled her chest and plunged into her mouth, hitting the back of her throat; she made gurgling sounds. The feeling of invasion and his crushing weight fueled her resolve at pushing back.

Let's not bet too much on his usual concerns about my boundaries... She dug her nails hard into his legs to slow him down while doing her best to relax and breath through her nose. She wouldn't be able to call red, but he would respect the traditional tapping signaling her limits. And if he didn't... then she would bite him.

"Why are you fighting me?" Honda growled. "Don't you trust me? Don't you have faith in me? Are you scared?" There was something in his voice, almost desperate. *What the hell happened tonight?*

Lana locked eyes with him, to show him she wasn't turning her back on him despite everything he threw at her. She let go of his legs and slid her trembling hands over his rocking hips, supple stomach and up to his flanks; she gripped him hard. Ten sharp and red half-moons appeared on his skin.

Honda hissed and grunted as she kept clenching until she drew blood. Pain was always welcome. It was something both expected and needed. His whole body shuddered, his roar of release reverberated in the air as his come filled her throat.

He had enough sense left to get up from her chest right away. Lana turned on her side to swallow his cum without choking on it. Panting hard and wiping her mouth with a shaky hand, she was confronted with his half erection. Breath irregular, he kept clenching and unclenching his fists. Jaw locked and face tumultuous, gaze unfocused, it was as if there was someone else in front of him, a ghost mocking him.

"*Goshujin sama...*" Her voice was reduced to a broken whisper by his invasive deep throating. "You are unwell. Let me help you..." Lana opened her hands in a non-threatening manner. *How about I caress him, comfort him...*

But she didn't have time to test her plan. Honda grabbed her wrists and with a surprised yelp, she found herself half sprawled on his lap.

"I have no use for your pity," Honda uttered with a flat voice, his grip tightening. "Give me your body and resilience, this is all I want from you."

His off-hand words poured oil on her resolve. She was in a vulnerable position, but she didn't attempt to pull away. She used her lower limbs' muscles while relaxing her upper body. Applying a technique he had taught her, she pushed herself up until she again faced him.

"You have my body," Lana whispered. "You can use it as you want. I will enjoy it and perhaps beg for more. But you are wrong. I am not pitying you. I want to make you... snap out of this haze. You are not yourself. Come back to us. *Oku sama* and I are not your enemies."

Honda pushed her backward in an impossible position, but she held her ground and refused to relent. He bit her earlobe hard. "Now is not the time to figure out things beyond your pay grade, little *mudansha*," he grunted. "You have one job, and it does not include getting inside my head. Get to it! Ride me!" he ordered, pulling her again back to him, and then grabbing her hips to make her straddle his hips.

Lana growled back, but let it go. She grinded herself on his lap and they fell into tense silence. Nearly desperate, she attempted to bring him a second time to closure, but it kept escaping him.

Nails raked long and bloody wounds on his spine and flanks. Teeth gnawed at necks, ears, and shoulders. His entire upper body was a mess of bruises, and hers wasn't in much better shape. Electric jolts shot throughout her body. Pleasure and pain, but also anxiety and frustration left them both panting hard.

He had recovered a bit of his self-control, but his face was still filled with a startling anxiety that left her even more confused and scared. It was much more disturbing than his carelessness and rough handling.

As she considered coming up with another approach, Honda grabbed something under the mattress. When a blade caught the moonlight in the dark room, she gasped and froze.

What the hell?

Honda caught her neck with his free hand. "Did I tell you to stop?"

Any pretense at submission was cast aside. Heart beating wildly, Lana stared him down, while her hand shot to catch his thick wrist to keep the short sword away. He was buried inside her, there was not much room to move. Tonight, many lines had been already blurred, and she was taking no chance.

Lila Mina

25

An Offering of Blood

"Should I call red already?" For more effect, Lana snarled and let her own steel pierce through as she applied a disarming technique.

His grip on her neck tightened, and he twisted his wrist free with a counter-technique. "This is not for you, or at least not until you ask for it. Keep still."

Before Lana could react, Honda slid the sharp blade on his left bicep, leaving a clean, long and bleeding cut behind. He let out a groan and hardened inside her. Her hand flew to her mouth in shock.

"No! Oh why... Why did you do this? Please stop!" Fear overcame her. *Something! I need something to stop the bleeding, some clothes, some tissue, anything!*

Honda dropped the blade and seized her chin. "It is nothing, just a flesh wound. Lick it. Lick the blood away like you have done in the past. Lick it, drink it, until it stops. Use your entire mouth, your lips, your tongue. I know that you enjoy the taste of my blood. Continue to ride me and heal me." He panted hard, his body quivering under her like never before. But whether it was from sexual tension, pain, or struggle to keep himself under control...

Lana searched his stormy face, trying to clamp down her panic. *Yes... I like it, I enjoy tasting his blood... but this is much more than a few drops! His words though... Healing him...*

She resumed rolling her hips and in slow motion, brought her lips closer to his arm, never breaking eye contact. As soon as her mouth touched his wound, Honda shuddered, and a new sound resonated from his chest, something different, a sob of relief, mixed with a groan of pure pleasure.

"Uh... yes! Faster now, ride me, ride me hard! And suck it! Suck it as you would drink my cum!" he urged her, his self-control once again reduced to shreds, but no longer by anger.

All her doubts and anxiety flew away. Her own caged monster roared and broke out of her confinement with a surge of dark relish, and a deafening rush of blood to her head shut out all other sounds. Her more assertive and dominant nature took over. Lana pushed him back down, dug her nails into his chest for leverage and launched herself into a powerful and fast ride. Turning into an animal feeding on her prey, her tongue flicked his cut, swallowing down the thick and hot liquid.

A violent and long orgasm, the first of the evening, washed over her and made her wet their locked pelvises. The added moisture made her sliding moves even easier. Sweat, cum, blood, saliva, all kinds of body fluids pooled between their legs and lower bodies. Honda answered her muted groans with other loud grunts, crushing her face to his arm, meeting each of her moves with his own thrusts.

"Yes! This is it! More... I need more... lap it, grind me, do not stop... your blood... will you give it to me?" That last part wasn't a command. There was hope in his rough voice, but also anxiety.

Scared and exhilarated, Lana grabbed blindly for the knife and straightened up to hand it to him, handle first. "Ah... All right..." she panted, trying to recover her wits. His blood was all over her chin, and she wiped it with the back of her free hand. "Let's try to do this... But please, a small cut..."

Honda pushed back the blade, declining it. His eyes were clearer, much more focused now. "No, you do it. You must be committed. I will not cut you, little *mudansha*. I offer you my blood, you offer me yours. You heal my wounds, I heal yours. This is much more difficult this way. And much more rewarding."

"I... I can't do it... I don't know how... Where?" she stammered.

Buried inside her, he took her hand handling the knife and brought it to her upper arm in a surprisingly gentle way. "When you are ready, hold still and press lightly. It is extremely sharp, you do not need strength but rather a steady hand. Do it here, on your bicep, where there are no arteries. You will not lose much blood and enjoy the way it hurts," Honda grumbled.

Lana watched him from behind hooded eyes, her mood turning grim. "This is what I fear."

"Do it only when we are together, for safety reasons but also because even if the pain is pleasurable, you will see: the feeling of my tongue licking your wound is even more exquisite."

You tempting devil... I should... shut my ears... run away... leave you here... not look back...

But her own beast heard him and hummed in feverish anticipation. Lana took a deep breath to stop her hand from shaking and applied the blade with a careful gesture, cutting her flesh over three centimeters. The pain was sharper than expected, and she hissed at the throbbing ache.

Honda's growl of desire and his hands tightening on her hips were enough to make her come again. That he needed her so made her head swirl. She licked his wound, his chest, up his throat, and nape to tug at his earlobe.

"Ahh, *goshujin sama*... Please..." Her voice was sultry and rough. She had slipped and fallen, joining him in his black and red world where their darkest drives ruled. "Drink my blood... And let me swallow yours... please fuck me hard while we lick each other..."

"I wouldn't do it in any other way..." Honda grunted before latching onto her arm and pushing her on her back in one fluid movement. The next second, he slid into her ass. Her legs locked on their own on his lower back and his renewed energy swept her away. Her eyes rolled back, body slackening as she screamed in ecstasy.

As soon as Lana had recovered her wits, she gripped his chest and pressed her mouth to his wound again. The next moments had them frantically thrusting against each other, their mouths locked on each other's bloody slashes. Caught in an erotic form of wrestling, they rolled outside the *futon* and on the *tatami*.

With their usual patterns set aside for once, both vied for dominance, refusing to submit, wanting to take and give it all. The air was permeated with their groans and rutting grunts, the metallic smell of blood, the pungent odor of their sweats mingling and the unmistakable smell of cum that kept flowing. Her mind shut down as her primal urges and darkest desires overruled her.

Later Lana sat up and rubbed her arm while watching her companion lost in deep slumber. Unusual lines of grim tension still creased his face. They had pushed it extremely far, and she had absorbed a lot of his overwhelming rage, but not all of it. Whatever he had told her, he needed comfort and a form of softer care. She nearly touched his face but dropped her hand. That wasn't her role.

Grimacing and limping, she got up, grabbed her panties and his discarded shirt, and buttoned it up. She found Yuki in the darkened kitchen, sitting under a lone light, lost in thought.

"*Oku sama*," she whispered as her throat was still sore, "I believe it would be best if you attended *goshujin sama* now."

Pale, Yuki stood so fast that her chair fell over. "Lana san. You are... in terrible shape! What did he do to you?"

"Don't worry," Lana shook her head. "I just need some water and rest. He needs... another kind of support now, and this... I can't give him." Lana gulped down two glasses of ice cold water then grabbed a bottle of whisky on the counter. She poured herself two shots for numbing the pain in her arm.

"But what about you?" Yuki exclaimed, growing agitated. Lana winced when her mistress grabbed her arm, brushing her wound without knowing. "Your health? Your body? You are covered in bruises... and is this blood? He was so... so rude and aggressive tonight! You should have said no! You are no punching bag!"

"I'm fine, Yuki sama," Lana tried to calm down her companion. "You should see the other guy," she chuckled to lighten the mood. "Maybe... later, you and me? We could relax a little together? But for now, let's get him back to normal again, shall we? It was like he was somewhere else, fighting a battle in his head. I could help and deal with the most violent outbursts, but I believe he needs something else, too." She shook her head. "And it's not my realm, *oku sama*, he made it clear."

Yuki remained silent and hung her head low, face showing her confusion and distress. Lana wondered if this had been the first time something like that had ever happened, if Yuki had any further insight but didn't want to share. *No matter, I'm way too tired for this conversation.*

"Let's get back together," Lana suggested. They went back to his room and approached his *futon*. Honda hadn't stirred. Yuki lay down next to him and wrapped her arm around his waist. Lana needed her own personal space.

"I will sleep over there on those covers. Wake me up if necessary, please," she whispered. She laid down on the fluffy covers, turned her back to the couple and, exhausted, was soon asleep.

Angry whispers woke her up.

"– stop, I don't want your apologies. It isn't me you should apologize to, anyway. How? How can you do this to her? She must handle the worst of you, your most monstrous and terrible side, and what, she doesn't deserve one moment of comfort with you? Why? Why are you so inflexible, so harsh with her? She is no robot or doll!"

"Enough! It is none of your concern," Honda's raspy voice replied.

"Yes, it is! She is in our home, she shares our bed, and I will not pretend there is no problem because you order me to. Don't you dare break her! I will order her to leave before it gets to this, and I will not care if you are pleased or not!" Instead of the expected explosive anger, there was a long silence.

"I am not breaking her, Yuki san," Honda asserted in a firm whisper. "I am giving her as much as she is giving me. It is not your place to criticize how I do it. She has all leeway to make me stop if she can't manage it. Not only can she handle a lot, but she also has enough steel to stand up against me. And I will not blur the lines between all of us for some unrequited emotional purpose. If you wish to bring her comfort, you may do it. I am providing her with other sources of strength."

There was the sound of bodies and bed sheets moving around. "Just make sure she always does it because she wants to, and not just by habit or mere wish to please you. I will not accept any kind of psychological or physical abuse, nothing where her consent is dubious."

"You know that I find abuse repulsive and unacceptable," he scoffed.

"I know, but it can happen because you do not want to see it," Yuki warned, but the anger was gone from her voice. There was another silence. "What happened tonight, *goshujin sama*?" Yuki continued with a low voice. "Who...?"

"Enough. I will not discuss it." It was a mistake to tread into those waters. Anger and tension were back in Honda's voice.

Yuki let out a frustrated hiss. "I hope one day you will learn to also accept my way of helping you. A lot could be different if you let me in. I am tired. Good night."

Without even waiting for his dismissal or any kind of reaction, Yuki trod out of his bedroom, stopping near Lana. Lana kept her eyes shut and attempted to regulate her breathing. Several minutes went by, and she was almost asleep again when a heavy hand dropped on her shoulder.

"Stop pretending."

Lana almost groaned aloud. Honda's silhouette was illuminated by the garden lanterns outside; she sat up carefully on her knees, trying not to grimace. Her body hurt everywhere. She was still wearing his shirt, but now it was stained by blood from her arm wound and all the smaller bruises he had covered her with.

"My apologies. I have a light sleep."

"Why did you go and fetch Yuki?" Honda asked, dismissing her apologies.

Lana sighed. "I thought there was nothing left I could do for you, that you needed additional... support, and that she was in the best position to do it. I didn't expect her to take offense on my behalf."

"You make wrong assumptions, about me and her. If I only included you tonight, I had my reasons, and not simply because you can deal with my more extreme demands. And I did not need any other kind of... support than what you gave me. Do not bring Yuki into this unless I say so."

He was stern and unflinching, but at least he seemed to be back within his normal parameters of temper and self-control. Lana sighed again and bowed to accept his criticism. It wasn't the time to argue or to ask what this madness had been all about. She found it hard not to yawn to his face.

"Now come, we need to dress those wounds, yours in particular." He went to a chest drawer and took out a first-aid kit. "Show me your arm."

He put on gloves, disinfected her cuts and arm wound, spread an antibiotic cream and put adhesive stripes on it with surprising expertise. Next, he asked her to do the same with his. She was less used to the process but managed to do a proper job.

He brought wet towels back from his bathroom and they used them to clean themselves up. Everything was done in an efficient manner, in silence, without any hint of seduction, just like when they were cleaning up the dojo and equipment. Any external observer would have had a hard time believing they had engaged in extreme sex that had shattered the limits of decency a few hours ago.

Cleaning herself up, Lana mulled over what she had overheard. There wasn't much new, rather mere confirmation of what he had told her at the beginning. She didn't try to guess what was amiss between Yuki and him. It wasn't just a question of physical strength and kinks. It seemed like every time she assumed something about them, she got it wrong.

"It is late," Honda broke the silence. "Thank you for your service, sleep well." He didn't suggest she join him.

This was fine with her, as even asleep, his presence could be physically and emotionally draining. As exhilarating and liberating as this last session had been, he had demanded enough for one night.

END OF BOOK ONE

Glossary of Japanese terms

Dogi: white pants and jacket used as training gear by aikido, judo and karate practitioners
Dojo-cho: leader of a martial art school
Genkan: entrance of a home
Goshujin sama: honored husband, honored lord/master
Hakama: black and flowing traditional trouser worn by aikido practitioners who hold a 'dan' rank (black belt)
Kohai: practitioner holding a lower rank
Kyu: grade conferred to Japanese martial arts practitioners before they achieve the first 'dan' rank
Mudansha: practitioner of a traditional Japanese martial arts who doesn't hold a 'dan' rank yet (black belt)
Neko: cat
Oku sama: (your, his) honored wife
- *san*: standard honorific put after a first or last name
- *sama*: respectful honorific put after a first or last name
Otoh sama: honored Father, your honored father
Seiza: Japanese traditional way of sitting on your knees and ankles

Sempai: practitioner holding a higher rank
Shihan: master, expert in martial art
Shintoism: the main, traditional religion of Japan, along with Buddhism. Shintoism is an animistic religion: everything (including non-animated objects and elements such as wind, swords or stones) possesses a spirit
Shodan: first black belt rank
Tatami: straw mats used in dojo and in rooms inside Japanese houses
Ukemi: rolling, falling
Uke: attacker and recipient of a martial art technique

Loved it? Please Review!

Did you enjoy TEMPER: DEFERENCE?
Can't wait to read the rest of the saga?

Share your love with fellow readers and leave an online review–it makes a world of difference.

Pick your favorite platforms:

Goodreads
Amazon
Kobo
Smashwords
Eden Books

Lila Mina

The Saga Continues!

TEMPER: DREAD
Book Two of the Saga

Available in paperback and ebook.

TEMPER: DELIVERANCE
Book Three of the Saga

Available in paperback and ebook.

TEMPER: DREAD

Dutiful Devotion Will Heal Cursed Bodies and Souls

An unexpected discovery leads our trio to rethink their relationship together, and Lana to confront buried trauma. Meanwhile, shapeless and mortal danger looms on the horizon, forcing Honda to finally confess to Lana why he chose her. Their boundless thirst has dark, cursed roots, and they have no choice: only together will they stand a chance to defeat the heinous monsters on their trail and put an end to the spiraling madness threatening them.

Desperate to protect her most precious treasure, Lana takes a radical decision in relation to Yuki and attempts to let go of her past.

But the time for secrecy is over: on top of their struggles against timeless forces bent on destroying them, the trio must come out clean with their powerful clans if they want a chance at a real future together.

TEMPER: DELIVERANCE

Compassion and Boundless Desire Will Set Them Free

Pure joy and sweet bliss mingling with utter horror and heartbreaking agony. Pristine snow turns red during the first hours of the New Year in the snowy countryside of Nikko.

Harrowing sacrifice allows a battered Lana and her mournful companions to begin a new life as a family. Healing is a slow process though, and Lana battles with herself to understand her new identity and family dynamics.

But true deliverance and peace will come only when she confronts her real enemy.

TEMPER: DREAD

Exclusive Sneak Peek!

AT THAT TIME of the day, the train was only moderately packed, and Lana found a seat right away. After checking her emails, her eyes wandered over her fellow passengers.

The car was quiet, something she still wasn't used to after years of commuting in noisy public transportation in Montreal. She welcomed the eerie silence with pleasure. It created a break, a transition between her work and personal spaces.

Trains were a complex affair in Japan, particularly in Tokyo. People were forced to coexist and share their precious personal sphere with throngs of complete strangers for long periods of time, something anathema to local social and cultural rules.

To overcome such a nervous and emotional toll, everyone locked themselves up in their own world, going online, playing games, reading books, often falling asleep or in a half-sleep, half-meditative state that surprised visitors. Commuters liked to pretend they weren't stuck in a steel box along with thousands of others, traveling alongside millions, crisscrossing the body of the restless Beast which was Tokyo. Silence was key to this affair, and disruption a severe breach of etiquette.

After three years in the city, Lana had yet to adopt those avoidance practices. People watching was one of her secret pleasures, and trains were perfect for indulging in it. Today, she was lucky.

Right in front of her, sitting on the other side of the car, a twenty-something woman wearing a sharp dark blue business suit carried a large shopping bag from an upscale department store with 'Fuckin' sales max 50% off' written in large, bold letters. Lana bit her cheek to stifle her bubbling mirth. Those slogans in hopeless English, French or Italian to make bags or shirts look cool were priceless. She shot a pic to upload it to one of her favorite Facebook pages that collected those treasures.

Further down on her right, three elegant older ladies in shimmering kimono were going to a formal event or maybe see a *kabuki* play. Their heads brought together, they were quietly sharing the latest gossips; how long had these three known each other? Forty, fifty years?

On her left, five teenagers coming home after a baseball game were snoring, sprawled on their seats, their pristine white uniforms now dirty. Yes indeed, trains carried the essence of Japan, its soul with its millions of facets.

Something touching her right foot broke her quiet contemplation. A plastic ball, red and white, had come to a rolling stop by her shoe. Lana picked it up. It was one of those *bikkurapon* — surprise-balls — children bought for 200 yen at the ubiquitous vending machines near the cashiers in supermarkets. It was hard to see what was inside, but it was the whole point. Usually, they contained stickers or erasers adorned with popular anime characters.

Lana took a peek on her right to identify its point of origin. From what she could see, there were no kids there. She quirked an eyebrow and put the ball in her bag. Probably, it had been rolling around the carriage for a while now. She would throw it out later. No need for a granny to twist her ankle on it.

Resting her head on the window behind her and closed her eyes, enjoying her favorite song. It was so tempting to fall asleep. But her station was four stops away now, and she'd hate to miss it. Her eyes shot open when something else hit her foot. Another *bikkurapon*, this time green and white. Lana picked it up, and this time she leaned forward, looking harder on her right.

Ah, there. Gotcha.

Two short legs covered in pink and purple high socks were swinging from the seat right next to the farthest exit of the carriage, on the same side as Lana. She couldn't see their owner, but she was young, bored, and unsupervised by the sleeping adult on her left.

Right then, the girl leaned forward and stared in Lana's direction. Her face was covered by a white and soft pink mask to protect her against air pollution and virus. Low bangs of unruffled black hair hid her brow and eyes. Lana raised her hand and showed the girl the green ball, asking silently if this belonged to her. The girl kept staring at her, her legs moving in quick rhythm, but showed no sign of recognition or acknowledgment.

Lana put the ball in her bag, alongside its red sibling. Eyes once again shut, she enjoyed the last stretch of her trip uninterrupted, softly rubbing her sternum. To her annoyance, her heartburns were flaring again. As the loudspeakers announced her station, she walked to the doors next to the girl, to give her one last chance to get her toys back.

"Are those yours?" Lana said, handing out the two balls. The girl gazed back at her from behind her bangs and didn't bother replying or making any move. Lana shrugged and stepped outside. *Whatever.*

As she headed for the escalators leading to the main concourse, a banging sound from the inside of the train made her glance back. What she saw turned her blood to ice. Shocked, she dropped the two balls that rolled away toward the tracks, but Lana couldn't care less about them.

The girl had moved to sit on her knees and bang the windows as if in a tantrum. She had taken her mask off and revealed the most horribly scarred face Lana had ever seen. She had no mouth, only a huge hole splitting the bottom half of her face from ear to ear, in a mock version of a smile, revealing irregular teeth and a black tongue.

Too stunned to look away, Lana gawked at the nightmarish vision. A part of her wondered at the lack of reaction of the people around the girl who seemed oblivious to her behavior. The doors closed, and the train took off, leaving Lana shivering and almost nauseous as she stood motionless among the crowd pressing toward the exit.

Right then, somebody pushed her from behind, and she lost her balance. There were no security barriers on the platforms of the old station. For a terrifying instant, unable to grab anything, Lana saw herself falling on the tracks. A hand seized her elbow and steadied her. She straightened up and faced her rescuer.

"Ah... thank you... thank you very much," she stammered.

The tall man holding her arm was also wearing a white mask, but his eyes smiled. "Please be always mindful of what is around you and watch where you are going. Those are yours, I believe," he added, putting in her hand the two balls she had dropped.

Lana stared at them, confused. "Well, not really, I found them on the —" She looked up and blinked. The man had already disappeared back into the crowd. The whole incident had lasted less than one minute, and she found herself alone on the platform, except for a couple of people waiting for the train running to downtown.

In a daze, Lana walked out the station. The incident and the afternoon's relentless heat had drained her of all remaining energy. Walking home like she usually did seemed an impossible task. She hailed a taxi instead. As the driver navigated through the small residential streets of the upscale neighborhood, her fingers played mindlessly with the two plastic balls, once again in her bag.

Staring outside, she wondered if her fatigue could be a bad case of *natsubate*, the infamous summer lethargy that plagued so many every year. It would be a first for her, but a double dose of those homemade pickled plums Yuki made and stored in the pantry would do the trick to boost her up. *Umeboshi* were sour and salty but beat an aspirin and an apple.

There was an unknown car outside the gate, and Honda's was in the garage. She came across an unfamiliar pair of shoes in the genkan. They had a visitor. Upbeat music in her ears, Lana took off her pumps, put away her business jacket and bag, and headed first to the kitchen for a large glass of chilled barley tea. She picked up her mail on the counter, and while she was busy opening it, she walked out to go to her room. As tired and distracted as she was, she was deaf and blind to her surroundings.

She slammed into a wall right as she stepped out the kitchen. While everything in her hands flew around and clattered on the ground, for the second time in less than one hour, someone deftly caught her and kept her on her feet. When she registered who it was, Lana wished she had hit her head unconscious on the floor instead.

"I... Inoue *shihan*, my... my apologies..." Lana blurted out in a strangled voice. With their respective status, she was supposed to kneel to greet him, but he had yet to let go of her. In the back, Honda and Yuki stood, somber and mute, startled by her apparition.

"Martin san. I was on my way out, but the coincidence is fortunate," Inoue grunted. "We can address this highly problematic situation once for all. I will talk with you now. Alone," he added with a slight head move toward the owners of the house, ordering them to stay put. Not waiting for her reply, he steered her to the nearest *tatami* room. Lana didn't even have the time to glance at her two companions. Panic squeezed her throat.

"Sit," Inoue ordered before closing the sliding door behind them and facing her. He waited several minutes in silence, and her discomfort grew with each breath she drew.

"Yesterday, you managed to be honest with me while expertly hiding the fact of the matter. My congratulations, you seemed to have adopted specific Japanese talents. Honda san's teachings are numerous," Inoue said with heavy sarcasm. "But no more games. I will demand the same from you as I did from him a moment ago: the bare, unedited truth. Answer me now. Are you here out of free will, or do you feel coerced to do... whatever it is you do?"

Silence fell again in the room. Lana stared at Inoue, dumbfounded, before finding back her voice. "Is this... Is this your main concern, Inoue *shihan*?" Lana asked, leaning forward. "My freedom, my consent? Not what I do, nor why...?"

Inoue growled with impatience. "I know exactly what you are here for, and why. I already told you: I know him. As for the rest, the only thing which matters is your full and absolute consent. Stop being so evasive! I will protect you and cut all bonds between the two of you if needed. I made this clear before you arrived, and he will not dare oppose me."

Relief washed over Lana who straightened up and bowed. "I am grateful for your concern and care, Inoue *shihan*. I swear to you I am here of my own will. Not only I have accepted everything freely, but my limits are respected and enforced at all times." Lana looked down, embarrassed. "The truth is, I realize I need this as much as he does. By far, not only his issues are being addressed but also mine."

Inoue pinched his lips and remained silent for a while, his piercing eyes assessing her critically. "This is what he alluded to; while he sounded honest, I didn't wish to take any risk. I had to confront you. It was fortunate you showed up like this. Do you live here now?"

"I do. Ever since the earthquake. But only a handful of people are aware of it, and nobody at our dojo or in our families." Lana hesitated. "*Dojo-cho*, may I ask you something?" He grunted. "How... how did you guess?" Her voice trailed off, her throat constricted. "Has anything like this happened before?"

Inoue's face softened. "No, never. But his usual mood and behavior have changed, which told me a lot given what I know. And then, I learned about your unusual training regimen and I had a hunch. Your fidgety behavior yesterday raised flags. My conversation with him today confirmed everything. All right, then. Honda san!" He called out with a booming voice.

Honda stepped inside and sat down next to Lana, head bowed at a slight angle. Inoue crossed his arms over his chest and stared them down.

"Honda san. You have here a loyal and dutiful lady, and I believe her to be sincere. I cannot approve that you chose someone among your students, a *mudansha* on top of it. But she is no young, gullible girl, she doesn't look like she can be easily impressed, and seems to have the necessary nerves and spine to handle you. It would have been more sensible to come to me at first for my permission. But what is done is done and... given that everyone involved — including your wife — is in agreement, I will stay away from this."

Inoue let silence settle in again. Honda was as still as a statue. "However, a word of warning, Honda san: I will keep a close eye on the dojo morale and above all on Martin san. If I have any doubt as to her well-being, this will end right away, and I will make you pay for it. Don't you forget your own duty toward her."

With those words, Inoue stood, and Honda and Lana bowed to the ground until he had left the room. Then Honda got up and followed him into the hall to see him out. Lana remained behind, trying to wrap her head around what had transpired.

Five minutes later, both Honda and Yuki joined her. She was pale while her husband's face was unreadable. The three of them remained silent for a while, mulling over the storm that had gathered over their heads in a few hours, only to dissipate like a morning fog.

"Lana san," Honda had never sounded so tired. "I wish to express my sincere appreciation for how you handled this situation. Inoue *shihan* came unannounced one hour ago, and it was impossible to let you know."

"Maybe it was for the best..." Lana mused aloud. "Everything was sorted out, and he could sense my heartfelt sincerity. But I should have waited for your return last night to share with you my trouble after my brief, yet intense conversation with him. I was clinging to the hope it was my paranoia talking. It didn't make any sense for him to have grounds to be so suspicious."

"You were not aware of the deep and complex ties binding us. As he was keen to point out, I should have come clear with him, and introduce you, at least when you moved here."

Lana was startled. "Ah, but forgive me for asking, but why is it all right and even important for Inoue *shihan* to know, but vital to keep it from everyone else, especially your families?"

Honda pinched his lips. Preempting his terse reaction, Yuki piped in. "Our families are another issue. We will cross those bridges if we need to. It will not go down like this with them, because the stakes and consequences are markedly different. But I am glad Inoue *shihan* is now aware of you sharing our lives."

Her husband stiffened with disapproval. Yuki sighed and bowed. "I beg your pardon for my poor choice of words. Aware of you entering *goshujin sama*'s service," she amended.

"While he made it clear you may count on his support, do not expect him to show you any special favor during your next test," Honda warned.

"Of course not. I am well aware of the specific scope of his offer."

Honda grunted and stood up. "I will go and engage in overdue meditation. Lana san, join me later in the dojo. There were several issues with your techniques yesterday evening." Lana hid her grimace and bowed in acceptance, watching him leave the room. This would be tough and would only work if she took a power nap right away.

"Well, I could use some relaxing green tea. I am going to prepare *sencha*," Yuki said. "Would you like a cup?"

"Not for now, thank you very much. Please excuse me for a while. I came home earlier than scheduled because I am exhausted today. Tea will be welcome before my practice session though."

Yuki moved to stand up but then changed her mind and sat next to Lana. Like earlier, she cupped her cheek and made her younger partner look at her.

"Don't fret or lose sleep over matters, which are out of your hands," she admonished her in a low whisper. "You are blameless for what happened today, for the choices and decisions made by others decades ago. It is important you grasp sensitive issues, but not every problem he must face is yours to solve."

Yuki's lips brushed her companion's. "I hope you haven't forgotten our plans for tonight, and that you will feel refreshed and be again full of stamina... because you will need it. I have a surprise for you, I will bring it to your room later," she added before catching her lover's bottom lip with her teeth and tugging at it.

Lana sighed and relaxed into her mistress' comforting and sensual embrace. "Thank you *oku sama*," she whispered. "I can't wait to see it." Yuki smiled against her mouth and left her alone. Lana sighed; after rubbing her eyes, she headed for her room.

She woke up less than an hour later and stretched her arms above her head. Sleeping had done wonders for her overall physical and mental state, and she put her earlier exhaustion on the stressful situation with Inoue, dehydration and her restless night. To her delight, she discovered cold-brewed sencha and some rice snacks next to her *futon*, another proof of Yuki's thoughtfulness. The precious beverage would help her focus during her upcoming training session.

There was also a small package beautifully wrapped in soft and silky paper, with a card on top of it. Yuki's elegant writing. 'Wear this tonight, under your little black dress, but don't open it now'.

Curbing her curiosity, Lana set aside the gift and took the time to enjoy two cups of tea while contemplating the stone garden outside her window.

She changed into her *dogi* and went to the dojo. Kneeling at the entrance, she proceeded with the ritual salutations and waited as Honda had yet to formally acknowledge her. Her instructor was practicing *jusan jo kata*, a solo performance combining a series of thirteen defense moves using a long staff. This was still much too complex for her to perform, as she knew four of those techniques, and then, only approximately.

She didn't know for how long he had been at it, but as she watched with utter fascination, Honda went through the entire motions five times in a row, each time faster than before, until coming to a halt in the appropriate final stance. He faced the main wall and bowed to the Founder, symbolically offering him his staff back, and replaced it on the weapon rack before sitting down and turning toward Lana. She hastened to join him.

"Lana san, yesterday your footwork and hip moves were hesitant at best on many forms of *ryote dori*. As a result, you still wrestle your way through the technique, using your strength to compensate for your poor execution. We will go through all fifteen defenses that you know, in both static and fluid stances. Let's begin, *onegaishimasu*."

Training went by in a blur and Lana ended up drenched in sweat, struggling to keep her panting in check. To her annoyance, her dizziness was coming back, even if much lighter than earlier.

"Let's stop here for today; you improved, but I want you to focus on these issues in the coming weeks, understood? Also, you should work on your endurance. The weather is getting uncomfortable and warm, and you are sensitive to it, but your stamina could be better."

"Yes, Sensei, thank you," Lana acknowledged and bowed.

She couldn't wait for a long and thorough cool shower as well as something to eat. Honda returned her bow, and this signaled the end of their training session. His body language shifted subtly, his physical presence became much more pressing; it was no longer her instructor who sat in front of her. A delicious tingle spread from her core.

"Yuki has planned something for us tonight," her master continued with a deeper voice. "It has been too long since the three of us spent an intimate evening together. After dinner, please prepare yourself and come to my bedroom." Lana bowed again, this time even more deeply.

"It will be my pleasure, *goshujin sama*, I am looking forward to it."

"As I am. You are dismissed."

About the Author

Readers will find behind the pen name Lila Mina a woman in her early forties who has been living in Japan for a decade with her family. After nearly twenty years of using her writing skills for drafting legal briefs and business reports, she went back to her first love: fiction.

These days, you can find her practicing aikido, writing or editing her manuscripts in local coffee shops, or sipping delicious green tea at home.

Inspired by the rich and complex Japanese culture and folklore, her stories feature strong and mature female protagonists facing their inner demons or ruthless enemies, and who are never shy to embrace their desires.

The TEMPER saga is her first major published work of fiction.

Follow her on social media and sign up to her mailing list on lilamina.com, and don't miss any new release!

> Facebook: @AuthorLilaMina
> Instagram: @lilaminaauthor
> Twitter: @lilamina11